Tall Tales at the
General Store

Mary Greene Lee

WestBow
PRESS
A DIVISION OF THOMAS NELSON

Scripture taken from the King James Version of the Bible.

WestBow Press books may be ordered through booksellers or by contacting:

WestBow Press
A Division of Thomas Nelson
1663 Liberty Drive
Bloomington, IN 47403
www.westbowpress.com
1-(866) 928-1240

Because of the dynamic nature of the Internet, any web addresses or links contained in this book may have changed since publication and may no longer be valid. The views expressed in this work are solely those of the author and do not necessarily reflect the views of the publisher, and the publisher hereby disclaims any responsibility for them.

Any people depicted in stock imagery provided by Thinkstock are models, and such images are being used for illustrative purposes only.

Certain stock imagery © Thinkstock.

ISBN: 978-1-4497-6261-2 (sc)
ISBN: 978-1-4497-6260-5 (hc)
ISBN: 978-1-4497-6262-9 (e)

Library of Congress Control Number: 2012914096

Printed in the United States of America

WestBow Press rev. date: 09/18/2012

To my children who believed in me—
Hollie, Mark, and Jeffrey

And my sister, Nancy, for encouragement and advice

TABLE OF CONTENTS

1. That No Account Man 1
2. The Wedding Serenade 7
3. The Jack Leg Preacher Arrives 13
4. Inquisition of the Preacher 21
5. Revenge—Righting a Wrong 27
6. Menopause Seizes the Mountain 31
7. The Checker Marathon 35
8. Behind Closed Doors 39
9. Entrepreneurs 43
10. Grief and Love 51
11. Snipe Huntin' 59
12. Music Here Tonight 67
13. Mountain-Style Punishment 71
14. Heaven Came Down 81
15. Simmerin' Apple Butter 85
16. Grandpaw Ought Not to Babysit 91
17. The Killing Tree 95
18. Help the Preacher with his Courtin' 101
19. What's in a Name? 109
20. By and By Arrives 117
21. Hearts 121
22. Changing Times 131
23. The Circle of Life 139
24. A Mountain Mourns 147
25. Formerly Known as Guthrie's 153
26. Too Many Udders—Too Few Hands 157
27. Wars and Rumors of Wars 163
28. Pay No Mind to Crazy Ike 165
29. High Fashion at the Baptist Church 173
30. Silent Night, Holy Night 177

31. Earthquakes and the End of Time 185
32. A Disastrous Easter Parade. 189
33. The Devil's Instrument Arrives. 191
34. An Unlikely Midwife 199
35. Wildflowers and Hope. 205
36. The Last Promise 213
37. Pennies in Mason Jars 215

THAT NO ACCOUNT MAN

Clyde purposefully drew the wooden match stick across the worn sole of his shoe several times before the flame ignited. He then touched the match to a half-smoked cigar. Afterall, the recent Depression taught the folly of wasting even a few good puffs. Rearing back, Clyde yelled across the general store to the sole shopper, "Bertha, git yourself over here, girl, and give account of yerself." Obediently, Bertha rounded the end of the dry goods aisle and stood before the group of regulars. She'd known this family her entire life.

The small community of Greenbed, North Carolina sat cradled in the secure arms of the western rugged mountain ranges. Guthrie's General Store served as the hub of the community where mighty tall tales were exchanged. Obadiah Guthrie managed the store in 1939 in the same manner as his father and grandfather, making only minor revisions.

"Howdy do." Bertha cast her eyes downward, softly addressing the six brothers seated by the front window. Bertha braced for whatever rude remark Mr. Willie might make. His bad eye drifted off to the left as he squinted the other one.

Willie fidgeted in his seat before speaking, "Girl, yer gettin' as dull as a mud fence."

Arville, the oldest brother, looked uncomfortable with Willie's comment; Clyde, a fun-loving man notorious for his colorful personality softly chuckled. Turner, always anxious to play a practical joke ignored the conversation. Lawrence, the more serious, rolled his eyes and shook his head. Most of the womenfolk steered clear of Mr. Willie with his high-pitched voice that tore at a person's confidence like a jagged knife ripping through the delicate fabric of feelings.

"I do believe ya done put on more weight than my fattenin' hog." Folks either loved Willie or hated him for his unpredictable comments.

Darrell, the youngest, small-framed and soft-spoken, kicked Willie's leg, "Leave her be. Ain't no call for bein' so dadburn insultin'," Darrell's salt—and-pepper hair meticulously combed straight back and slicked down with a heavy oil.

The family included three sisters, Flora, Creolla, and Bessie. Upon occasion, these sisters produced the same disruptive behavior.

Bertha crept down the aisle, looking far older than her years. A beauty in her teens, she married young, and commenced making babies with her husband, Homer. The Brothers referred to him as her "no-account husband." Bertha worked the dirt like a man, stacking hay bales on the flatbed wagon, shoveling manure, planting crops, plowing the fields, milking the cows, as well as performing the duties considered "woman's work," which included tending a huge garden to feed her family. Since marrying Homer, she'd known blistered hands, bearing babies, and many lonely nights. Homer frequently yielded to his wondering ways.

Turner asked, "Where's Homer? None of us see'd him in a coon's age."

Bertha shook her head, "He done run off agin. Left me tendin' the farm," Bertha motioned toward the window where her three small girls sat stoically on the front porch, "and feed them".

Earnestly, Clyde inquired, "Want us'ns to fetch him fer ya'? We'll scrub his hindquarters raw with a corncob doused in kerosene. That'd make 'im think twice before he up and leaves youins next time." Bertha knew this was not an idle threat. If she gave the nod, he'd get a good lesson, but he'd also know who to ultimately blame. He'd never struck her or the youngins in a drunken stupor, she wanted to keep it that way. "Wouldn't it do your heart good to see Homer lookin' like he'd been drug through a knothole backwards?"

As tempting as it sounded, Bertha declined, "Naw, won't do nary a bit of good. He'll come back when he gits a mind to. That man's got wandering blood, cain't stay put for long. Seems he's got it in 'im to break western every couple months, goes on a toot for a week or more. Then he be comin' back, tail twixt his legs like a beat hound dog, lookin' a heap pitiful. Them youngins'll latch hold of his legs so's he can't half walk up the steps. Ya' know, when he's a mind to, he's a good worker."

Willie wouldn't relent, "What's yer Momma and Poppa say about that sorry fool leavin' you? If'n he was to do that to one of my girls, I'd be takin' it out on his no—account hide."

"Mr. Willie, my Momma and Poppa drilled into me the Good Book says to forgive." She paused. "But if'n I was to up and leave him, they'd take us in, and Poppa said there'd be nary a question."

Darrell, anxious to change the subject, interjected, "You needin' anything, Bertha?"

"I reckon if ya pass my way and could lend a hand hitchin' up that rusty plow, I'd be obliged. Soon's it dries out, we oughta plow that east field for plantin' corn, or turn it over to the weeds and be done with it. This wind'll dry it out right smart."

Darrell nodded and assured Bertha he'd come in a day or two. All the Brothers exchanged smirks knowing that Darrell would draft them.

Willie seized the opportunity to meddle, "How do ya' know he ain't shacked up with some low-down huzzy? I say, if ya lie down with dogs, ya get up with fleas."

"Homer Tyson, Jr. hankers for the juice, can't leave it alone for the life of 'im. That man knows ever' still in these here parts. If'n he's got a woman, I feel rightly sorry fer her, cuz when he drinks, he's mean as a snake. I stay a far piece away when I catch a whiff of that stinkin' ole bootleg whiskey. It's the devil's juice and turns 'im into a devil."

The Brothers also knew the locations of the stills, and occasionally patronized them. The wandering ways were no stranger to them either. The previous year, Clyde almost died from impure whiskey from a still. He vomited blood for days. When the doctor arrived, he told the family, "If he makes it through the night, he'll survive."

Willie straightened before speaking, "Bertha, ya ever think of runnin' him plum out of this county? I'll tell ya, I'd not put up with his tomfollery n'more than I'd sprout wings and fly over that mountain into Tennessee. Ya've got a few good years in ya'. Git ya' a man who'll be good to ya' and yer youngins. Now, I'll tell ya . . . ."

Clearly, Bertha didn't intend to hear anymore. He sparked the spitfire in her and she retaliated. "Mr. Willie, ya' need to either sprout them wings and fly away or mind your own beeswax. Ya' don't know 'bee from bulls foot!"

Satisfied with this reaction, the Brothers erupted into laughter. Once again, Willie lived up to his reputation. The Brothers were delighted that Bertha shot back at him.

Turner patted Willie's back. "I reckon that thar little woman set ya straight, Brother."

The Brothers could not quote more then ten scriptures between the lot of them, but they lived the faith. They knew the Creator and expressed a genuine concern for their fellow man. They knew how to walk in the shadow of the cross, which meant taking care of their loved ones and neighbors.

Guthrie inquired about a matter of great concern, "Has anybody heard when the new preacher is supposed to show up? We been without far too long. The flock is apt to stray if the shepherd don't get here fast."

Clyde responded, "By the way, Guthrie, I know he's your preacher, but I heared some mighty odd tales about him. He ain't married and don't take to the women folk. Don't that seem a tad strange? A preacher oughtn't to be, you know, that 'way'. All the preachers I ever knowed had 'em a wife. People won't stand for that. It ain't natural and he'll be run out of Greenbed if it's true."

Guthrie shook his head. "How come tales get goin' before ya see the white's of his eyes? Give the man a fightin' chance."

Bertha finished gathering the few items which she had money to pay for—hoping to stretch the food. The Brothers continued exchanging jabs among themselves as they awaited the next victim to enter the general store. Bertha clutched the small bag of seeds to her breast and prayed they would produce fine vegetables. She felt compelled to get the seeds in the ground quickly, so they could germinate and become viable food for her table. Too many nights they all went to bed hungry.

Bertha believed Homer would come home, but only when he got good and ready, and not one minute before, like always. She hated to admit how accustomed she'd become to his irresponsible behavior. Her major concern now was that he returned before the strenuous work needed to be done. She'd work alongside him, but knew the babe growing within her limited lifting and tugging at the heavy machinery. Nary a soul knew the secret of this baby, but it couldn't be concealed much longer since she'd felt the quickening. A smile played across her weary face, imagining the general store gossip if these Brothers knew. Perhaps the girl curse was broken, and she'd bear a man child. A son may create a bond strong enough to keep Homer away from the whiskey stills. The Good Lord knew she and the three girls hadn't altered his wayward ways one iota.

The Brothers tipped their hats to Bertha as she left the store with a small parcel. They were already spinning another tale about the deplorable condition of Joe Neal Watson's barn. Turner passed by Watson's place earlier in the week, "I'll tell ya the truth, we oughta be takin' bets on when that roof collapses. The cows'll sense the danger and stampede out." Turner shook his head in disgust. "That outhouse down by the barn leans toward the orchard, it's gonna go anyday. I wish we could be there to see that happen!" They all cackled at the thoughts of such a show. "And what if . . . ."

Bertha let the screen door slam behind her as she exited.

Little did the Brothers know the outhouse would indeed collapse with an unsuspecting occupant inside, nor how this calamity would impact the remainder of their lives.

"When we hitch that plow for Bertha, I'll take a slab of meat from the smokehouse. We got a crock of pickled beans in the springhouse, we'll take some of them too," Clyde announced. They all nodded in agreement. "Arville, are them layin' hens of yours doin' any good? How 'bout bringin' a hat full of eggs?" He paused, a devilish grin appeared, "Bring extra eggs; we'll take turns hurlin' them at Watson's barn. Who knows, an egg might finish off that eyesore and put it out of misery. Who'd think a blamed ole chicken could be credited for savin' Watson's herd?"

The laughter floated out the general store, off the porch, into the dirt road. Guthrie, the Proprietor, knew this served as a welcomed sound to one and all. Curious folks were always drawn to the store to investigate the source of such uproarious gaiety. Even though hard work frequently dampened the spirits of the mountaineers, this band of Brothers always managed to afford a hearty laugh. Many a night Guthrie thanked God for these lively friends.

Shortly, the lives of everyone in the mountain would be touched by this new Preacher in ways they never anticipated.

THE WEDDING SERENADE

Sixteen-year old Tiny Carlton ran home, anxious to ask her Momma, Ole Tiny, about something she heard at the general store. Ole Tiny had sent her daughter to fetch a spool of white thread. After all, crafting a wedding dress for Baby Tiny could not be trusted to a spool of aged, maybe rotten, thread.

When Baby Tiny entered the general store, she saw the Brothers, Arville, Turner, Lawrence, Clyde, Willie, and Darrell, sitting by the front door. Today, each Brother whittled with their sharpened pocketknives. The shavings of the crooked sticks fell carelessly into piles onto the wooden floor.

Turner spoke, "Baby Tiny, whatcha doin' out and about this early? I heared tell you folks don't never get up 'til the sun is high in the sky." The Brothers knew that was not true. The Carlton's kept their noses to the grindstone season after weary season. The Carlton's had two sons and after ten years were blessed with a daughter, Baby Tiny. The sons built small houses in the clearing of the 'new ground.' The community helped prepare the land by cutting trees, grubbing up roots and bushes, and hauling off large stones. The highlight of the laborious task occurred at the end of the days with a bonfire to burn the cut brush. The tales spun around those fires fascinated young and old.

Ironically, in school Ole Tiny weighed about the same as a young heifer and was dubbed the name of 'Tiny' due to her ample size. The name stuck throughout her brief years of schooling, education being considered a low priority for a mountain girl. Common knowledge was that 'it don't take no book learnin' to raise a family.' When she bore a daughter, she became Ole Tiny, and her daughter inherited the name of Baby Tiny.

Much to the delight of the Brothers, Baby Tiny turned scarlet and visibly uncomfortable as she answered, "Momma sent me for somethin' she be a needin'."

The gathering of men exchanged looks, as if to ask, 'who's gonna jump on this easy prey?' Arville took the challenge, "What's so all-fired important to walk to the store for this morning?"

Baby Tiny tried ignoring the men as she made her way past the fabrics and threads. She hoped they'd let it go. Her fate had been cast. Mr. Guthrie moved closer to offer assistance. "They're just funnin'. What can I get for ya?"

"Momma needs thread." She quickly added, "White thread."

He held two white spools, "Does Ole Tiny want heavy cotton thread or this finer thread?"

"I don't rightly know. Momma didn't say."

Mr. Guthrie offered, "What's she sewing?"

Without thinking, Baby Tiny blurted, "My weddin' dress! I'm gittin' married Sunday after next, directly after the altar call. And that new Preacher better show up by then! He's movin' here any day now." Her proud smile faded as she realized the announcement was loud enough for every set of ears in the general store. She bit her bottom lip, but couldn't retract it.

The Brothers erupted into laughter, anticipating the fun this promised. Turner spoke up, "Baby Tiny, ya ain't no more than a baby, ain't got no business gettin' hitched."

Willie chimed in, "Ya ain't even a woman yet. Ya oughta stay on at your Daddy's farm til yer growed up, then go to lookin' at the men folk."

"I am too a woman," she snapped.

He continued, "Yer still wet behind the ears. Who ya marryin' up with anyhow?"

Defensively, she told the curious men, "I'm fixin' to be Mrs. Claude Moretz."

The brothers felt it necessary to chastise her for that foolish decision. With sincerity Darrell said, "Girl, that ole coot's old enough to be yer Paw! What are ya' thinkin'? Surely to goodness, ya can do better'n that."

"I'm marrying Claude Walter, the son, not his Poppa. Do ya think I'm looney in the head?" she spat in frustration at the meddlesome Brothers.

Defensively, she stamped her foot, "You can smoke that in yer corncob pipes."

Relieved to hear she wasn't marrying someone nigh onto their own age, Clyde told her, "Well, I thought ya'd be crazy if ya tied the knot with the likes of that ole man. If he'd got you, I'd declare him to be the slyest fox sniffin' round the chicken coup."

Willie could scarcely contain himself to add to the gossip, "Ya know that new Preacher may not even perform a weddin'. He might not believe in it. It's said that he don't take to the man and woman kind of love."

Guthrie defended the absent Parson, "Willie, shame on you! That's an ignorant thing to say, even for you!"

"Well, I'm just saying . . . I heared tell that he . . . ."

Guthrie halted such talk, "Hush your mouth! I don't want to hear another word 'bout that mess. Nobody say another word about that or I might run ya outta the store . . . for good." They knew Guthrie would never do such a thing, but they let it drop—for now.

Tiny turned back to the business of purchasing the thread. Momma instructed her to hurry and not dillydally. The green beans had to be picked and canned today. Those rows of beans seemed to go on forever as they'd hunker down to start the back-breaking chore. Momma promised to put up some jars for Claude and her. Momma's theory, 'these'll taste mighty good when the snow blows hither and yon. A wife's gotta keep her man happy. There ain't never been a man happy when his belly growls from hunger pangs.'

With the precious bag containing a single spool, Baby Tiny made her way toward the door. With an innocent smile she asked the Brothers if they would come to see her marry up. The men were noncommittal. Clyde told her, "But don't ya be a frettin' that pretty little noggin of yer'n. We'll see ya' later on your weddin' day."

Puzzled, she inquired, "If ya ain't comin' to the weddin', then when?"

Clyde stopped whittling, and let loose a belly-shaking laugh, "At yer serenade, girl! Wouldn't miss it for all the bear hides roamin' these hills."

The first words out of Baby Tiny's mouth to her Momma when she arrived home, "Them Brothers at the general store laughed at me and said something 'bout a serenade. Momma, what are they a talkin' about?"

Momma placed the wooden spool of white thread on the table after inspecting it. "Baby Tiny, we got all day to chew the fat whilst we work. Grab them bushel baskets in the woodshed and let's hit the garden, lest it gets any hotter. Fetch my straw bonnet off the hook in the shed. I don't want to cook my brains." As they made their way to the garden, Momma continued, "Your Poppa and brothers are mendin' the fence where that blamed jersey cow busted out again last night. The grass seems greener on the other side of the fence. She was grazin', jest the other side, as if to say 'ya can't build no fence to keep me in' when they went to drive in the herd in this mornin'. If she didn't give the richest milk in the herd, I'd be tellin' your Poppa to butcher her. That'd teach that whipper snapper to get out ever' chance she gets." Ole Tiny slapped the worn hat on her head. "Lord knows, there's always a dozen things to do in a day's time. On the Great Judgment Day, we won't be done with our work." Ole Tiny paused and drew a labored breath, "We'll probably still be chasin' that hard-headed jersey cow when we hear the trumpet."

As Ole Tiny and Baby Tiny began their task, the conversation between Mother and Daughter ensued. "Momma, now tell me, what's a serenade? What are them ole men talkin' about, why'd they take on so?"

While Ole Tiny was a fine worker and loving Mother, she was not a diplomatic communicator. Ole Tiny added to the stress when she snickered, "Serenades are more pleasure for us'ns, than for you'ns. Ya gotta bear it."

Determined for answers, Baby Tiny pryed, "But what the dickens is it?"

Ole Tiny began, "Been goin' on in these mountains long as I 'member. On your weddin' night, a gang of men folk and their women show up at yer house, 'bout half an hour after you cut the lights off. They'll beat on the door 'til ya open it. They nab the Bride, put ya in a big galvanized washtub, won't be no water in the tub though. The men hoist the tub onto their shoulders and beat the sides of it with sticks as they carry ya off."

Baby Tiny gasped in horror, "Claude ain't gonna let that happen."

Momma appeared proud as punch to complete the story, "He can't. They plop Claude smack dab on a big log and the men put the log on their shoulders and carry him off into the woods too. They jerk and bounce the log, so's to make it a powerful rough ride for Claude's manhood. 'Course there's a lot of pokin' fun at ya both as yer jostled along." Ole Tiny spit a stream of snuff and wiped the corner of her wrinkled mouth with the back of her dirt-encrusted hand. Remembering her own serenade brought a smile to her sweaty face.

Baby Tiny stood, defiantly placing her hands on her narrow hips, "We ain't gonna open the door when they come. That'll put a stop to them rowdy shenanigans."

"That'd be like tryin' to stop a stampede, girl. It won't do no good. They'll take the door plum off the hinges to git to drag the lovebirds straight from the nest. That'd make it worse."

"Momma, that's awful! I don't want them to do that."

"It ain't so bad. We've all lived through it. You're spring chickens, it won't hurt ya's none. Ya know, there ain't much to celebrate here in these hills. We cain't none miss a chance to frolic and kick up our heels. Love oughta be a thing to celebrate."

"But, Momma, it don't sound like no celebration!"

"No. No. It is! They tote ya to somebody's house and drop the washtub and log. I'm here to tell ya, they won't be droppin' it none too gentle, but then there's a weddin' feast. Ever'body brings their best grub."

Baby Tiny resumed pulling the ripened beans from the vines. She expelled a long, slow sigh, resolving to accept her doom. If every other couple survived this humiliation, she reckoned she and Claude Walter could.

Momma added one last thought. "Just ya's remember this, Baby Tiny, and it's the gospel truth. If'n the folks didn't love you'ns, they'd not be serenadin'. You and Claude Walter will 'member the weddin' night the longest day ya got breath. These here families have know'd ya both since ya were sprouts. It's just the mountain way of showin' how much they care for both ya two youngins."

Baby Tiny rolled her eyes and gritted her teeth. There was no changing mountain tradition. She'd witnessed that fact her entire life.

3

THE JACK LEG
PREACHER ARRIVES

The anticipated arrival of the new preacher consumed the conversations of the mountain residents. Word spread that the young Preacher was moving from a northeastern city and had 'peculiar' ways. Expectation grew to the point that when two met, regardless of where, after the customary greeting they'd say, 'here yet?' The reply: 'Nobody's seen hide nor hair.' Some included, 'reckon, he turned tail and run smack dab back to the highfaluting city life?' The nameless Parson agreed to serve as Pastor of the flock at the Greenbed Baptist Church while authoring a theological study and assist with teaching duties at the one-room school. Many of the old timers remained loyal to the Primitive Baptist Church. Nothing changed in their church in sixty years; they liked it that way. After all, God didn't change, and human nature didn't change.

The Brothers were members of the Primitive Baptist, however, their attendance waned and waxed more frequently than the winds varied throughout the rugged mountain ranges. The new preacher provided hours of speculation, especially among the Primitive membership frequenting the general store. Although the Brothers knew nothing about the new Parson, they referred to him as 'The Jack Leg Preacher.'

After all but dismissing the hope of getting to meet him, the Brothers gathered in the store, sitting in a semi-circle in wooden straight-backed chairs to exchange tall tales and engage in a checker game. They noted a young stranger heading to the general store. His dark wavy hair, piercing brown eyes and a pleasant smile permanently plastered upon his face. He took the steps two at a time. The Brothers ceased their conversation in mid sentence to listen. Leaning closer, they raised their heads and looked straight at the newcomer, scrutinizing his every movement with a keen interest. The young man felt the sets of eyes on him and turned to face the Brothers, tipped his hat and smiled at the gaping men in the semi-circle. Clyde, Darrell, and Lawrence nodded at him in unison, listening, watching and waiting.

With an extended right hand toward the Proprietor, "Mr. Guthrie, pleased to meet you. I'm Gerhart Lawson, new Pastor at the Baptist Church. Word on the street says you're the first person I need to meet for a few supplies for setting up my meager housekeeping. I'm not much of a cook but need a little grub to get by on." Reverend Lawson did not miss the raised eyebrows of the Brothers when they heard the confirmation that there wasn't a Mrs. Preacher.

Pumping his hand with a hearty shake, Mr. Guthrie greeted his new Preacher, "It's a pleasure. We've been without far too long. Our congregation attended the Primitive Baptist. It left something to be desired. I missed the music somethin' awful. Music is like the angels joinin' in on the service." Guthrie looked toward the Brothers, "Sorry, fellers, it's just the way I feel. Ya' all can keep your Primitive ways and we'll still be on speakin' terms."

"Mr. Guthrie, I'm honored that you're in the flock I'll shepherd." Small snickers escaped from Willie and Turner. Anytime Turner was caught stepping over the line, his eyes widened, and at this moment they were twice their normal size. Reverend Lawson picked up the items on his list, paid, and headed toward the door.

As he walked across the creaking wooden floor, he debated the best way to handle "the Brothers." Forewarned of their sarcasm, he took the middle road and stopped to greet them, "Pleased to meet you. I'm sure we'll be running into each other. As you already know, I'm ..." for emphasis he deliberately paused, "I'm the new . . . Jack Leg Preacher at the Baptist Church."

Willie cleared his throat before making his observation, "I thought you'd be a might older and settled. Why, Preacher, you're still wet behind the ears," one of Willie's favorite clichés.

"I'll take that as a compliment to my youthfulness. Sounds as though you expected a dried up old prune of a minister." Willie had no idea how to respond. He couldn't decipher if the Preacher joked with him, insulted him, or simply made a statement.

The Reverend smiled at the gathering of men and exited the general store. As he closed the door behind him, he offered a quick prayer, "Lord, forgive me. The temptation to get the upper hand with the Brothers from the 'get go' proved too much to resist. I promise to do better at showing Your love . . . next time."

At first, the Brothers sat stunned, then laughter erupted. Clyde said, "I wish the Primitive Baptist could've grabbed the likes of that little feller. He'd bring life into religion."

The town continued to be a buzz over Reverend Lawson. Curisoty ran rampant. The rumor mill worked overtime. The Parson posted signs announcing seven days of tent meetings for the following week. The upcoming tent meetings dominated every conversation. It had been fifteen long years since the last tent meeting. The older mountaineers recalled the vivacious preacher that preached 'hell fire and brimstone' messages, slamming his fists on the makeshift pulpit. Back in the day, the congregation sat mesmerized for endless hours.

The second time the Brothers saw the new Parson at Guthrie's General Store, Willie, Clyde, Arville, and Darrell occupied the chairs. Reverend Lawson entered with a hearty wave of the hand and smile to match.

"Mornin' Preacher," Arville called out.

"This is the day the Lord has made, let us rejoice and be glad in it!"

Silence. They'd been taught to respect the Lord's Holy Words. They feared the wrath of God, and held a healthy respect for His punishment. The Primitive Baptist frequently preached about the wrath of God, seldom mentioning the love of God.

"Are you gentlemen going to join us at the tent meeting next week? I trust the weather will cooperate."

Willie spoke up, "All depends."

"Depends on what?" Reverend Lawson asked. Distractedly, he studied his crumbled list.

Willie twisted in his seat before responding, turned his head sideways, squinted his bad eye tightly closed, "Depends on what kind of a show ya put on. What can ya do?"

"A show? The only 'show' is what we all present to our Lord. We are all there to worship Him, and He should be the only spectator, the worshippers are doing the presentations."

Willie continued, the others snickered, "How many times a night are ya gonna jump it?"

"Jump what?" The perplexed young Reverend asked.

"Last Preacher holdin' a tent meetin' in these parts jumped the pulpit. That feller never missed. He'd do it onct a night, and if he got extra fired up, he'd do it twice. That's what ever'body went to see. I'm here to tell ya, it'll draw a crowd. Word travels like wild fire here and they'll come early to git a front-row seat."

"The Good Lord can draw His own crowd without my jumping anything! I hardly see how that fits with worship. I'm curious, how does one jump the pulpit?"

"Well sir, he'd be preachin along, and you'd never know when it might come. All at onct, in the middle of a word, just like a scared rabbit flushed out of its nest, over the top he'd leap and land clear down on the tother side. Lickety Split!" He smacked his hands together for emphasis. "What's more, he always landed square dab on his feet. It was somethin' to behold."

Reverend Lawson looked puzzled and only managed to say, "I don't know why anyone would be compelled to do such a thing."

The Brothers laughed. They felt his tent meeting would be a flop, but respected the young Preacher's enthusiasm. One thing for certain, the pulpit jumping drew folks away from the typical back row choice seats.

Willie did not relent, "Why would anyone go and sit on them hard benches with no backs without the Preacher puttin' on a show? I'm tellin' ya, that other Preacher used to cut a shine. The folks loved it, looked forward to it. Preacher, you're gonna break hearts if'n ya don't jump that pulpit. You're young and spry. I bet ever' penny in my pocket that ya can do it if ya's to put your mind to it. Shootfire, ya got all week to practice. Think how good ya'd be, better'n that other feller if ya' was to practice right diligently. He had short stubby, sawed-off legs, you got them granddaddy long legs."

Unamused, he shook his head, "I appreciate your concern, but there will still be no pulpit jumping, leaping, or any other carnival sideshows at this tent meeting. Why don't you come, bring your families, and see for yourselves. Change can be a good thing if you give it a try."

One of the Brothers grunted. No promises were made. Reverend Lawson selected his items and made for the door, but not before extending one final invitation. "I would consider it a favor if you would attend just one service. I'm not sure what you expect of a Jack Leg Preacher, but I'll do my best to live up to it."

"I tell ya, I like that Jack Leg Preacher. I'll declare, if he ain't got the spunk, I don't know who does," Clyde said.

Arville asked, very sincerely, "Do ya' think we oughta go and see what it's all about?"

Darrell immediately answered that he wouldn't be going, whether or not the Jack Leg jumped the pulpit. Turner and Clyde both shook their heads, "We ain't' goin' neither. He's gonna preach hellfire and get people to come forward, and then he'll take 'em down to the creek and dunk 'em. Nothin' against him, but I'm not wastin' my time. Besides, I'm still not clear on that . . . that . . . other business we ain't supposed to mention in Guthrie's presence. You know, the funny business."

For the next several days, the Reverend Lawson made house calls, working his way through the community inviting folks to the revival tent meeting. He visited from practically sunrise, to after sunset. He diligently met and greeted the community. The mountaineers admired his persistence and dedication. He walked from homestead to backwoods shack, covering as much territory as possible in the remaining days. It didn't matter which congregation folks were aligned with, if any, he invited them, without apologies. His winsome way appealed to every generation, his charismatic personality attracted the young and old and all in between.

Following the first night of the meeting, everyone was interested in getting the scoop. Curiosity did about kill all those not in attendance. The unofficial word was that the meeting was poorly attended, but the Reverend delivered his sermon without discouragement, and he 'carried on' with great enthusiasm, although no pulpit jumping or the likes.

The Preacher didn't appear at the general store for several days. He continued to visit and invite up and down the dirt roads, long lanes, crossing fields, knocking on screen doors. On the fourth day of the revival, Darrell and Clyde paused from their conversation out front of the gas station. The gasoline pumped, yet they continued to chew the fat with the owner, Hubert Cheeks. Hubert never disappointed his patrons. They suspected Hubert conjured up these tall tales rather than sleeping at night, but the tales always served as great entertainment. Hubert always displayed a broad smile which covered his round face. He was a gentle giant of a man. He abruptly halted, "Darrell, look yonder, the Jack Leg Preacher hightailin' it like his britches are on fire. Let's find out the meanin' of this."

As soon as they entered the general store, they covered their noses to stifle the foul, disgusting odor, radiating from the Preacher's direction. They dared to edge forward a few steps to make the final determination. Sure enough, Reverend Lawson reeked! Clyde asked, "Preacher, what've ya been

17

doin'? Ya smell worse than my barnyard." The Brothers noted that Rev. Lawson retrieved a large box of detergent for washing clothes from the shelf and made haste to the front of the store to pay. His clothes were, indeed, the source of the pungent odor. "What in the world happened?"

Reverend Lawson turned to face Clyde and Darrell, the front of his clothes covered with the awful smelling deposits of what they first assumed to be manure. Holding their noses, they backed away from him.

Without a moment of hesitation, Reverend Lawson answered. "If you'll bring your whole family, brothers, sisters and their husbands, wives, children, in-laws and outlaws, everybody but the family dogs, to the meeting tonight, I'll tell you a true tale that you won't believe. First, you must promise me, or you'll never know what happened this afternoon. Besides, your families will fill the tent and I can take the rest of the day off from visiting and promoting the meeting and start scrubbing myself and clothes."

Darrell and Clyde exchanged looks. Darrell quietly said, "I don't hold much stock in church goin'. Churches are for hatchin', matchin', and dispatchin'. Takin' the new babies, marryin' up and sendin' people to the grave."

The young Reverend turned back to the counter, "Well, then I don't hold much stock in telling you the best account you'll hear this year." He noted their interest peaked.

"Come on Darrell, it won't hurt ya to go to church jes' onct, whata ya say? It looks like a mighty good tale."

Darrell relented. Reverend Lawson extended his hand to shake hands to seal the deal. Both Darrell and Clyde quickly withdrew their hands and stuffed them safely in their pockets. Clyde ventured, "We ain't much wantin to touch yer hand, Preacher. Ya gotta take our word for it. Guthrie'll vouch for our word. It's as good as gold."

"Alright then, I consider it a gentleman's promise." Darrell and Clyde nodded in agreement, anxious for this story to unfold. Even Guthrie expectantly dared a step closer, not to miss a word. Unconsciously, Darrell fanned the air beneath his nose to draw a fresh breath.

"Well, you know I've been calling on all parishioners, as well as everyone else in the mountain and valley, inviting them to the revival." The Brothers nodded. Their anticipation dulled their sense of smell to the point they could stand beside the Preacher without pinching their noses closed. He continued, "I went to call on Joe Neal Watson. We sat down out in the field by his old barn. After a while, well, gentlemen, it's a little embarrassing to admit. Nature called. Joe Neal told me he had an outhouse behind the barn for such emergencies. I went in, sat down, and after a few minutes, I heard a crackling sound. I wasn't in a position to run out and see what was happening, if you know what I mean. So, I sat there, still as a mouse. That old outhouse began leaning more and cracking. Before I knew what happened, it collapsed, and down I went into the . . . the . . . the storage area."

Clyde held up his hand to interrupt him with a question, "Preacher, are ya tellin' us that ya fell in the poop heap?"

Guthrie gasped at the crudeness, but all three men knew it was the truth. Not a one of them could control the outburst of laughter upon the realization. The Preacher nodded, confirming. All were wiping tears from their eyes. No one minded the smell now.

"Don't forget your promise. I expect a full tent tonight. I kept my end of the bargain. I'll be looking for each one of you and yours."

Still laughing, Darrell said, "Ya gonna have time to scrub up before tonight, aren't ya?"

"The Lord shall cleanse me whiter than snow." That initiated a second round of laughter.

Clyde confirmed the promise in between gasping for breath, "Preacher, count on us bein' there. It takes a real man to confess that story. Ya' won't even have to jump the pulpit. Ya done won the grand prize for the best Preacher show ever . . . hands down. And, to show our goodwill t'wards ya, we'll be obliged to take ya snipe huntin' soon." Reverend Lawson nodded, Darrell snickered. Mr. Guthrie sighed and shook his finger at Clyde although wild horses wouldn't keep Guthrie from this particular snipe hunting adventure!

4

INQUISITION OF THE PREACHER

Reverend Lawson leaned his trim, muscular frame across the scratched, thick glass top of the counter in the general store. "Mr. Guthrie, how long have you run the general store?"

"Preacher, what kind of question is that? Tarnation! That's the same as askin' a man how old he is," Guthrie chuckled. "Cuz, ya see, I was born here in the back room, raised in this store started helping my Paw stock these same old wooden shelves when I was nothing more than a pollywog."

"Have you seen many changes throughout the years, changes with the community?"

Guthrie pensively rubbed his chin, "Funny thing about folks living in the mountains. I'll declare, the mountains get into your system and you'd never think of livin' no where else. Most of these folks been here for generations, on the very same plots of land, no need to ask nobody where he's from, he'll look at ya' strange like and tell ya' he's from down the mountain a piece, or a hop, skip and a jump down the tother side."

The door to the store opened, in strolled Nathaniel Green and two of the Brothers. It didn't matter which combination of the six brothers, all were labeled 'the Brothers.' Reverend Lawson lowered his head and allowed a slight sigh to escape, representing his disappointment. He hoped for a few private minutes of Mr. Guthrie's attention. It hadn't taken long to surmise Guthrie to be a straight shooter, who served as an ally to everyone. On the other hand, he'd concluded 'the Brothers,' could, and would, prove to be a challenge.

Guthrie looked at the Reverend, winked and immediately greeted the men, calling them by name to help reinforce the Parson's memory. "Nathaniel, why are you hangin' out with the likes of Clyde and Turner on this fair-to-middlin day?" Each man in the general store knew he meant no disrespect. They'd been fast friends since childhood. They were beholding to each other, and remembered the lean years of the Great Depression, banding the tight-knit community even tighter as they assisted one another.

Nathaniel smiled, displaying the wide gap of a missing front tooth. He removed his tattered felt hat by the brim and covered his heart with it. "Guthrie, be kind to my old companion. It's Turner's birthday and he's gettin' up thar in years—way, way up thar," he pointed toward the ceiling.

Reverend Lawson turned to face the three men, and extending his hand to shake Turner's. "Happy Birthday to you, Mr. Turner. I'm not going to ask how many years you been celebrating birthdays since Mr. Guthrie just finished raking me over the coals for that today."

Clyde walked toward the stools and chairs around the checkerboard, "Preacher, come over here and sit a spell. We'll talk turkey." Clyde noticed the questioning expression slowly creep cross Reverend Lawson's face. "Oops, I forgot, you're a city slicker. Let's talk business, preacher business." Clyde waved at the others, "Come on, join us. It's a good chance to find out what kind of pumpkin juice the Preacher's made of, gather 'round." Clyde pointed toward a stool and Reverend Lawson felt summoned to the witness stand, facing the three men.

Reverend Lawson looked at Guthrie and clinched his eyes shut for a second before joining this inquisition. Guthrie smiled and gave him a slight nod, which he interpreted as his sanction.

Clyde wasted no time in opening the line of questioning. "Preacher, you're an educated man. Ya know, not many of us went to school much past the fourth or fifth grade. How do ya' think God compares us?"

"I'm not sure I understand that question, because God doesn't compare any two people. He desires a personal relationship with each one of us, as an individual."

"But, Preacher, you read the Bible and don't get stuck on them five dollar words. Don't ya think God 'preciates that more than the likes of us who can barely read?"

"Well, Sir," the Reverend was very careful not to appear condescending as he truthfully answered, "God isn't as interested in the words that spill out of our mouth, or how many chapters we read in His Word, or even how many verses we can quote. He's interested in what is in our hearts. It's my belief that He very much cares how we treat our fellowman. Each of His creations is special. He loves each with the exact same love. You know, Jesus died on the cross for every single one of us."

Clyde pondered that for a moment, shook his head slowly in agreement before formulating his next question. "Before we hitch our wagons to any horse of yours, I got somethin' else I need to know. Ya didn't bring no wife with ya. Why is that?

"A good reason for that, because I don't have a wife."

Not quite the information Clyde fished for, "Why ain't ya got one?"

"A straightforward question, deserves a straightforward answer. It isn't my time to have a wife. I haven't met the right woman yet."

All the men in the store beamed. Clyde looked relieved, "Preacher, ya don't know how glad I am to hear that. There's been suspicious talk about ya and questioning if ya were interested in women . . . or men."

"Why would anyone say that? You all don't even know me! Thank goodness, we cleared that up today."

Clyde did not admit that many speculated about that. Satisfied that he had the truth, it could be put to rest now. He left the subject and forged on. "I've heard it said, and I'm not saying I hold to this, that only white people have souls."

Guthrie took immediate offense to the question, "Shut your mouth wide open! Ya' mean to tell me ya' don't think Elihu and Willamae; and Shad and Annie Fisher and their boys and the little youngins don't have souls? I'm ashamed to the bone how our ancestors treated the blacks, not just here, but all over."

Reverend Lawson shook his head, "Oh no, I do not hold to that idea at all! As I understand the Bible, God created us equal. The ground was level at the foot of the cross. Again, no one person is better than the next, regardless of wealth, power, knowledge, or color. All are equal in God's sight as far as His loving care for them. By the way, I wasn't aware of any any black families in the area?"

"Good people, keep to themselves, never bother nobody," added Nathaniel.

"How do they live? Why haven't I seen them at the store, mill, or the school?"

Guthrie uncomfortably squirmed. "Preacher, it's like this. We worked out a deal, and mind ya', it ain't 'cuz I minded at all, but when they need somethin', they tap on my back window after I've closed down the store. I never do nothin' but read or listen to the radio at night, it don't make no never mind to me to be interrupted. They seem to like doin' their tradin' that way. If there's any mail for them, I hold it 'til their visit."

Clyde interjected with an additional thought, "I 'spect I got just one more question for ya. It's a humdinger too."

To ease the tension, the Preacher said, "We may as well have it. I'm about to commence to preaching here any minute."

Shocking all of the men with his brazenness, Clyde retaliated, "Shoot fire and save the matches, we don't want none of that monkey business. I reckon I'll jump right on in then, and git up the gumption to ask it." The men laughed at the good-natured humor. "What do ya' think of war? Do ya' believe in it? I mean are ya' for it, or agin it? All that killin' and takin' of lives? I listen to the radio every night, seems to me to be gettin' worse every week."

"Let me see, what do I think of war. Mr. Clyde, you strike me as a no nonsense kind of man, so I'll be blunt with you. I hate war, same as the next man. Am I for it or against it? It has a place in our history. There are times it cannot be ignored. Justice must prevail, and unfortunately, sometimes that means at the cost of declaring war against a country. It is our duty to defend freedom, our country, and our citizens, and . . . ."

Nathaniel interrupted, "Preacher, have ya ever kill't a man?"

Shocked, he retorted, "Absolutely not!"

"How would ya defend anything lessen ya could shoot to kill? Way I see it, protectin' is shootin', and that don't mean woundin' 'em. It means killin' 'em dead as a doornail." Nathaniel expressed pride in contributing a question that caused the Preacher to wiggle on the small stool.

"I have never even shot at anyone! My uncle once showed me how to load and hold a gun." He noted an immediate exchange of snears from the gathering of men. "Let me put it this way, I feel it's every able-bodied man's duty to protect this great nation, whatever it takes. Besides, God equipped men in the Bible to fight, and win. He gave the battle plans to Joshua and guaranteed victory for the Israelites, as long as they faithfully served Him. Some of those battles, God specifically instructed Joshua to kill every single thing that drew breath, every man, woman, child, cow, goat, everything. That's some serious killing. Our Lord is a God of justice. If the time presents itself, I would trust Him to lead me through making those decisions."

Guthrie shook his head, "I hope all this talk of war over yonder never comes about. I listen, same as ever' one of you, ever' night to the President on the radio. It don't sound none too hopeful to me. If war breaks out, I hope we stay out of it."

Each man was lost in thought of the conflicts broadcast daily and wondered how, or if, it would affect their individual lives. Reverend Lawson broke the pensive gray cloud heavily hoovering over the room. "Did I pass? I answered every single one of your inquiries, now tell me how did I do?"

Clyde slapped the Parson on the back, "Ya done good. We needed to know what we were dealin' with here. Don't hold it agin' us."

"No offense taken, Mr. Clyde, I welcome all questions and wish everyone would be as straight forward and honest. It seems only fair that I get to ask you a question about religion."

That might have intimidated most men, not Clyde, "I'm ready. Let's have it, square between the eyes. Shoot. Well, no, don't shoot! Now that ya' told me ya think ya could shoot a man, I'll be more careful in sayin' that to the likes of you."

"How important is religion to a person's life?"

"Preacher, I ain't talkin' for nobody but myself. Ever person ought to come up with a different answer, I reckon."

"You're right about that, Mr. Clyde. Let's start with you?"

"Me and mine try to do what the Good Book says. We raised our youngins by them rules. Way I see it, it's 'tween me and God. He knows my name and I know His. It needs to be simple enough for a little one to understand, but bold enough for the strongest man on the mountain to grab with his mighty bear-claw grip and hold tight. It's gotta be good enough to get me through all the storms of life; and walk hand-in-hand with me through the valley of the shadow of death, 'cuz that's when it counts the most. Yep, if I can be happy with bein' with God out in the fields, and visitin' with Him ever' day; knowing He made ever'thing my eyes behold, and be ready to look Him in the eyes and call Him my Friend after I close my eyes for the last time in this life, then I got braggin' rights on a good religion. That old-time religion we heard our Grandpaws talk about can't be beat with a stick. I don't reckon I see any need to change it."

Reverend Lawson felt his throat constricting, "I couldn't have said it better. Would you mind if I used that in a sermon sometime?"

"No, Preacher, help yerself. Anytime ya' want me to help with a sermon, jest come over and I'll dish up some more good stuff that'll preach from the pulpit. Fellows, bet ya' a plug nickel ya' never thought I'd be writin' the Jack Leg Preacher's sermons."

All the men enjoyed the joke, including Reverend Lawson. His laughter was joy overflowing from his cup. He'd never heard anything expressed more perfectly, or more succinctly. Today, he learned a valuable lesson. He knew these mountainfolk, while having a simplistic faith, were much deeper than he imagined. He smiled as he thought, 'this shouldn't just be preached from the pulpit, but taught in the finest theological schools in the world.' This was a faith not described in a textbook, or preached to a congregation. Today, he'd sat at the feet of a wise teacher and heard a great truth at the general store, the greatest truth.

5

REVENGE—RIGHTING A WRONG

Early spring, the appointed time to repair and reinforce fences around the perimeter of the fields in anticipation of the planting season, their livelihood depended on the security of the fence.This created heavier business and commotion at the lumber yard, conveniently located cattycornered from the general store. The lumber yard always geared up for the extra business by stocking up on fencing supplies. Today, a group of men stood at the end of the aisle complaining about the increase in prices. Of course, some of the older men equally focused on how much more difficult digging with the post-hole digger became each year.

Jim Green entered the store and rather than joining in the conversation, selected nails and barbed wire. His entire adult life, folks compared him to Honest Abe Lincoln for two reasons; his lanky heighth and deep set eye sockets created a hollow look to his thin face. His whisper-soft voice complimented the gentle personality. Secondly, he was as honest as the day long. Young and old referred to him as Uncle Jim. His pale blue eyes typically twinkled, accompanied by an inviting smile. This day, he appeared visibly upset as he mumbled under his breath, and uncharacteristically kicked a scrap of wood out of his path.

Clyde left the group of men to inquire. Putting his arm around Jim's shoulder, "What's wrong with ya t'day? Jim, ya don't look right. Ya look lower than a snake's belly in a wagon rut." When Jim looked up from the bag of nails clutched tightly in his hands, his eyes reflected a mixture of anger, frustration and defeat. Jim, a bachelor who lived with his aging Mother was the one child, out of seven brothers and sisters, to care for his Mother. They got by, with nothing to spare. Jim's hands shook as he poured another scoop of nails into the paper sack for weighing.

"Clyde, I'll tell ya the God's truth, ya know this to be true too, I'm a peace-lovin' man, never bother nobody. But today at the mill, I believe I coulda kill't that Claude Taugel. For some time, I been suspecting he overcharges for chop for the cows; and cheats me at the scales when he weighs the corn and grain I bring in to sell. But today, I caught him red handed and I called him out on it. Know what he done?"

Clyde shook his head, anxious to hear the details. Jim continued, "That lowdown man looked me right in the eyeballs and lied to my face. Now, tell me how could a man do such a thing? I never cheated a man in my life, best I recollect. It was all I could do not to pick up a shovel off the ground and bash him up side of his lying head."

They stood in silence for a moment, unaware that other men migrated closer to hear. Without acknowledging any of the group, Jim said, "I don't know what I'll do. Taugel's got the only mill to grind the corn into chop for the cows; but with God as my witness, I don't see how I can go back there and let him cheat me again, like I knowed he done today. He didn't weigh that corn right. I know he's been keeping some aside and not givin' me all of it back in feed. I work too hard to give it to the cheatin' likes of that sorry excuse of a man. Besides, it's gonna be a long stretch 'til the next crop of corn is ready for pickin'. I can't afford to give him a dried up corncob and certainly no corn for him to resell for profit." He adjusted his hat, "I ain't even got the seeds in the ground yet for a new crop and my corncrib is gettin' bare."

Clyde listened to every word, hurt to see his friend upset. And if Jim said he'd been cheated, you could stake your life on that being the absolute truth. "Those thoughts crossed my mind a time or two about Taugel. He's a slick one. I thought he'd cheat any one of us if'n he thought he'd get away with it. Anybody that shakes hands with him ought to count their fingers quick to be sure they still got 'em all. I'm gonna put my mind to this and talk to my Brothers. We'll come up with somethin' to right things fair and square. Now, don't ya worry none about it." They shook hands. Neither man counted their fingers after the trusted handshake.

As promised, the Brothers discussed it as they sat in the familiar semicircle at the general store. Guthrie chimed in, totally disgusted, "I don't know how Claude Taugel could cheat his neighbors like that and ever look 'em in the eyes again. I hope to live long enough to see this come back to Claude and hit him square in the head."

Turner widened his eyes to give his statement more emphasis, "We could see to it that it comes back to Taugel, sooner than later, if'n ya know what I mean. When we take corn or grain to be ground, we ought to make certain it weighs a plenty. I got a rusty ole anvil I can scarcely lift. Somethin' like that ought to be tucked down under in ever' load we take. For cheatin' Jim, he deserves every piece of junk we can find. We'll leave all the busted pieces and let him worry about disposin' of them." The Brothers agreed that would give Taugel a dose of his own medicine. Besides, he'd probably cheated other unsuspecting patrons. They felt obliged to even the score. They'd share their idea with other selected, trusted neighbors. Yep, Claude Taugel would be plenty sorry he ever cheated Jim, or anybody for that matter. Furthermore, they determined that if several went together each time, Taugel would not have the courage to challenge them or make an accusation. And by the time he caught onto what happened, they'd be ready to call it even. Taugel would weigh the loads of corn or wheat before grinding it, and he'd pay a pretty penny.

Needless to say, after two weeks, it was amazing how accurate Claude Taugel's weighing devices became, and the 'extra' income each farmer received was gladly passed onto an appreciative recipient, Jim Green. Turner added, "Have ya noticed that Taugel has been scarcer than hen's teeth of late, ain't nobody seen him. He's ashamed to show his face." While most of the men congregated in Guthrie's General Store laughed and enjoyed the victory, Arville scarcely smiled.

"What's the matter with ya, Arville, didn't it serve Claude right? Ain't it good to see Cheatin Claude get his what's for? We done his Momma a favor, somethin' she never accomplished, we made an honest man outta him," Luther said as he patted Arville's back.

Arville nodded, "It's good to see a wrong made right. I'm right proud we had a hand in it. Ain't nobody ought to be cheated, but 'specially a man like Jim Green." The men exchanged glances, each person noticed Arville's pale, solemn face. Something wasn't right. They felt it in their bones. The tight-knit Brothers hoped their imaginations tricked them.

6

MENOPAUSE SEIZES
THE MOUNTAIN

After exchanging a few tall tales at Guthrie's General Store, Clyde and Turner settled into a game of checkers as the others observed and offered advice. An uneasy look claimed Clyde's face. He snuffed out his cigar on the bottom of his shoe and abruptly stood to take his leave. Turner looked up at his brother's tall frame in surprise, "Clydie, where's the fire? Ya' can't be a leavin'? We're jest gettin' warmed up on checkies." As customary, every word Turner spoke his eyes opened wider. The crystal blue eyes appeared larger than the checker his forefinger rested upon. "Nobody walks out on an unfinished checker game."

"Don't be blaring them big eyes at me, Turner. I gotta head for home and I mean right now. Lickety Split! Look out yonder. See what's creepin' up the mountain, like a thief in the night?" Clyde motioned toward the fog slowly engulfing everything in its path, one inch at a time. "Emmer hates that blame fog worse 'n anything, 'cept maybe snow. Besides, she ain't' been right lately."

Mr. Guthrie held the greatest respect for Clyde's wife, Emma, known by all as a quiet, loving woman. Her Grandfather served as the mountain doctor for many years, and his compassion to care for the sick passed through and landed smack dab onto her fraile, but capable shoulders. When she heard of a sick person in need, she immediately offered to tend to them, or toted food for their families. In 1918, most every family in the mountain suffered with the flu epidemic. Mrs. Emma left food on the porches of the ailing, which saved many a life and the mountainfolk continued to express their gratitude to her. She came down with the flu, and gave birth to her second child while sick. It was nothing short of a miracle that she and the baby boy survived. Guthrie was sincerely interested to know if something ailed Mrs. Emma. "Seriously, what seems to be her problem, Clyde?"

Clyde let out a long sigh before offering an explanation, shaking his head slowly from side to side, "I wish I could figure it out. I'm tellin' ya, and I swear it to be the truth on a stack of Bibles, when she sees the fog rollin' in, like it is right now, she bout loses her mind. She walks them floors, wringing her hands, and goes from window to window. She don't say much, just keeps moaning and watchin' out the window, looking like she's gonna burst into tears and cry a river. She hates the mountains, says they're too lonely for anyone to endure. I've heard her carryin' on 'bout how that fog sneaks up like the death angel to claim its victim. She scant takes her eyes off it for fear of what it might do if'n she ain't watchin' out and guardin' her loved ones. That far away look in her eyes sends a chill plumb down my spine. I can't make heads or tails of it."

Darrell squirmed on the makeshift barrel he used as a stool, cleared his throat, "I'll put my two cents in, same sort of thing happenin' at my house. Wife's been actin' powerful weird. One minute she's workin' at something and the next she commences to swoonin' and carryin' on, you never heard the likes. When those days come, it don't make no never mind what I say or do, ever' word I say is wrong. Days on end, she sits gawking out at nothin'. I come up behind her and look out the window, and know what I see? Nothing. She don't even blink her eyes, keeps lookin' straight ahead. She'll do it pert nigh all day, then jump up like there's a bumble bee in her bloomers. Maybe the next day she'll mope all day, and not muster up a speck of gumption. She won't even fix me nothin' to eat, I tell ya, I don't dare open my mouth to complain neither. These spells overcome her, and the next day she's fine as frog hair."

Lawrence shook his head before confessing, "This is downright spooky, as I listen to you talkin' and tellin'. They couldn't all be goin' crazy at the same time, could they? And cranky as a wet hen wantin' to flog somebody, don't forget that! Reckon it's somethin' in the air, like a disease they done caught, or in the spring water?"

"You fools! Aren't your wives near the same age?" Guthrie inquired. "Didn't your own Mothers go through *the change*? It's a natural part of life."

"There ain't nary a thing the least bit natural 'bout it," Darrell spat back.

Guthrie continued, "I never thought I'd see the day that I, the only bachelor in the whole lot of ya's, would be educatin' a bunch of men about their wives. I've heard tell, it can be hard on a woman when they reach that age. It's the end of childbearin' years, and the passage into another phase of life. Sure enough, some women do go mad."

"Well, we're all gettin' older every blessed day; but I ain't cuttin' no shine like she does," Lawrence argued. "Ain't there nothin' can be done for a woman? Guthrie, ya know so blamed much 'bout it, and you got more book learnin' than the likes of us, ain't ya' got a pill they can take for it?"

Clyde attentively listened to the conversation, hoping for a glimmer of understanding as to what he witnessed the past couple of months. Every time his eyes caught a glimpse of the fog out the store window, he edged closer to the door and became noticeably more nervous. "I think I heared tell of a recipe that helps most everything. Three or four drops of turpentine in a teaspoon of sugar."

"Good Lord, Clyde, these women don't have a belly full of worms! That's all it's good for curing. I don't want none of you doctorin' me for nary a thing." Mr. Guthrie picked a worn book off the shelf, 'Home Remedies.' Every eye glued to him, trusting that he could find something to ease the miseries that baffled them and disrupted their home lives. Guthrie wet his forefinger on his tongue and began flipping page after page, intently searching the sections. His finger followed along a line in the book as his lips moved repeating the words, "Says here, a Cure-All Preventive is a Spring Tonic made by taking wild cherry tree bark, yellow poplar bark and yellowroot boiled, strained and mixed with white liquor. I wouldn't hold no stock in that curing nothin', not even a thirst for bad liquor. Besides you fellers would drink up all the medicine 'fore your wives ever tasted of it."

"Well sir, I don't 'member our Momma goin' through nothin' like this, do you?" Lawrence looked to his Brothers for confirmation. "We woulda 'membered any such thing as this." All the Brothers agreed they did not recall their Momma suffering in quite the manners as their wives. This 'change' thing was beyond their comprehension. They just knew they didn't like it, had no tolerance for it, and prayed it would be a short-lived ailment with their womenfolk.

"Ain't there no help? How 'bout them city doctors, reckon they've got some newfangled medicine a woman could swaller?" Darrell asked.

Guthrie shook his head, "Afraid not. It won't last forever, may seem like forever, but they'll return to their old ways. This is a good chance for you men to reach down into your entrails and pull out a speck of understanding for your women. After all, they deserve it for stayin' with the likes of you all of these years." Guthrie knew full well that he would be scorned for such a statement.

"Listen, from the man who says he'd rather have a John Deere tractor than a wife." They laughed at Lawrence's observation. Guthrie nodded. It was true, and he expressed no shame.

Guthrie continued flipping pages of the book, "Aha, I found it! Here's what I was looking for, the answer to your problems! Get some paper to write down this recipe. The Brothers dug into their pockets for scraps of paper, Clyde pulled a posted announcement off the general store's front window. They quietly waited, poised with paper and pencil. Guthrie read, "For goodness sake, get this right, I don't want you making anybody sick by muddlin' up the recipe, and come cryin' back in here laying blame to me for your silly mistake." He cleared his throat and began slowly reading. "It says here that this is for the husbands of the women, gather the roots of mayapple, cut out the joints, dry the middle of the root, beat it to a powder, add a tablespoon of castor oil, roll it into pills. Take two or three ever'day."

"Castor oil? Ya must've read it wrong. What kind of cure is that? That'll have us all squirting like a goose," Clyde declared.

Guthrie looked up from the book with a cunning grin on his face, "Well, if you fellas would take that ever'day, you'd spend more time in the crapper on your royal thrones takin' care of your own business, worryin' about your own butts, and less time fretting about your womenfolk! You're probably makin' them worse by aggravatin' them half to death all the time about something being wrong with them. Maybe it's a good recipe to cure the Ignorance of husbands."

Clyde wadded up the paper and threw it in Guthrie's general direction, and left, slamming the door of the general store behind him, muttering under his breath as he went down the steps. Before he hit the bottom step, he chuckled. Guthrie had successfully pranked the prankster.

THE CHECKER MARATHON

Most every man and boy in both the mountain and the valley were expert checker players. The checkerboard filled many hours during the long winter evenings and days not fit to work the fields. Some could look at the board and visualize the next several moves, while others played defensively, responding to their opponent's moves, never initiating an attack. Some men enjoyed telling tall tales the entire time, throughout the game, others scarcely grunted a response of acknowledgement.

The general store served as the primary checker arena. On chilly, damp days the checkerboard balanced on the top of any crate or nail keg near the pot-bellied stove for players to soak up the warmth. Warmer days players favored the front porch of the general store. Men leaned on the front rails to view the game, and offered unsolicited advice. From time-to-time the over emphasized throat clearing signified the strong disapproval of a move. The opponents would glare at the perpetrators for such coaching.

The third Saturday in August marked the annual Greenbed Founder's Day Celebration, including the traditional Checker Marathon. One could enter the Marathon by signing the posted paper taped to the window of Guthrie's General Store for fifty cents. Challengers played until they lost, and thus eliminated. However, if a player opted to challenge another winning player, he could pay an additional fifty cents to play again. At the conclusion of the day, the winner received the entry money. During this annual checker match, strict rules were enforced, forbidding throat clearing or signaling in any manner. Such actions disqualified the game, forfeiting the fifty cents of both players.

The womenfolk busied themselves with a jam/jelly contest. No entry fee, no rules or regulations and the winner proudly received a blue ribbon sampler created by the Methodist Church's quilting group. Most of the older women brought along tatting, or knitting projects, depending on the temperature. Quilting was reserved for cooler seasons. The youngsters busied themselves with races and games.

Several years running the young men had participated in a tree chopping competition. The spectators were entertained by the contest, however, the previous year a tree fell in the wrong direction, narrowly missing a group of little girls playing tag. Greenbed now excluded that competition.

In the grassy area beside the general store, Guthrie placed a large wooden table to hold the prize pies to be judged. Guthrie made certain that he reserved the honor of judging the pies for himself along with two other men. Every year, an abundance of volunteers pleaded with Guthrie to help judge. He refused to relinguish that distinction, declaring, "Fellas, there ain't many pleasures in life as sweet as pie judging and I don't want to miss out on this treat. I don't have a wife to bake me pies. I ain't givin' up this chance for pie!"

With the checkerboard set up, the rules recited, the first players hunkered down over the board as if it were the most serious thing they'd ever done. Throughout the day, first one and then the other would be turned away in defeat. The Brothers made a good showing of themselves, and at times brother was pitted against brother. This didn't concern them in the least. After all, they'd spent a lifetime playing checkers together.

Tempers occasionally flared during the course of the Checker Marathon. The familiar ring of the day was the demanding call, "King Me! How long does my checkie need to sit in that king row 'til he gets crowned? That checkie's done sprouted roots, he sat there so long." And the most common of all delcarations, "I hadn't taken my finger off my checkie yet," and debates ensued. The witnesses always prevailed in such matters. Most of the participants proved good sports, of course, there were some that desperately wanted the prize money.

Much to everyone's surprise, Mr. Willie, the most unpredictable Brother, was the last player to be challenged. As he sat on a stool looking out over the crowd that gathered to see the final game, the two winners of the day were to square off. Mr. Willie shut his bad eye and squinted at the crowd anticipating who would be his final opponent. Guthrie checked and verified the paperwork and called out, "Looks like we need Reverend

Lawson front and center." Guthrie patted the Parson on his back as he took the seat. Reverend Lawson smiled at this peculiar character across from him, sporting an impish grin on his face, wiping away the remnants of dripping tobacco juice at the corner of his mouth. Mr. Willie nodded at the Parson and studied the checkerboard as if he'd never laid eyes on one before.

The game began with intensity, both men displaying an aggressive approach. Willie immediately regretted never inviting the Reverend to play checkies with him in the store. Knowing the Reverend's strategies would've helped him feel more secure. Lord knows, the Reverend had watched Willie play many a time. Willie never thought Reverend Lawson paid any attention to the games as he'd played. He suddenly regretted ever playing in front of the Reverend. Willie felt that it surely gave the Reverend a distinct advantage. Unconsciously, he pursed his lips together and shook his head, squinting the one bad eye shut.

It turned into a long game consumed in concentration. Both men played the game with passion. Each fought for every checker they removed from the board. Willie studied his remaining two checkers on the board, both kings. Reverend Lawson had three kings left and was cornering one of Willie's kings into an impossible escape. Willie turned his head from side to side, stared at the board, squinted his eye tighter as he looked into Reverend Lawson's piercing brown eyes. Reverend Lawson did not blink, just returned the stare. Willie wondered how the Reverend knew to bluff like this.

Willie slowly stretched his hand across the board and placed it on the king in jeopardy of elimination. He lightly touched the top of his checker, suddenly pulling his arm back slapping at his own neck, sending his knees into the overhanging corner of the bottom of the checkerboard. The checkers scattered across the ground. Reverend Lawson looked up in astonishment as Willie stood, rubbing his neck. "What happened, Mr. Willie?"

"Dad-blamed ole hornet! That's what happened. He done popped me on my neck shooting his venom into my hide. Hurts like the thunder too!"

Some of the onlookers encouraged the two men to re-set the board and finish the game. The spectators knew exactly the placement of the five kings, as did the players.

Reverend Lawson stood to inspect this 'alleged' hornet sting. Willie would not remove his hand from his neck. The perceptive Reverend announced, "Mr. Willie, you better attend to that sting, and put some medicine on it. Hornet stings are bad. Yes, Sir, they need immediate attention."

Willie smiled at him and agreed that he best be gettin' along home to do just that. Willie appreciated the Reverend allowing him to save face.

The Reverend called after him as he walked away, "Mr. Willie, since we didn't finish the game, shall we call it a draw and split the prize money?" Willie's smile broadened. The Reverend added, "Would you be willing to donate your winnings to the Widows and Orphans Fund? That's what I'm doing with my winnings."

Trapped, Willie responded, "Sure. You take care of it for me, Preacher." Willie mumbled and complained under his breath as his old pickup truck chugged along the dirt roads toward home. Nothing ever worked as he planned, and now this Jack Leg Preacher stole his rightful winnings right out from under him. He kept shaking his head and repeating, "That blame busy body."

Founder's Day ended. There wouldn't be a reigning checkie champion to hold the honor, but there would always be next year. The Greenbed community would debate and discuss the alleged, mysterious appearance and the disappearance of the hornet throughout the long winter.

BEHIND CLOSED DOORS

The newly married Baby Tiny Carlton Moretz dreaded this particular trip to Guthrie's General Store now that the growing child within her could no longer be kept a secret. She conceived the first week she and Claude married up. She expected unmerciful teasing. Up to this day, she concealed this baby in every possible manner. Old Tiny reprimanded her for wearing the constricting garments to conceal the protrusion of her belly. Baby Tiny knew today she'd be forced to face the townsfolk and allow the world to openly gawk at the obvious. She wished family could make the trip to the store with her. She felt her condition was all Claude's fault, and never missed an opportunity to tell him about it.

The day dawned too warm to wear the baggy sweater she'd pulled around her mid-section lately. She tried to rehearse all the possible comments she might hear for a quick comeback. There was no way of predicting what the men at the general store might be capable of saying. She silently prayed, 'Lord, don't let my face turn beet red.' She hoped that only Mr. Guthrie would be in the store. She knew and trusted Guthrie not to cause her any embarrassment.

She attempted a pert demeanor as she climbed the steps and pushed open the door with as much false confidence as she could muster. She mustn't let them see her apprehensiveness. Three men sat there, two focusing on a game of checkers and one observing the game. The men barely noticed her and called out absently, "Hey Baby Tiny!" She swept past them and down the aisle to gather her items.

Mr. Guthrie stocked the shelf behind the register and called to her, "Baby Tiny, holler if you need me. How ya' been gettin' on? Haven't laid my eyeballs on ya in nigh unto a coon age."

"We been good. Momma said to tell ya' she'll be comin' for jar tops next week. Me and her is gonna pick blackberries and make jam. We found the biggest thicket ever, back off over."

One of the checker players called out, "Ya best watch out for them chiggers. They're powerful plentiful this year. Your hands'll be so busy scratchin' ya won't have no time to stir that jam." Snickers erupted. She felt a warm flush creeping to her face.

"Mmmm, ain't nothin' better than blackberry jam," Darrell confidently announced. "And blackberry cobbler is food fit for a king. I'm gettin' hungry just studyin' on it. Tiny, you best bring us some."

Without responding, Baby Tiny moved around the store quickly. If she were lucky, she might actually exit before anyone noticed her being with child. For months now, she made Momma and her brothers promise not to breathe a word of her motherly way. They honored her secret for nigh onto five months.

Mr. Guthrie turned to make the final tally. As he noticed the fullness of her midsection, he smiled broadly. Tiny frowned and put her finger to her mouth, signifying her desire to keep that a secret. Mr. Guthrie nodded and gave her an acknowledging wink. He dared to whisper, "Ya needn't be ashamed of a blessing such as that." She'd have to face the inevitable soon, but everyday she put it off, was one day more not to 'to face the music'.

With a pained expression she replied, "I don't want 'them' to know," she tilted her head in the direction of the checker playing Brothers.

"Why?" asked Guthrie.

Tiny felt the familiar red warmth oozing up her neck to her face, "Cuz they'll know what we been a doin' behind closed doors!"

Mr. Guthrie stifled his desire to laugh, "They already know." She let out a gasp, louder than intended. "Baby Tiny, every person in this world got here the same way. You. Me. Even those old checker-playin' fools. Besides, they're farmers, and birth and death represents a natural part of life to them. It'll be ok. No need to be a frettin' yourself needlessly. You ain't doin' the little one no favors by takin' on."

She paid for the items and sheepishly headed toward the door. She paused at the door to speak to the men. They looked up from the checkerboard, tipped their hats and greeted Baby Tiny. Clyde distractedly spoke, "How's

Claude Walter doin'? He's been scarcer than hens' teeth. Tell him we said hey." Tiny turned to leave. Strangely, she felt letdown that no one noticed her babe. Clyde broke the spell, "Baby Tiny, you'll make a fine Mother, cuz ya' had one of the best in these here parts. Ya best be takin' lessons from Old Tiny." She left. Whew. She survived. That wasn't bad at all. They didn't gawk, tease, or laugh. That was nothing like the conversations she'd rehearsed in her mind for this dreaded day.

As her foot landed on the last step, she heard the door open and Mr. Clyde stepped outside, lightly closing the door behind him. "Hold up there Baby Tiny." She froze in her tracks, afraid to face him. "Turn yourself around here and look me square in the eyeballs when I'm talkin' to ya, girl."

Baby Tiny knew her face and neck displayed a full-fledged scarlet now. Reluctantly, she turned and looked up into the soft blue eyes which shockingly displayed a tenderness. "Baby Tiny, ya can't saw no sawdust."

"Mr. Clyde, whatcha talkin' and tellin' about? I got no idea what that means," she innocently declared.

"What's done is done. Ain't no need troublin' yourself now. Put your head up and be proud. This here is a happy thing," he pointed to the baby. "Your Maw and Paw are gonna love the pitter patter of little feet in their house again. It's the nature of life and you oughta be peach pleased and proud to be a doin' your part. Don't ya never be ashamed of that little 'un." He turned to go back up the steps. "One more thing."

She braced herself.

"Tell Claude he best be treatin' ya special good now, and pamperin' ya, lest he'll be answerin' to us." He disappeared behind the closed door to rejoin the checker game. Tiny stood frozen, peering at the closed door, unable to believe the kind advice Clyde delivered.

Just a short time later, sure as bears poop in the woods, Baby Tiny Carlton helplessly scratched chigger bites for weeks just as the checker players predicted. And a brief three months and two days later, Baby Tiny gave birth to a 5 lb. 6 oz. premature baby. Word spread throughout the mountain that the tiny infant fit in a shoebox. The child immediately dubbed at Guthrie's General Store as "Teensy-Weensy." Baby Tiny knew that her beautiful, blue eyed daughter with brown curly locks would seldom hear her rightful name—Annalee Jewell. However, she would respond to Teensy-Weensy before her first tooth broke through her gums.

9

ENTREPRENEURS

Arville and Darrell sat on the front steps of the general store whittling while the womenfolk fetched supplies. The Brothers knew they had plenty of time to kill because their wives dared not leave before inspecting every bolt of the calico material. Typically, the women converted the colorful feedbags into pillowcases, quilts, and sometimes dresses, making bought material a luxury. Feedbag prints were limited and sometimes one waited a spell to get enough matching feedbags to complete a project.

The Brothers brought along 3 ft. branches, unusually straight with a 90° curvature at the top. These held the potential of becoming perfect walking sticks, after the whittling knives performed their magic. Darrell made short, staccato cuts with his knife, leaving small patches of the bark intact. Arville made long, smooth cuts, pealing away the bark exposing a near pure white piece of wood. The men exchanged childhood tales as they whittled in the warm sun.

Both men paused to study a well-dressed couple heading toward the general store. The woman's elbows pumping as she hurriedly marched three or four feet in front of the man. Darrell leaned toward Arville, "Who's that comin' yonder? I never seen the likes of them 'round these parts. I'll eat my hat if she ain't a wet hen 'bout to flog somebody."

Arville shrugged his shoulders. Times like this, he missed the outspoken Brothers, who'd stayed behind today to tend crops. The Brothers tipped their hats at the lady as she briskly ascended the steps. Her focus on the door to the store, she didn't acknowledge the whittlers. The fancy dude stopped at the bottom step, propped his right foot on the second step and leaned onto his knee to light a cigarette. After exhaling the first puff of smoke he looked toward the Brothers, "Howdy do. I'm Lance Thurston and that little whirlwind shuffling past is my wife, Eleanor Juliet VictoriaAnn Wesley Thurston. She's as complicated as her name!"

"She always like a fart on a skillet?" asked Arville.

Thurston balanced the cigarette on the rail and allowed it to burn. He laughed as he removed his hat and smoothed his wavy, straw-colored hair, "Afraid so. Keeps me on my toes."

Arville and Darrell introduced themselves, resisting the urge to ask a string of questions. Luckily, Thurston volunteered further information to ease their curiosity. "We're spending a week here, looking at property for a city get-away and eventually retirement. City life gets weary, always busy, noisy, rushing here and there. This slow, easy, laid-back lifestyle fits me like a glove. We're staying at the boarding house," he motioned toward Etta Trivette's home, the slate roof just visible through the tree branches. For extra income Etta rented out two of her upstairs spare bedrooms. The Brothers never heard anyone refer to it as a boarding house. Etta Trivette had not rented a room in years. "The only sounds we hear are birds singing and the breeze rustling the leaves. Mighty peaceful."

Arville nodded in complete agreement, "Yes sir, right peaceful, but we've not been to your city to know what that'd be like. From what I hear, I don't much think I'd take to it."

"No, I don't expect you would, not after living here in paradise." He replaced his hat and adjusted the brim, "What are you making with the wood?"

Darrell held up his stick for Mr. Thurston to see. "A walkin' stick. They work real good. Can't get this wood but only in one field 'round these parts. This wood will hold a whoppin' 300 pounder. A feller can't hardly break it." He stood to demonstrate leaning his weight on the unfinished stick. "Never heard of one of 'em bucklin' or breakin'. We make 'em outta good hard wood, a special hickory. For some reason the hickory trees in that field are the toughest wood with a right purty grain runnin' through it."

Mr. Thurston took the stick, to closely scrutinize. "I must say, you do excellent workmanship." He held it straight out before him and turned his head slightly to study it. Darrell and Arville exchanged curious looks, puzzled at Thurston's extensive examination. After all, didn't everyone whittle walkin' canes? It was just a stick, nothing unusual.

"How much would you take for these?"

"What do ya mean?" asked Arville.

"Would you sell these?" Thurston laid the stick on the palm of his hand, allowing it to roll freely back and forth as he continued to rub the smooth wood.

"Sell 'em? Why? You don't strike me as needin' a walkin' stick. You're a young whipper snapper and spry in your gait," Darrell spit his tobacco over the porch rail. "Reckon ya gotta be spry to keep up to that thar woman."

Thurston shook his head, "Well, thank you for the compliment. I think. No, I don't need one, not yet. I am an entrepreneur of sorts and there may be a market for these in the city."

Mrs. Thurston rushed out of the store juggling a large bag and her purse. "Lance, here! Help me! Make yourself useful." Mr. Thurston immediately leaped up the steps, reaching for the bag and attempted to take his wife's elbow. She jerked free of his hand, but placed her bag into his outstretched hand. The Brothers exchanged a look, Darrell winked. Both were thinking the 'city fella was well trained by this little woman.' No question who wore the pants in that family.

"One minute, Dear, I'm attempting to make these gentlemen entrepreneurs."

Eleanor Thurston gave Arville and Darrell a side glance, without speaking to them. She crossed her arms and stood beside her husband nervously tapping her dainty size five foot, while gazing at the sky. Her smooth, young face exhibited irritation at this further inconvenience to her schedule.

"How much?" Thurston inquired.

Darrell spoke up, "The truth of the matter is, we've never sold one and wouldn't know what to tell ya. Ever' man makes his own. Arville, what do ya think?"

"Ain't got a ghost of an idea. What's it worth to ya?" Arville responded.

Mrs. Thurston shattered the magic of the spell, "Lance, I am ready to go back to the pitiful excuse referred to as our room, if we must. Could you possibly conduct this conversation another time?"

"One minute, Dear."

Mrs. Thurston released an exaggerated sigh and turned toward the Trivette home. Surprisingly, Mr. Thurston did not immediately fall in to obediently trail behind her. "How about $1 a stick?"

Darrell and Arville laughed. They'd never been offered money for whittling, besides they did it to pass the time of day. They couldn't believe anyone offered to pay good money for the likes of a common stick from a tree. Darrell said, "Are ya kiddin'?"

"How about $1.25? You drive a hard bargain," Thurston counter offered.

Darrell looked Thurston in the eyes, "You're not funnin' with us? Ya mean it? Ya wanta buy these for $1.25? Sold!"

Thurston smiled, "Wonderful. How many can you make while I'm here this week?"

Arville asked, "Ya mean to tell me ya want *more* of these contraptions?"

"I'll buy all you produce in the time I'm in Greenbed."

Darrell immediately thought of his other Brothers. "We got brothers who do fine whittlin'. Ya want that we should tell 'em and get 'em busy too?"

"Absolutely. The old saying goes, 'the more the merrier.' I'll take all you make this week. If they sell as well as I think, I'll come back for more the following week." Mr. Thurston grabbed their hands to shake. He pulled out $2.50 handing it to the brothers. "Congratulations, gentlemen, you're officially genuine entrepreneurs. Consider us business partners now." He turned and rushed down the street in a half run after Ms. Eleanor so and so Thurston, leaving Darrell and Arville speechless as they gripped their $1.25 as if it might mysteriously disappear as easily as it appeared.

Arville muttered, "Imagine that. A city slicker comes rollin' into these parts and hires us to make sticks. And what'd he say we'd be if we made sticks? It sounded somethin' like manure, but I don't remember the rest of it."

Throughout the next several days, Darrell and Arville thought of little else other than their new careers in creating walking sticks. After the farming duties were attended, each sat on their respective porches whittling. Piles of shavings gathered around their boots. Being conspicuously absent from visiting with any of the other Brothers, Willie went to see Arville to find out what preoccupied he and Darrell. Arville told his brother about the walking stick arrangement with Mr. Thurston. Willie looked at his brother in disbelief. "Shut your mouth wide open! Ya know there's no truth to that. God never created nobody that naïve, not even a city slicker."

Arville raised his right hand, signifying that he took an oath. "Arville, do ya' know what $1.25 will buy? Three pounds of coffee, or a gob of miles worth of gasoline," he studied on that a minute, "or at 8 cents a loaf that'd be enough bread to feed us for a feast. Is that man plum crazy?" Without so much as a good-bye, Willie left. Arville laughed, knowing that his brother, whom everyone recognized as the biggest tight wad in these parts, would do nothing else but whittle until Thurston left town.

And right he was. Willie spread the word to the other Brothers, then tackled the challenge. He calculated how he could make the most of his time. Trips into town, visits to the general store, playing checkers, calling on his Brothers, all would be put on hold for the remainder of the week. Willie whittled every possible minute, not to let this golden opportunity slip through his whittling-capable fingers.

Darrell and Arville took their masterpieces into town at the end of the first week to meet with Mr. Thurston and receive their payment for the week's work. The other Brothers kept too busy with farming chores to bother making more than what they carved out in the evenings while waiting for bedtime. Besides, they were skeptical of such a deal.

Darrell and Arville kept their sticks separated to guarantee each would receive his just wage. Darrell held out five sticks to show his Brother while Arville managed to produce three. "I was too blamed tired at night. When I sat down after supper first thing I knowed, I done went and fell sound asleep." While they compared walking sticks,' they saw Brother Willie. His old truck rolled to a slow halt, he threw open the door before the pickup completely stopped. He hustled down the street, dragging a burlap feedbag filled with walking sticks. The Brothers laughed as they saw two sticks find their way to a hole in the bag and lay on the road. He struggled to get the bag up the steps to the store and fumbled with the door.

"What's so blame funny with you'ns?" he grumbled at the smiling Brothers.

"Brother, it's mighty kind of ya to leave two fine lookin' canes in the road for finders keepers."

Willie whirled around and squinted at the two canes left behind. He dropped the burlap bag just inside the door and scampered down the steps cussing at the two delinquent walking sticks. He moved faster than they'd witnessed in years. He snatched the canes, lowered his head like a bull preparing to charge, and made straightway for the general store.

Upon entering, he proclaimed, "If'n any of ya open his big mouth, so help me, I'll be a shuttin' it for ya!" The Brothers looked up in surprise. Their eyes settled on the big bandage haphazardly wrapped around his middle three fingers on his left hand.

Clyde and Guthrie sat hunched over the checkerboard deep in thought. Clyde spotted the bandages. Laughing, he inquired, "What'd ya do to them fingers?"

Willie snapped at him, "I done told ya, I don't aim to hear it. Mind yer own bees wax." He knew he'd be the laughing stock of Greenbed once they learned about his mishap.

Lawrence inquired, sincerely interested, "Willie, all jokin' aside, what happened?"

"I'll tell ya, if'n y'all, promise fair and square to shut up 'bout it and don't be runnin' yer mouths to nobody else." They nodded in unison, knowing full well that Willie did'nt expect them to keep a juicy tale to themselves.

"I was whittlin' away, holding a slicker 'n snot stick in my left hand, reckon I dozed off, the dad-blamed knife slipped and sliced a hunk outta all three fingers. I ought to throw that knife into the river. There, ya' know. Are ya' happy, ya lazy fools?" The room was dead silent for ten seconds before the laughter erupted. Willie knew his fate was doomed, he realized every man, woman, child, and cow would hear this ridiculous account before bedding down tonight. Suddenly, he wished he'd lied and said he caught the fingers in a piece of farm equipment. He pursed his lips tightly in immediate regret for not preparing a believable account. Thinking a head of the game had never been Brother Willie's forte.

As promised, Mr. Thurston showed up at the store to assess the production. His smile stretched from ear to ear as he handed over the money to the entrepreneurs, unceremoniously gathered the walking sticks and disappeared in the direction of Etta Trivette's. Arville and Darrell counted their money while Willie jammed his into his pocket and left in a huff, arguing with himself as he made for the door. The Brothers knew the nature of the urgency for Willie to make haste. After receiving a taste of 'easy money', he rushed straight home to start whittling all over again. Turner was the first to catch his breath and comment, "If that Thurston feller don't leave these parts soon, Willie ain't gonna have no fingers left to count his meager earnings. He'll be buttonin' his shirt with nubbins." Willie's rapid departure spared him from further humiliation.

Arville and Darrell declared their resignations from the walking cane business, neither had time to spare after tending to their farms. Besides, whittling for profit took the pleasure out of the calming pastime for the men.

Willie abandoned every possible farming duty to dedicate more time to cane production. He grumbled at the cows as he milked them, "I wish you'ins could do this for yerself and not deprive me from a money-makin' proposition." The cow responded by shifting her weight onto the other side, and swishing her coarse tail across his face as a further insult. "Dad-Blame, ungrateful hussy! You are just like every other woman on the face of the earth. It don't matter if females got two legs or four, yer all made out of the same confounded mold—contrary as a mule." Willie could boldly say such things without worry since his wife passed two and half years ago. Her notoriety that she conveniently suffered from fainting spells, however, only if she stood in close proximity to a handsome man and could swoon in his direction. Always the same pattern, she coughed slightly, put her hand to her forehead, then fanned frantically with both hands fluttering in the air. After the attention shifted to her, her long eyelashes fluttered as she rolled her eyes, and stumbled in the direction of the snared man. As soon as she felt the strong arms wrap around her, she gracefully folded like an accordion.

At the conclusion of the second week, Willie still wore the bandages as he waited in Guthrie's General Store for Mr. Thurston. He experienced a more tolerable mood these days. In fact, the anticipation of another pocket stuffed plum full to the brim of money made him downright tolerable, even jovial. He managed to laugh along with the others as they razzed him about his dedication to whittling and the knife and fingers collision course. "A man oughta be dedicated to something, which is more than I can say for some of youins," he spat back.

They talked among themselves, and visited with every person shopping at the general store. The store and church presented the only opportunities to hear the local news and gossip. Guthrie managed to stay in the know, and part of the reason mountainfolk looked forward to talking to Guthrie was to obtain the latest. Eventually, everyone needed supplies of some sort.

They waited and talked and talked and waited. Willie retrieved his old pocketwatch and lightly pecked his finger on the cracked crystal. "Reckon this thing done give up the ghost and quit running? What time does your watch piece say?" After Mr. Thurston was two hours late, the Brothers encouraged Willie to call on him at the Trivette's and see what detained him. He secured his prized canes in a safe corner of Guthrie's store and made everyone swear not to touch them. The screen door slammed behind him. He didn't bother to stop and chew the fat with anyone, he walked directly to Trivette's, head turned sideways, eye squinted, pumping his elbows, and mumbling with each step.

Shortly, Lawrence spotted Willie coming back toward the general store, talking to himself, throwing his hands into the air, shaking his head. "Where's your wad of money, Willie?" he asked.

"Ain't none! That low-down, no good, snake in the grass is gone! Hightailed it outta here."

Clyde choked back a laugh, "Gone? Where'd he go?"

Almost too angry to speak, Willie shot back, "To the blame, stinkin' city, I reckon. Mrs. Trivette said they had a screamin' match. His wife hated it here, and wasn't staying one more day with us 'hillbillies.' Said she was leavin' with him or without him and he'd have to manage gittin' back to the city the best way he could figure out. That weak-livered, spineless feller let her drag him outta here. He may as well have a bull's ring in his nose the way she pulls him around."

Turner chimed in, "Willie, you're jest jealous. You need a little filly like Mrs. Thurston. It might do ya good and help ya too."

Everyone laughed more at the disgusted look on Willie's face than the failed opportunity and betrayal he felt. No one imagined that in less than a week Willie would meet a special lady, and he too would obey the whims of a feisty little filly, growing accustomed to the ring in his own nose.

10

GRIEF AND LOVE

Guthrie leaned against the doorframe for half an hour enjoying the bantering in the store, occasionally adding his two cents worth. He generously offered to purchase the walking canes from Willie, giving Willie 80% of the sale. Willie felt Guthrie keeping 20% was unfair, and accused Guthrie of taking advantage of the situation. Everyone else recognized the offer as very generous. Everyone, except Willie, realized that Guthrie would not sell a single walking stick. Afterall, every man and boy made their own, maybe not from the hickory wood, but something that sufficed as a cattle driving stick. Thurston had been the first visitor in over two years. Greenbed remained a quiet, remote little community hidden among the rugged mountain ranges, far off the beaten path. After much persuasion, a deal was finally sealed with a handshake, and this time Willie could be assured the handshake was a binding agreement.

Guthrie shook his head, "I'll declare, Willie, I never worked that hard to do a man a favor in all of my life. You're one knot-headed man! Did you take a right hard lick to the head, or are ya jes' plumb dimwitted."

Willie immediately tuned out the conversation and concerned himself with, again, mentally calculating the profit of the walking sticks. "Look, ain't that the Widow Carlton. They say she's not been off her place since that cow kicked J.C. in the head. I heard tell, she still grieves something awful for him. Ya' know he died right there in the barn. They say she ain't never shed one tear over him to this day. How could that be? Not nary a one."

Another shopper in the store added, "Anybody out yonder to help her?"

Mr. Guthrie typically knew the wherewithal about everyone in the vicinity. "She gets by, Carlton had done OK for himself. They made it through the Depression and aren't hurtin' bad for money. Their three boys live on plots of land Carlton gave 'em when they married. They look out for her."

Widow Carlton slowly made her way to Guthrie's General Store. She walked as if a 60 lb. bag of potatoes were strapped to her back. She didn't acknowledge anyone, kept her eyes straight ahead and with trembling hands retrieved the tattered list from her pocket. Mr. Guthrie approached her, "Mrs. Carlton, I'd be pleased to help ya."

Her worried, confused face looked back at him with a hollow expression, "I'd be obliged. The girls done this for me for a spell." Looks were exchanged among the others in the store. Finally, Clyde pushed back the wooden chair he sat straddle in and went to her. Putting his arm loosely around her shoulder he spoke softly, yet firmly, "Sarah, ya gotta get a hold of yourself. A person can't keep grievin' right on. Ya know good and well J.C. don't approve of ya carryin' on like this. It ain't doin' nobody no good."

Sarah Carlton displayed a look of total defeat. She'd aged far beyond her years, "You don't know nothin' about grievin'. If I'd jest a gone to the barn to check on him when he didn't come in for supper, I mighta saved his life. I made him die in the barn with them cows."

"J.C. was our friend too. We miss him. I know it musta been the worst shock of your life. But, I do know about hurtin' and feelin' guilty as sin over one's death."

"What do you know about it? Ya got your wife, youngins, and Brothers sittin' right over yander," she motioned with a slight nod of her head. "Ya get to see them anytime ya want. I can't see J.C., never again."

"Sarah, you're partly right on that account. If ya' but remember, when I was a young man, I ventured out west to mine for gold and insisted my brother, Harvey, go along. He didn't want to go, but I wouldn't let him be 'til he agreed. We was in a saloon in Colorado when we heard the awfulest noise startin', growin' louder and louder in the basement. The boiler rumbled and somebody shouted, 'She's gonna' blow.' We all made for the door, stumbling over chairs and pushing people to get out of our way. In a panic, we stampeded for the door. We wuz scared for our lives. A bad feelin' like something awful was about to happen took hold of me, sent goose-egg-sized chills up my spine. We ran from the saloon, across that muddy street. Let me tell ya, sure enough, that ole boiler exploded. A chunk of the metal hit my brother, Harvey, right smack dab in his head. He died right there in that mud and dirt.

We brought his body back on the train. Don't ya never think for a second you're the only person in the world to grieve. Lots of people in Greenbed grieved one time or another, but they keep goin'. It 'bout killed me to see Harvey layin' there, bleedin' to death in a strange town, dyin' in the dirt, no betterna helpless animal. He had no desire to seek his fortune huntin' for gold, but I'd insisted. It hurt bad. How do ya think my Maw felt? But she went on, had to, people depended on her. We got no choice but to go on with life."

Widow Sarah Carlton stood in silence, looking down at the wood floors.

He waited before continuing, "Ya gotta keep on livin', and ya've been actin' as if you wuz the one put in a hole in the ground. There wuz only one funeral, best I recollect. Ya know mountain folk wanta help ya' get back to yourself, but ya run people off with that grievin' and carryin' on. A person can only take so much of it."

"I loved my husband, Mr. Clyde."

"I know. And I loved my brother. That train ride home with his poor body all mangled in that wooden box was one of the worst times of my life and me feelin' it my fault. For a long time, I'd close my eyes and see him laying there dyin'. I had to make myself stop thinkin' them thoughts, and remember the fun times. Mulligrubbin' over it, wouldn't bring him back, no matter how hard I wanted to change it, he wuz dead. Seems to me that all this carryin' on ya been a doin' ain't provin' to nobody that you loved him. Ya ought to put your mind to thinkin' about the good times, the family ya raised. Get a hold of yourself, woman! Nobody can do it for ya."

It might have seemed like a cruel lecture, but he concluded the harsh words by gently wrapping her into his arms, drawing her to his chest. She buried her head in his barrelled chest and cried. Finally letting go of the remainder of the grief she'd carefully harbored.

She walked out of the store without collecting her supplies. Clyde paid for the items, and took the bag. He told Guthrie he and his wife would visit Sarah tomorrow. It was long past the time for someone to shake her loose from that farm.

The following week, the Brothers congregated at the general store to catch up on the news and whereabouts of everyone. As usual, Mr. Guthrie shared the scoop. Guthrie wasn't a gossip, but freely passed on the information he knew to be a fact, but only when asked. Willie, Arville, and Darrell leaned on the counter, peering through the glass at the assortment of pocketknives.

Turner called from the front of the store, "Willie, maybe if ya spent some of that money ya been hoardin' away, and buy a new knife, that fancy city slicker might come back and buy more walkin sticks." That instigated a chorus of snickers from the other Brothers.

"Ya think you're so blamed funny! Mind yer own talkin' and tellin' over there."

Lawrence asked quite seriously, "Fellas would ya do it again if'n someone offered ya money for your whittlin' efforts?"

Willie snorted the response, "If my knee could be hinged on the back of my leg, I'd kick myself in the butt for the time I spent a whittlin' them sticks. I'll tell ya the truth, I don't think I'm never gonna whittle nothing else the longest day I live." Everyone laughed, not so much at him, they knew that statement wasn't true, and that he'd probably already whittled.

Several more good-humored jabs were exchanged, before someone spotted Reverend Lawson and a lady coming toward the general store. Mr. Guthrie adjusted his wire-rimmed glasses for a better inspection.

Darrell quietly asked, "Guthrie, who is that woman with your Parson? Did he up and find himself a woman?"

"I'll be snookernosed if I know," Guthrie mumbled. "Mighty good looking woman, but a smidgen old for him."

A typical Willie outlandish remark, "Maybe the Reverend is gettin' desperate up here in these hills and she's all he could find. Ya know, fellas, it ain't easy to marry off a preacher. Most of 'em has got weird ways." The giggles and conversations hushed as the Reverend opened the door for the lady and stepped aside to allow her to enter the store. Smirks remained on the faces of the men, as they continued to ponder Willie's observations.

Reverend Lawson enjoyed the few moments of intrigue. He sensed the curiosity peaking, and he relished in it. He briefly had the upper hand on this gathering. He walked to the counter and addressed Willie, Arville and Darrell first, "Gentlemen, I would like to introduce the new school teacher, Miss Daisy Moretz. With Miss Daisy taking over the teaching duties, I can devote more time to my writing." Prior to the Reverend's arrival, the community depended on volunteers to instruct the students a day or two a week in the one-room school house. Most of this time, schooling amounted to nothing more than encouraging the few students who showed up to read in their primers. One of the first school duties, Reverend Lawson promised was to visit the families of children and encourage parents to send the children now that Greenbed had a full-time teacher.

The men tipped the brims of their well-worn felt hats and smiled. Miss Moretz browsed through the store, lightly fingering merchandise. Willie never took his eyes from her. She was a beauty, as she appeared to float on air gracefully traversing the aisles. "Miss Moretz, shall we walk to the schoolhouse where you'll spend happy hours teaching Greenbed's youngsters?"

Willie moved to the window to watch as the Reverend escorted her down the steps. He uttered, "How come we never had no teacher that looked like that? I'll tell ya the gospel truth, I wish I wuz back in school. I could look at the likes of her all day, and beg to be kept in at recess." Willie fell in love—hook, line, and sinker.

Guthrie broke the magic of his spell, "If you want, Willie, I'll arrange a meeting for you and Miss Moretz." He gave Willie a sly wink.

Arville laughed. "A school teacher? Willie, what would ya even talk to a school teacher about? Ya could tell her about how much milk that Holstein cow ya bought from the Hopper's gives; or yer whittling advenutres. She'd be amused to hear that saga unfold."

"All's I'm saying is, seein' a woman like that makes a feller as lonesome as a polecat at a Sunday school picnic!"

Darrell leaned over, as if to whisper to the Brothers, excluding Willie.

"Go on, Darrell say it out loud. I know your 'bout to bust the seam outta your britches to say some smart remark."

"Well, Willie, ya know ya were so ugly when ya was little that Maw had to tie a pork chop bone around yer neck to git the ole dog to play with ya'."

Giving the Brothers the reaction they desired, Willie stood and stormed out. He heard the laughter inside the store. More important matters consumed his mind. Indeed, he wanted to meet Miss Moretz. He began plotting the best way to obtain information about her. He came up with a scheme, which involved going to Reverend Lawson's Sunday service to pry any tidbit of information, or at least to gain a formal introduction to this vision of beauty. Willie felt confident in his capabilities to woo a woman. Pursuing this relationship felt right, clear down to his toenails. Once back to his farm, he jumped out the door of his rattletrap truck and took aim at a stone to kick it out of his path, much the same as when he was a lad. Just seeing Miss Daisy made him feel like a kid again.

Willie wished Mr. Guthrie had been privy to any information about Miss Daisy. It would have made life easier for him to get the details from Guthrie. But, this woman was well worth his best, most creative and cleverest plan to finesse the delicate situation properly. Willie remembered the teasing he'd dished out to the Jackleg Preacher. He knew his Brothers would have a hay day teasing him, and embarrassing him in front of Miss Moretz. He must brave going to the meetings that he'd heard rumors about since he was a youngin'. He heard one best watch out for them Baptists, they'd give an altar call, and people get to cryin' when they get saved. He heard they'd kneel at the mourner's bench—praying, singing, wailing and it became a regular snot-slingin' time as they prepared their hearts for the kingdom gates. Willie dreaded this alleged Baptist meeting; but the thought of not seeing or meeting Miss Daisy Moretz was a far worse notion.

For the next week, the Brothers didn't see much of Willie. Nine or ten days later a group of the men gathered on the front porch of the general store, Turner, Willie, Clyde, and Darrell among them. Willie sat with his chair leaning back against the wall, propped on the back two legs. As they discussed the draught, someone added, "My corn ain't gonna be fit to cut! It ain't gonna make, if'n we don't get some rain, and get it soon." The group commented on the critically dire need for rain.

Lawrence noted Willie suddenly flopped his chair down onto all four legs and turned white as a ghost as he looked straight a head as if in a trance. They turned to see the cause. Down the road strolled Miss Daisy Moretz. She crossed over the road and headed toward the general store. Although she still appeared to be floating, she bore a determined mannerism. She immediately looked to her right and smiled when she saw Willie sitting with the group of men. The men tipped their hats and nodded a polite greeting. As she climbed the steps, she only focused on one person in this group of men and with a twinkle in her eyes, she greeted only one person. "Good morning, William." She passed on into the general store. Without any explanation, Willie immediately left the group of men and trailed her into the store.

Willie heard the laughter and was thankful to escape before any punishing comments were heard by Miss Daisy. He could well imagine the conversation, but it didn't matter. All was right in his world. He knew full well that he'd be teased about her addressing him as "William." Right now, that didn't much matter either.

The whirlwind romance began when Miss Daisy had witnessed a strange man picking flowers from around her house. Fear built in her small body. How she missed having a neighbor close enough to call on for help! The man moved from one area to the next, determined to pick all the flowering plants around her small cottage. She peered out the side window and he had vanished. To her surprise this bold man knocked on her back door. When she opened the door, he thrust a huge bouquet of sunflowers and rhododrendron into her hands and said, "Here. These are from me. I reckon you are the purtiest woman I done ever seen in all my live-long days." He turned to leave her porch. She opened the screen door and smiled as William introduced himself to the beautiful school teacher. The birth of the most extraordinary courtship Miss Daisy ever encountered spun out of control. Something about this unusually honest, unpretentious man intrigued her.

It must be true that opposites attract. Willie, who had never read a book in his life, and the educated school teacher joined right hands four months later standing before Reverend Lawson as Miss Daisy pledged her love to 'William.'

The local widows shed no tears over the loss of an eligible bachelor snatched out from under them; none of them wanted him. However, there were a great many unanswered questions as to why or how this unlikely union came about here in the Greenbed community. Typically, life in the hills is totally predictable. They assumed this gave even more validity to the old clique, 'love is blind,' indeed.

SNIPE HUNTIN'

The new Preacher adjusted well to the mountain community, he survived his first revival, conducted two weddings, and officiated his first Greenbed funeral. Clearly, the funeral service was a disaster. Four year old Sally had slipped off a log while crossing the swelling river with her Grandmother and drowned. The community was distraught. Willie tutored the Preacher, informing him that every funeral followed the same format: 'read the Bible, pray, say nice things to make the family feel better, then sing Shall We Gather at the River.' Willie assured the new Parson, 'it never varied and if the new Preacher knew what was good for him, he'd not try anything fancy at a sad time like this, but follow the same course.' Sure enough, Reverend Lawson followed Mr. Willie's advice. However, when he announced they'd sing 'Shall We Gather at the River,' the grieving Grandmother fainted dead away, the child's Mother screamed and swooned, and the entire congregation shot the Reverend angry looks. The following day the Parson questioned Mr. Willie. Willie rocked back and forth holding his stomach, laughing, slapping his knee with his hand. Reverend Lawson inquired why he'd given that particularly cruel advice. Willie gave him an honest answer, "You're supposed to be so blame city smart. I didn't think you'd be that dumb witted." The young Reverend realized winning the confidence and respect back after this innocent mistake would be an arduous task to accomplish.

The gathering at the general store hungered for excitement. As they studied the next moves on the checkerboard, they hatched the idea of taking the Jack Leg Preacher snipe huntin'. He earned his place on the social ladder and it may help lighten his guilt over the blunder at the funeral. Besides, every man in the store had been treated to a snipe hunting trip upon coming of age. It served as a ritualistic passageway for boys to enter manhood. Since the Jack Leg Preacher didn't know about snipe hunting, it seemed, only fittin' to properly indoctrinate him with this little joke.

Mr. Guthrie didn't approve; nor did he strongly object. Snipe hunting always held the promise of great entertainment for the 'seasoned' snipe hunters. Guthrie remembered his own snipe hunting episode, and besides no real harm would befall the Parson. It was all in fun.

The next debate was whether to do it in the light of a full moon, or wait for the darkness of a new moon making the woods darker and harder to traverse. They decided to wait for the new moon in six days. None of the men had been afforded the opportunity to snipe hunt with a minister. The part-time preacher at the Methodist church led in services sporadically. He made it abundantly clear he didn't intend to perform weddings, funerals, or any special services. If a wedding or funeral could be conveniently combined with a Sunday service, he might consider conducting it. Clearly, he was not to be inconvenienced. The preacher at the Primitive Baptist Church barely managed to climb the seven steps at the side of the small church. The Brothers joked that when the rapture occurred, he'd best be out in the open, otherwise he'd never make it to the door and down the steps in time. Willie readily accepted the assigned duty of extending the personal invitation to the Preacher. Afterall, he was the only Brother claiming membership at Reverend Lawson's church since his marriage to Daisy and Willie's facial expressions being such that one never knew if he teased or was serious. The others might not be able to sound convincing if the Preacher saw the unmistakable gleam in their eyes as they anticipated the Jack Leg Preacher hopelessly lost in the woods on a dark night.

Willie watched for the Preacher to pass the general store and he shuffled out of the store, crossing over to him. He wanted to catch the Reverend out of ear shod of anyone else who might ruin the fun.

"Reverend! Wait up." Willie strolled nonchalantly toward him. "Hey, Preacher. Me and some of the menfolk started workin' up a snipe huntin' trip. You in?" When Reverend Lawson cocked an eyebrow at Willie and gave him a suspicious look, Willie quickly defended the invitation. "Oh come on! Ya ain't still mad at me for the funeral advice? One of these days you're gonna look back on that and see how slick I got one over on ya'. I don't want no hard feelins'." Willie struggled to make an exra attempt to sound sincere yet casual. He certainly did not want to let on that the preacher was the main attraction of the trip and without him there would be no snipe hunting trip.

"No hard feelings. I take the blame. I knew better than to take any advice from you. Sure, tell me when and where and I'll be there."

Willie managed to keep his excitement under tight wrap, "Fine and dandy! How 'bout meetin' up out at Solomon Jordan's next Tuesday night, at 8:00 bells? Them snipes don't get to movin' much until after dark. They feel safer to come out then. Blame near impossible to catch one before pitch black." He patted Reverend Lawson on the back, "But that's OK, we'll be a lay waitin' 'em. By snort, we'll get 'em. We'll out smart 'em. We know their conniving tricks, but they don't got no idea of the tricks up our sleeves." Pleased with himself for such an eloquent sales pitch, Willie left good enough alone and headed toward his old pickup parked haphazardly by the side of the dirt road.

As soon as the Reverend was out of sight, Willie forced himself to slowly walk back to the general store, not to cause suspicion if the Preacher happened to spot him. As soon as he entered the store, he became the center of attention. He was in hog heaven when the men begged to hear verbatim the entire account. If they met up with Reverend Lawson they wanted to have accurate details to confirm the outing. Willie doubled over laughing, "I feel like I robbed a little youngin' of its candy. I ain't never done nothin' no easier! I'm tellin' ya, I pulled it off without a hitch." He relayed the 'who said what' to the gathering of men. They congratulated Willie on a fine performance.

The snipe hunting adventure occupied the men's minds for the next six days. There wasn't a mundane day as they anticipated the fun awaiting them. They tackled chores with a merry heart, and all during the long days in the fields, they worked with the hint of a smile. Anticipating the amusement of the hunting trip lightened their burdens.

Tuesday evening finally arrived and they made their way to Solomon Jordan's farm. His backyard adjoined a dense portion of the mountain, containing the roughest, most uneven terrain. This portion of the mountain literally went straight up. Climbing the thickly covered mountain, they had to grab onto small saplings, or tree trunks, and pull themselves along, lunging for the next bit of vegetation and hoping it was strong enough to support the weight. The only way these men would be able to climb the mountain at this point was on the sheer adrenaline in expectation of the trick they plotted for the Jack Leg Preacher.

As they struggled up the steep incline, Arville explained to the Preacher how one goes about catching a snipe. "Preacher, since you don't know what you're lookin' for, we'll go on a head and find their hidin' places and shoo them in yer direction. Ya better stay squatted down and ready, holdin' yer bag wide open. They're powerful skittish creatures. When you hear the rustlin' in the bushes, brace yerself 'cuz they'll be a comin' any minute. Ya gotta be ready. We're countin' on ya. Rest assured, we'll be a doin' our part. It ain't hard, bein' ready, that's the key and keepin' quiet."

Reverend Lawson asked, "Did you bring something to tie the top of the bag? And, if we get more than a couple at a time, do you have another bag to use, so the first ones caught won't get out?"

Without hesitation Clyde answered, "We don't want to wipe out the whole population, so we'll just keep a few." The others were grateful for the darkness; to conceal their broad smiles. This promised to be great! In all their snipe hunting adventures, they'd never had a person ask such a question. Granted, most first-time snipe hunters were boys about 13 years of age. The men rehearsed in their minds how they'd embellish and retell this tale. They started to get winded a third of the way up and slowed their pace. However, Reverend Lawson steadily progressed forward. They attributed it all to the difference in their ages, not the extra forty to sixty pounds each had on him.

They ceased talking, and trying to catch a good breath became laborious. Reverend Lawson chatted and asked questions all the way up the mountain. Willie piped up, "Preacher, how long ya had that ailment?"

"What ailment?"

"That diaherra of the mouth!" The Reverend laughed louder than they'd ever heard him laugh, not the least insulted. Nor did the comment curtail his conversation. The others only grunted answers to his array of questions about the mountain in general, the plants, elevation, and so forth. They wished he'd shut up. The thought crossed their minds, this wasn't as much fun as expected if they had to endure this quiz.

Finally, they reached semi-level ground. In the darkness they took a minute to get their bearings. They crouched down and slowly walked toward a thicket and handed the burlap bag to the Preacher. As planned, in a whisper Darrell said, "Here, take this and edge your way 'round this thicket to the yon side. We're gonna spread out and circle the thicket, gotta be quiet as field mice. Ya gotta hold that bag open, down on the ground 'til ya' hear them snipes headin' yer direction. When ya' feel the bag a jumpin', ya know one or two done run in it. Then, quick like, hold it tight at the top." Without any further instruction, Reverend Lawson tiptoed around to the far side of the thicket. The men stood there in the darkness several minutes, pressing the backs of their hands to their mouths to keep from laughing. Willie bit into his own flesh hard enough to cause pain. Somehow, he smothered the hoot he wanted to produce.

After ten minutes, they began rustling some branches on the bushes, and called out, "Here it comes! Git ready, Preacher! One's a comin' your way ligity split." Then they'd walk away from that thicket to the next patch and repeat the actions. "Did ya git one yet, Preacher?"

Reverend Lawson barely audibly answered, "Nope. Somehow, I missed it."

"Preacher, ya gotta hold that bag down at ground level and don't move a muscle. Don't even let 'em hear ya breathin'. Them snipes ain't gonna jump up in the bag if they see ya so much as bat your eyes."

"I am holding still. The bag's flat on the ground."

"It might be that them snipes hear ya whisperin'. Ya best think about hushin' up."

After the next thicket, the men stood in silence for a few minutes. They enjoyed knowing the Reverend finally stopped talking and obediently followed instructions. They edged their way over to a fallen tree, putting more distance between the Preacher and themselves. They sat down in the darkness and listened to the night sounds, envisioned the Jack Leg Preacher out there—somewhere—waiting for the snipes to run into his burlap bag. They dared not speak above a whisper and they struggled to stifle laughter.

After three-quarters of an hour, they headed back to Jordan's, thankful that Solomon was with them. The path was difficult to find in the darkness, even plenty treacherous for a mountain goat in broad daylight, and next to impossible in the darkness. Willie called out, "Whoever is behind me, take a hold of my hand."

"Brother, you're on yer' own. I can hardly keep on my own two feet," Darrell responded.

Willie grabbed for the next tree, missed, and tumbled down. He screamed the minute he hit the ground and rolled about fifteen feet, before thumping into another tree. He grabbed the tree and pulled himself to his unsteady feet and clung onto the tree for dear life. Disoriented in the darkness he called out, "I mean it. Help me! I cain't see my hand in front of my face." He felt the strong arms of Turner and Clyde wrap around him, one on each side. They all waited for several minutes while Willie got his footing. Rolling down the mountain, even the short distance made him dizzy. It was a dangerous descent, but they finally made it without a further incident.

They limped toward Solomon's porch. The humor of the evening returned as they imagined the Preacher still up yonder, dutifully holding the burlap bag open. They wondered how long he might stay put, if they didn't go back for him.

Forty feet shy of the porch, Solomon threw his arm out to halt the men in their tracks. He pointed in the direction of his porch and whispered, "Something's there, in the shadows. Lookie, sittin' on the step. They froze as each strained to make out a figure in the darkness. They saw movement and knew someone indeed squatted on the porch steps. They cautiously edged another step closer trying to focus in the darkness.

They jumped when the 'something' spoke to them. They recognized the Jack Leg Preacher's voice, "Where've you been? I gave up and came on back down to wait for you. Anyway, we got our limit. So, no need staying up there any longer. I called for you, but didn't hear nary a peep."

"How the blue blaze thunder did you beat us'ns back and us not hear you," said Lawrence.

"You do recall telling me to be quiet? Well, I was," Reverend Lawson answered.

As the startled men edged closer to the porch, they noticed the burlap bag at his feet, knotted tightly at the top. They dared not comment on the bag. They stood speechless as the Reverend got up and thanked them for the adventure and for letting him tag along. He called back over his shoulder, "I once visited a friend of mine that had a parish assignment in southern Georgia. Those folks really do snipe hunt. Snipe aren't indigenous to these mountains, nor did we catch snipe in a burlap bag, but this was certainly an interesting experience." He stuffed his hands deep into his pockets and leisurely strolled off down the road, whistling a happy tune. The burlap bag continued to move. They stood in a semi-circle curiously focusing on the squirming bag.

One of the men whispered, "What do ya reckon he bagged?" Carefully, Solomon loosened the knot. They watched more movement from within. Solomon nudged the bag with the toe of his boot. Out strutted an irritated polecat which wasted no time positioning itself perfectly in line with the men. The skunk raised its tail and sprayed a stream of repulsive scent covering Solomon Jordan's front porch and hitting some of the men. The snipe hunters scrambled over one another in an attempt to avoid the pungent oily spray.

This would not be a tale to repeat at the general store after all. A major disappointment.

Reverend Lawson knelt by his bed that night, "Father, again, I ask for forgiveness." He chuckled a little before continuing, "One thing for certain, Lord, I've asked for more forgiveness since I met these Brothers, than I've needed in the past five years. They're keeping me humbled before You. Bless them, Lord. They need it."

MUSIC HERE TONIGHT

Hand lettered posters plastered the window fronts of the general store and lumber yard.

It read simply:

MUSIC HERE TONIGHT

To the mountain folks, no other explanation was necessary. Life in these mountains proved a hard life, with few celebrations. In many households, laughter came as a rare treat. The day-to-day struggles necessitated a serious lifestyle. Any opportunity that afforded an escape from the norm was embraced. No tickets sold, no chairs set up, no elaborate sound system installed, no programs printed for distribution. The music would be as simple as the announcement.

It was a clear day with a balmy breeze. Families would bring their own quilts both to sit on and throw around their shoulders for protection against the brisk night air certain to arrive following the sunset. At the completion of the evening milking and chores, the spectators arrived settling in next to friends and neighbors for a rare time of relaxation and socializing.

Anticipation had grown during the day. The doldrums disappeared as they hurried through mundane tasks to guarantee early arrival prior to the music making. Many of these ballards they'd heard their entire lives. The familiar tunes provided a certain comfort. Most times the music evoked childhood memories from the past, as care-free children roaming the green fields of Greenbed. The music lifted the heavy burdens off tired, stooped shoulders, refreshing spirits as nothing else could.

The Bairds placed their quilts next to the Lowes. Even though their lands were adjacent, they hadn't seen each other in months. A long list of chores to accomplish took every hour from sun up to sun down for the households to survive.

Josiah Baird asked Thomas Lowe when he'd last seen their neighbor, Jake Hicks. Thomas chuckled, "I'm gonna tell ya a story, happened last week. I'd put my hand on the Good Book to swear it to be the truth. I was fixin' to mow the back pasture and I drove on over to Hicks' farm whilst I was right under his nose. I beat on the door. No answer. I hollered. No answer. I walked 'round to the back of the house. What do ya reckon I spied? I'll tell ya." Thomas stopped to enjoy a chuckle, slapping Josiah on the back. "There was Jake, facing mason jars set up on the fence posts. He was havin' a shoot out with them jars. He'd swear at 'em, threaten 'em, then pull his gun and shoot at the jar. He'd tell 'em he was powerful sorry it had come to this, but he'd done give 'em ever' chance to mend their wicked ways. He'd put the gun back and start talkin' to the next jar. I never see'd nothin' like that in my life. I stood there and watched that blame show for four jars and then I thought my insides might bust wide open if'n I didn't laugh. And I'm here to tell ya', I let loose a roar of a laugh. You wouldn't believe the wild look on his face!"

Josiah and Thomas rolled backwards on the quilts laughing. Josiah could scarcely speak, "What'd ya do? Hattie woulda, for sure, shot him if she'd but known he was breakin' her cannin' jars."

"I busted out laughin', that's what I done! Tell ya the truth, there for a minute, I feared that ole cowboy might point that gun at me and shoot. He lowered the gun, but he looked powerful mad that somebody done caught him out there bein' a gunslinger, marshal, or whatever from the wild west." Another round of laughter, before Thomas continued, "He looked me square in the eyeballs, and told me if'n I breathed a single word of that to anybody, he'd hunt me down and put a bullet in my hide, same as if I was a varmint raidin' his henhouse."

Josiah quickly sobered up, "He threatened ya, like that? For real? What're ya gonna do 'bout that?"

Thomas let loose the loudest cackle yet, "I'll tell ya what I been doin' 'bout it. I been tellin' ever livin' soul I see. It gets better ever time I git the chance to tell it."

"Ain't ya scared he might hunt ya down and shoot ya, like he threatened?"

"Don't forgit, I saw the way he shot. I don't think he'd be lucky enough to hit me, besides I doubt he could hit the broad side of a bright red barn on a clear day. I ain't a bit scared."

Dusk closed in on the Greenbed gathering. The children busied themselves chasing lightning bugs emitting squeals of delight. The chatter hummed continuously on every quilt as neighbors reacquainted. Thousands of brilliant stars blanketed the dark backdrop of the sky. Couples that rarely looked across the table at one another sat arm in arm as lovers.

The musicians gathered on the porch of Guthrie's General Store. A hush spread over the crowd as they hungered for the first sounds of music. The musicians tuned their various instruments and foot-stomping, hand-clapping music soon filled the air, transforming the quiet little community into a well-deserved celebration of lively, joyous, music. The weights of their burdens and the hard life were alleviated with the first strum of the five-string banjo. No doctor, no medication, no home-brewed whiskey could work this kind of charm on the mountaineers as completely as the sounds of the strings and beloved old songs.

The first song to warm up the gathering was 'The Country Blues'. The group hooped and hollered at the amusing lyrics of friends being friends as long as one has money; but as soon as the money ran out, the friends couldn't be found. They knew the words to be true. The fiddle player stepped forward and began playing another lively tune well known by the group.

The crowd sat motionless anticipating the next song, and it was the upbeat rhythm that they had longed to hear. The banjo player's fingers flew across the strings producing magical sounds. He occasionally plucked individual strings for emphasis as he played Rambling Hobo. Although the song was barely one minute in length, it sufficiently circulated music through the veins of every listener. The performers felt the crowd in their hands, as always, at a singin' in the mountains.

There needn't be a set format for the Music Nights. It flowed freely, like a river meandering gently through the community. First one, then another, would step forward and play their wonderful instruments, singing until their voices strained to reach the notes. The musicians would lay one instrument aside only to retrieve another. They went from six string guitar, harmonica, banjo, twelve-string guitar, juice harp, hammered dulcimer, regular dulcimer, mandolin, autoharp, spoons and jugs, and back to the favorite—the fiddle. They sang a mixture of songs dating back generations, and made up songs about recent events there in Greenbed. And, of course, the old gospel songs always proved a favorite, even to the residents who never darkened the door of a church.

The foot stomping that accompanied "I'll Fly Away" was so vigorous that at the conclusion of the song the performer yelled out, "Guthrie, where are ya?" Guthrie waved his arm from within the crowd. "Are ya' frettin' that we're gonna put a hole through the General Store's porch?"

Guthrie yelled back from his seat on the grass, "Go ahead. We'll patch her up if'n ya' do. It'll be worth it!" That was the feeling of the entire crowd—'it was worth it,' worth it to forget the worries of an ailing family member, worth it not to worry about the money for the tractor tire, worth it to escape the concern over the dry fields begging for rain. Whatever heavy burdens they'd brought on their backs to the 'Music Tonight' were mysteriously absent on the trip home. Even though the same problems and struggles would be there with the sunrise, they'd be a tad easier to cope with for yet another day.

For two hours the music filled the mountainside, the laughter rang out as freely as the notes. The spectators clapped and kept time to the contagious beats until their red palms became sore. The last song of the evening was announced and a man came forward from his sitting position from within the center of the crowd, moving toward the porch. He picked up a fiddle and solemnly overlooked the crowd, stretched his right arm and bow out toward the heavens and held that pose until a hush settled over the entire crowd. Reverend Lawson lowered the bow and slowly pulled the bow across the strings to produce the moving notes of Amazing Grace. They lingered there, sitting as though mesmerized. The rich notes filled the night. The mountaineers joined in and the words of praise lightly floated upward, to kiss the bright stars in the heavens, greeting and praising the Living Lord. When he completed the last note of the song, again he outstretched his long arm and bow towards the heavens. He held that pose. No one spoke, not daring to break the magical spell. God was present in their midst.

The Parson had delivered the most powerful sermon of his life, without uttering a single word.

MOUNTAIN-STYLE PUNISHMENT

Reverend Lawson headed toward Guthrie's General Store with a burdened gait. He held the banister rail and slowly traversed the steps, deep in thought. On this chilly autumn day, the Brothers enjoyed the warmth of the general store's potbelly stove and the companionship. These days, the uncertainty of the brewing war abroad occupied most conversations, whether the general store, church, or lumber yard.

Clyde shared what he heard on the radio the previous night, "I'm afraid we are headin' lickety split for war. It's getting' bad over yonder. I don't know what's next, bound to be something mighty big. That Hitler feller marched them troops right into Poland. He cain't keep doin' such."

Concerned, Lawrence inquired, "Preacher, are ya tryin' to carry the weight of the world on yer shoulders. Are ya' worried about this war too? Ya' look like a whipped puppy draggin' in here. What ails ya?"

"Sure, I'm concerned about the war. Those nations won't stand for the injustices the Germans continue to dish out. I'll tell you this, mark my words, if our country gets involved in this mess, I'm going." The Brothers didn't respond. The Preacher surprised them with his fervor. Reverend Lawson surveyed the store to see who might be within ear shod. He forced a smile at the men congregated in the front by the windows, and cut his eyes toward the women shoppers. The men surmised he wanted to talk to them, but only after the ladies exited. The minutes seemed to drag by as the women strolled up and down the aisles inspecting first one thing then another. After a long ten minutes, the two ladies finally left and only with a five pound bag of coffee beans each. The tension in the room could be cut with a dull knife.

Unconsciously, the men scooted their stools and chairs closer to where the Parson stood.

As soon as the door shut behind them, Willie said, "I think them two womenfolk fingered ever' blame thing in the whole daggone store twice before leavin.' Now tell us what's got ya lookin' all down in the mouth, Preacher?"

Reverend Lawson cleared his throat, "Now, listen, this must remain within these walls. I am bound by an oath of my profession not to divulge this information, but perhaps I need to ask a question in a matter that would not break the confidence of the parishioner."

Lawrence spoke for the group of men when he said, "Preacher, what in the sam hills are ya talking about? I ain't got a ghost of an idea what ya just said. Cain't ya do plain talkin' to us'ns?"

He tried again, "It's delicate and potentially dangerous. Give me your word you won't repeat this outside these walls." Spontaneously, they nodded in agreement. Any man worth his weight in salt kept his word. Reverend Lawson knew if this group gave their word, they'd go to their graves with a secret. "I went to call on one of my parishioners. The wife weakly called through the closed door that her husband was not home. It's a rule of mine to never go into a lady's home unless the husband is there. I won't be accused of being in a compromised situation, if you know what I mean." He noted the confused look on their faces. "Anyway, I asked if she could come out and we could sit a spell on the front porch. She began hemming and hawing with one excuse after another. I felt uneasy about her at this point. I sensed something was amiss, and wanted to know things were on the up and up. After much persuasion, she opened the door and came out. One look at her told me she'd been beaten. The goose-egg knot on her head, black eye, cut and swollen lip, she could hardly move her right arm, and she was holding her side. The way she was bent over and whispering, I suspect she suffers from a broken or cracked rib or two. I asked her what happened and she said she clumsily tumbled down the cellar steps. I knew by the cowed look on her face, that was no accident. She couldn't look me in the eyes. She became hysterical and refused me when I suggested that I'd take her to see a doctor. She's living in fear of whomever did this to her."

He paused for a minute. "To tell the truth, I never dealt with anything quite like this before. I don't know if it's more my duty to talk to the law and let them handle it, or guard the confidence she placed in me by allowing me to see her. I'm asking your advice, how are things like this handled in the mountains? I can't just turn my head and pretend not to have noticed."

"No! Don't take it to sheriff," Guthrie said. "I've seen firsthand how that goes, and it's never good. It makes matters worse, like throwing gasoline on a raging fire. Besides, the law won't do nothing about it. It's private business."

The young Parson put his head in his hands, running his fingers through his dark hair, and shook his head. When he removed his hands, tears clouded his eyes. "I can't sit by and allow that person to continue using her as a punching bag. Nobody deserves that life."

Darrell asked the obvious question on everyone's mind, "Who is it?"

"Darrell, you know I can't tell you that. That would be a total breach of confidence. I've said too much already. I feel that my hands are tied."

Turner asked, "Reckon her man done it to her?"

Reverend Lawson slowly nodded. "That's my guess judging from the way she reacted. Plain to see she was scared to the bone but still protecting someone. No one else lives there with her. I assume he is the culprit."

Turner continued, "There's different ways of dealing with things in the mountains. We don't fool with no trial and juries. There'd not be no witnesses, wouldn't do no good to have a trial. We go straight to the root of the problem, and take care of things. Then it's over and done with, it's a sure-shot cure."

Reverend Lawson looked up appalled, "I in no way wish to be involved with any type of revenge, nor condone any further violence. Not after dedicating my life to a way of peace and forgiveness. I pledged to be a beacon of light in the darkness and to show a better way." The Reverend turned to take his leave. "If you have any ideas, please let me know. Mr. Guthrie, that goes for you too. Something needs to be done, but I don't have a clue." Without another word, he left the general store, as encumbered as when he entered.

Although the gathering of Brothers felt chastised, they still determined to smell out where this trouble brewed and spring into action. They weren't as young as they used to be when they'd taken such matters into their own hands. Father Time taught them as they aged, they needed to give this more thought to plot out; whereas in younger years, it didn't matter. They would have accosted the abuser regardless of where he was, or who was with him and gave him a beating he'd not likely forget.

Guthrie stealthily joined the Brothers and spoke just above a whisper, "I didn't let on to the Parson, but first thing yesterday morning, soon as I opened, Ella Mae Thompson was hiding 'round the side of the store. She came creepin' in, kept her head down. I clearly saw when we settled up, a split lip and eye swollen nigh onto shut. I asked her what happened. She mumbled a response, about taking a tumble. I doubt a fall did that. Poor soul, already embarrassed to death. She took her purchase, slapped down the money and left. Nary another word. I'll betcha that low-down husband of hers is the culprit. That Jasper is no good."

Clyde shifted in his seat adjusting himself, as if he prepared to deliver a speech from a podium. "I heard what the Preacher said, and that's OK for him. It ain't gonna cut it for me. Jasper can't keep beatin' her. She couldn't weigh more than a sack of feed. He's apt to kill her in a drunken stupor. Likely, he came home drunk as a skunk when he done that to her. He needs a lesson he won't be forgettin no time soon. Brothers, who's in with me?"

As expected, all the Brothers, plus Guthrie, readily agreed. They knew Jasper visited the still located down the mountain from his place, in what was commonly known as The Flower Patch Still. This clearing acquired its name many years earlier when sunflowers voluntarily sprang up, and covered the sunny bare patch on the side of the mountain. Beyond the sunflowers, the still was located about 500 ft. into the dense trees, down beside the stream. All stills required a water source and the nearby stream was far more convenient than a piping system to which some stills resorted. The Bass brothers operated this still, notorious for producing one of the lowest qualities and cheapest white lightning in the vicinity. They consistently rushed the process to turn a quick profit. They didn't mind the reputation of being gallivanting ruffians producing the worst moonshine in the area. As long as the customers kept coming, they didn't care about cleanliness or quality. The Brothers heard tales about the disgusting conditions in which the Bass moonshine was brewed. They didn't use copper piping, but rather settled for sheet iron, causing the liquid to frequently burn which produced a most unpleasant taste; nor did they stir it as it heated. More than once, they hadn't properly strained the whiskey and several of the men became violently ill. Yet, these same men returned to purchase more the next time they hankered for the powerful juice.

The scheming men plotted, and ideas bounced around from first one Brother and then the next. "We could jump Jasper as he heads to the still."

"Ya know good and well, all the stills post a lookout man. He'd go to ringin' the warnin' bells or blowin' a horn, or worse yet, shootin his shotgun. I tell ya', we might get blown to kingdom come if we mess with them crazy Bass boys! They've always shot first and asked questions later."

"Besides, them other men would come runnin' onct they saw we weren't revenuers. It'd be a brawl to go down in the history books. More 'n likely, they'd kill us before we could hightail it outta that den of thieves."

Another Brother suggested, "If we waited for him at his home, he might be too drunk to remember, or worse yet, might think his wife had done him harm. Not to mention, it'd scare Ella Mae to death, and who knows, she may grab Jasper's gun and blow us to the pearly gates."

They decided to wait at the edge of the sunflowers and jump him as he came off the path. Jump him how? Would they pummel him? How would he know this was a revenge flogging? He needed to learn a lesson, or it would be a waste of time and energy. They discussed a number of possibilities. They agreed to hide and wait among the sunflowers, hoping he'd consume enough snorts of whiskey before he reached the road, at least enough to dull his senses. They'd sneak up behind him and throw a burlap feedbag over his head and quickly drag him to the other side of the road. They'd have dug a shallow grave and put a makeshift open wooden coffin in the hole. They knew Jasper came from a superstitious family and was mighty fearful of boogers, haints, and goblins. Without showing their faces, they'd position Jasper with a view of the coffin, warning him not to move. They'd cover their heads with sheets and dance around the grave. They knew he'd soon jerk the burlap sack off his head as soon as he freed his hands. If all went well, they wouldn't hurt him, but scare him into mending his wicked ways. Surely, the haints would sober him up enough to realize his life hung in jeopardy with the great beyond.

They carefully practiced the speeches, 'We've been sent to claim your soul—dead or alive. Your Maker is ready to meet you face—to-face for your final judgment. Jasper, ya cain't no longer live in this world 'cuz ya are a mean cuss of a man and y'er married to a Saint. It's your time to stand before the Almighty and confess your actions toward Saint Ella Mae 'cuz she deserves better than the likes of y'er sorry soul.' They'd also flash long, sharpened, huntin' knives and make threats until he solemnly promised not to lay a hand to her again. A bucket of cold water might serve well to sober him up.

Clyde offered, "Full moon's tomorrow night. We could dig the shallow grave first light and make a wooden coffin and be ready for him 'fore he seizes a chance to strike her again. Whatcha say?" Content with this plan, they dispersed toward their respective homes. Clyde reminded them, "Don't utter a word of this, to nobody. Understand?" They all nodded. He called back over his shoulder, "You in, Guthrie? Can ya meet us there about 7 PM and we'll wait. Full moon out, he'll for sure pay a visit to the 'farm in the woods'." He used the familiar bootlegger term. They all knew what 'farmin in the woods' represented and hastily nodded in agreement.

Guthrie called out, "Good Lord willing and the creek don't rise, count on me." He shut the door and questioned if telling them about Ella Mae was a wise decision. What if this scheme didn't unwind as planned? What if he were responsible for someone else being injured, or worse yet, killed? The more thought he gave this scheme, the weaker it appeared, success relied on too many uncertainties. Looking at the battered Ella Mae, he knew she didn't deserve such treatment and her life could be in jeopardy. Guthrie felt, unless they stepped up to help her, Clyde was right, it wouldn't be long until that crazy Jasper would take her life, and probably get away with it. With shaky hands, Guthrie began stocking the shelves, but his mind ventured into the next twenty-four hours. He wished he could consult with the Reverend to at least enlist his prayers for this scheme. After all, it wouldn't hurt to have God in their corner. Guthrie sensed God would be in their corner, even without the Reverend standing by in a prayer vigil.

Long-bladed—hunting knives were carefully sharpened and shined, hoping when the moonlight hit the knife, it might add to the confusion, and fright for ole Jasper. Willie, Turner, and Lawrence took care of digging the fictitious grave among the mountain laurel. Darrell, Clyde, and Arville constructed the makeshift coffin from scrap lumber. Clyde kept reminding them, "No need takin pains with the workmanship, with luck, Jasper'll be beyond noticin'. I hope he recognizes it as his coffin and not a cozy place to sleep off his toot."

The conspiracy was set in motion as they concealed themselves among the tall, gently swaying sunflowers. They watched and waited. About 8:10 they spotted Jasper moseying down the dirt road from the direction of his farm. He paused looking both ways to be certain no one followed him before entering the woods. The Bass boys warned all the customers to use a different path each time they came and went. The sunflower gang's hearts pounded. They realized loopholes existed in this loosely concocted scheme.

Clyde felt their anxieties, he whispered, "What we're doing is a good thing. We *can* do this. I believe we got the Good Lord on our side." The pep talk squelched a little of the uncertainty. In Jasper's haste to get that first taste of the white lightning; he didn't so much as glance in the direction of the rustling sunflowers. So far, the plan unfolded right on track. Guthrie whispered, "Looks like the Good Lord is smilin' down on us."

They remained concealed for another half hour, lay-waiting Jasper. The challenge became keeping Willie's mouth shut. His Brothers threatened him several times.

Jasper and the Bass boys were cut from the same mold, they were probably exchanging useless jibberish now. Willie asked, "How we gonna know if Jasper had a good nip 'fore we jump 'im?"

Clyde had already been concerned about that, but confidently responded, "We've ever one tipped the bottle with Jasper before, liquor goes straight to his head. He'll come swaying like a chicken with its head cut off. Don't matter no way, we're here to take care of the business we came to do." He secretly hoped that held true. In the soft moonlight he looked up to the heavens and offered a silent prayer for help.

They heard voices coming. Singing. Guthrie whispered, "Ut oh, sounds like Jasper met up with a drinkin' buddy. Now what? We weren't countin' on two of 'em."

Arville responded, "There's just two of them, seven of us'ns. I say we take 'em by surprise. It won't matter."

"Only thing is, I brought one burlap feedbag. We gonna have to see how wasted they are first," Turner said. They watched for the first signs of Jasper and his drinking companion. Jasper staggered out into the clearing with his arm looped carelessly around the shoulder of someone. Both men carried a jar that shone in the moonlight.

Clyde rose a little from the crouching position, "It's now or never. I say it's now. Arville's right. We'll surprise 'em and they won't know what hit 'em. Put them sheets over your heads now and let's go a whoopin' and a hollerin', grab 'em fast and get 'em to the other side of the road, where you dug the grave before Basses' gang gets suspicious. We best move like greased lightning. Basses won't risk crossin' over to the other side of the road out in the clearing to investigate. They'll be a guardin' their interests back at the still if'n they hear any commotion. Come on." With that, he threw the sheet over his head and left the security of the sunflower patch. With white bed sheets flapping, they attacked the unsuspecting men. Clyde wondered what the wives would think next time they used the sheets and saw two big eyeholes cut in them.

The haints quickly circled the two surprised men, the slurred singing immediately ceased. The sheeted group forced the two across the narrow road and into the cover of the woods. In the moonlight they recognized the second imbiber as Ray Clemmins, a harmless, timid gent, whom they'd all shared bottles with at one time or another. Right off, Ray began crying, "Oh, Lordie, Lordie, Lordie! No! I know what this means. Have mercy on me." Confused, the sheeted haints said nothing, hoping Ray might expound on his theory, which he did. "Lord, have mercy on me! Jasper, 'ain't ya' never heard tell of the rapture? This is the rapture and ya better commence to beg for y'er sorry soul, b'fore it's too late. We're gonna be throwed into the Lake of Fire. Forever!" The goblins took their lead from Guthrie, who began flapping his sheet like crazy, and he loosened his grip on Ray's shaking arm. Ray jerked his arm free and ran through the woods lickety split, as fast and far as his shaking legs could carry him. Not once, did he look back. They witnessed in amazement Ray's speed, as he wobbled through the woods, bouncing off tree to tree. Somehow, he miraculously jumped over a fallen tree trunk like a deer. They knew he wouldn't return to help Jasper. Ray saved himself.

The ghosts kept a tight circle around Jasper and edged him closer to the prepared grave. They pushed Jasper toward the make-shift wooden coffin and surrounded him. His eyes widened at the sight of the coffin. Drink may have clouded his ability to logically think, but there was no mistaking what the wooden box represented. His face showed the fear of that recognition. Thus, began the Day of Judgment.

Surprisingly, Jasper stood in front of the makeshift box serving as his coffin. He looked at the ghosts around him as the moonlight flashed on the metal of long knives. Jasper was paralyzed from fear. The accusations began, Jasper was called upon to confess his guilt, and he did. He confessed to drinking, swearing, lying, cheating, laying out of church, and stealing a pig from old man Reynolds. He never once mentioned the afflictions he showered on Ella Mae. A mysterious voice from under a sheet spoke, "How ya treat yer wife?"

The bootleg whiskey provided a false courage, as he responded indignantly, "Leave her outta this. She ain't got nothin' to do with it."

Another hooded haint spoke, "We're here to judge ya. She's yer responsibility to take care of, seems like ya been falling down on yer job. She ain't been treated none too good. Hold out yer hands." Obediently, Jasper outstretched one hand in the moonlight. "Yep, sure enough. She got them marks on her from yer very hands."

"She ain't got it so bad. She complains and nags."

Another of the sheets joined, "We oughta cut yer lying tongue outta yer mouth. Then we need to cut off yer hand so ya never hit her again. How do ya like that, Mr. Big Tough Man?" Instinctively, all the sheeted creatures raised their long knives. "And if'n yer still bad-mouthin' her and bein' mean, we'll come back and carve yer wicked heart outta yer chest and feed it to the dogs for supper." The sheeted creatures couldn't believe how well this inquisition played out. They read the fear on Jasper's face and knew he began to comprehend his guilt.

Jasper, indeed, grasped the severity of his situation and commenced to beg for forgiveness and swearing he would change and never raise a hand to Ella May again, he'd be good in word and deed.

The sheeted beings with their arms hooked together, began slowly circling the grave, proclaiming their threats to Jasper 'if he ever so much as looked cross-eyed at Ella Mae again.' Willie stepped on the edge of his sheet and lost his footing and felt himself slipping, he didn't unclasp his arm from Arville or Clyde, who hadn't broken the hold they had on the ghosts next to them. Too quickly to recover, all seven men fell into the grave, with Jasper at the bottom of the heap of haints. They all began a mad scramble to get out, stepping on Jasper, elbowing, kicking, doing whatever it took to escape the grave and free themselves from one another. It was one thing to put a drunken Jasper in a grave, but quite a different story when they found themselves sharing the same grave. After scrambling out, they peered down at the motionless Jasper. They gasped when they spotted a pool of blood forming by him. Apparently, one of the knives sliced his arm.

"Reckon he's dead? Did we kilt 'em?"

"Somebody best check," said Darrell. As if on cue, Jasper let out a low groan. It was time to get out of the sheets and beat it home. Jasper, just momentarily knocked out, would likey come to and leap straight out of the grave.

The moonlight haints did not reconvene at Guthrie's General Store for two days. They made a pact not to discuss that night with anyone and not even talk about it among theirselves. Reverend Lawson saw Lawrence and Darrell walking toward the store and quickened his gait to catch up with them. Unable to contain the boyish grin on his face, he greeted the Brothers.

He squatted on a stool next to them in the store and joined in the small talk about the weather.

He waited for the opportunity for the store to be empty of other customers before speaking his mind, "Did you hear about Jasper Thompson?"

The color faded from Lawrence's face as he stammered a response, "We a . . . a . . . been powerful busy. Did something happen to 'im? I don't believe we saw him for, oh, I don't know. But it's been a long time."

Proud as a peacock the Reverend continued, "Jasper got religion! It is nothing short of a miracle."

The 'retired sheeted haints' managed to keep straight faces while Guthrie asked, "No, hadn't heard that, Preacher. Do tell." The Brothers and Guthrie exhaled a sigh of relief and tried to force a smile onto their solemn faces.

"Sure enough! Jasper came to see me, got me out of bed. He'd had a near death experience. It left him with a sore ribcage, two black eyes, a gash on his arm, and a lump on his forehead bigger than the one Ella Mae sported. It seems he got involved in some sort of rapture occurrence. Jasper told me one of the tallest tales I've ever heard in my life. He couldn't quite get the details straight, but he definitely knew he needed to get right with the Lord. He knelt right there on my kitchen floor and prayed for forgiveness and turned his life over to the Lord. Jasper shed tears of shame, mixed with tears of joy. He promised he would be in church alongside Ella Mae every time the church doors opened. I believe he is genuinely a changed man. The Lord moves in mysterious ways, His wonders to perform. Ella Mae is mighty grateful to those haints, goblins, for whatever happened. It is an answer to prayer. Ella Mae is beholding to the haints and sure wants to shake their hands." The Preacher didn't say another word. He left Guthrie's General Store with a smile on his face.

14

HEAVEN CAME DOWN

Lawrence didn't like what he saw in Arville's face, "What's ailin' ya t'day, Brother?"

Arville slowly shook his head, "Blamed if I know. I'm weak as pond water. I don't know when I ever felt this puny."

All the frivolous jokes and tall tales ceased. The mood turned serious as they noted his swarthy coloring. Willie engaged his mouth before his brain, "Have ya consulted old sawbones yet?"

"Nah, ain't no use. I'll get to feelin' better one of these days."

Clyde looked at his Brother, "Why don't we go into town to one of them city doctors, and let him take a look? See what he says."

"I'd have to have one foot in the grave to do that!"

Clyde dropped it, but far from forgot it. He remembered the pain of losing his other brother. After all these years, each Brother grieved and felt the guilt for Harvey's death.

Several weeks passed, they saw less and less of Arville at the store. Coming to the store required more energy than he could muster. Individually, the Brothers called on him at his home and were shocked to find him in bed resting in the middle of the day. His crops needed attention, the Brothers along with his neighbors, took turns tending to the farm's immediate needs.

A crisp, clear morning, Arville walked slowly into Guthrie's and assumed his usual seat by the window. As the Brothers and other shoppers dribbled in during the mid-morning hours, they were shocked to see a frail Arville sitting in his typical spot. The men sat in silence, each staring out the front window, or lightly running their fingers along the ragged hems of their coveralls. They wanted to look anywhere, but into the hollow face of Arville. He broke the silence, "Fellas, I reckon I got bad news."

Lawrence placed his hand on his Brother's shoulder and looked him squarely in the eyes, "Arville, what is it?"

Every eye in the general store turned to Arville, "The doc says I got cancer, it's apt to take me."

"What doctor done told ya that hogwash?" Willie hoped the doc was wrong, but felt Arville shared the truth.

"The city doctor, he done told me. He's a smart feller and 'sides them tests done proved it."

Clyde asked him, "City doctor? When did ya see any city doctor? How'd ya get there? Yer old truck can't pull the noll at Coome's Junction without sputterin' and rollin' backwards. You'd never get up and down the mountain."

"Preacher Lawson took me. He know'd of this doctor and said if'n any man could fix me, it'd be him. He set it up and took me and Della. I'll tell ya, we ought'n to tease that Preacher feller. He's a good man, and smart as a whip. Ya oughta heard him talkin' up to that city doctor, like he know'd ever'thing the doctor was a talkin' and tellin' about, askin' all manner of questions."

Again, the Brothers were speechless. This huge boulder crushed their hearts and spirits. What could be said? Words couldn't alter the inevitable end result. It was Arville who broke the intense cloud engulfing the general store. "Now, don't ya be all down in the mouth. I don't wanta be a lookin at no ugly, sourpuss faces from now til I'm called outta this world. We've had good lives. We been Brothers and best friends, like no brothers I ever heared tell of, it'll be alright. I done talked to Reverend Lawson and I'm right with my Maker."

Darrell spoke with a shaky voice, "But Arville, we ain't near ready to give ya up." All the Brothers dabbed at tears, including Arville.

None of the Brothers came about Guthrie's General Store for several days. And for the next three weeks, Arville was conspicuously missing. Each of the other Brothers faithfully stopped by his house to inquire, helping Della with anything that she needed. Della and Arville had been invited to move in with their oldest son, Joshua, but Arville insisted on staying in his own home until the end. Joshua and his wife lived at the end of the lane. It wasn't like they'd even leave the farm.

When they finally visited the general store, the Brothers exchanged tall tales about growing up, and mischief they performed in years gone by. Laughing was therapeutic. Many in Greenbed envied the unique relationship the Brothers shared. From the time they were small, if you messed with one—you dealt with all!

Mrs. Hickem questioned the Brothers as to how Arville was getting on. Clyde told last he saw him, Arville made the comment he 'felt like a sack full of possum heads.'

Much to everyone's delight and surprise, Arville seemed to rally slightly and was determined to whittle at the general store again with his Brothers. The perfect day donned, warm with streams of sunshine and the air brisk enough to refresh. He felt a tad stronger this morning. He slowly climbed the steps to Guthrie's General Store and Clyde and Darrell moved to make room for Arville to sit in the most comfortable chair. Darrell said, "Arville, ya look right pert today, ya gettin' better?" They hoped for a different outcome.

Arville shook his head, "No, Brother, 'fraid not. I've got one foot in the grave, but the other is a kickin' and fightin' for dear life. Mind ya, best I can tell, it's scarier to live than to die. But, then again, I ain't never crossed over Jordan before, I may be talkin' out of my head. Hand me one of them sticks, I might finish one of them fancy walkin' sticks and sell it to the city slicker." Arville chuckled and glanced toward Willie, who feigned embarrassment, pleased to see his Brother making light of anything, even at his expense.

The Brothers relished this special time with Arville, and everyone that came into the store, expressed joy at seeing him. It became the social event of the season. Old tales were rehashed and new tales spun, a wonderful spirit of remembering special times and celebrating their lives. Tears of joy, right along with tears of sorrow were shed unashamedly in the general store that day. Guthrie was proud to house this blessed event.

Darrell coaxed Clyde to divulge a tale he had shared with few. Today was a different kind of day though, and no attempts were made to guard secrets. "Tell us 'bout that late night visitor."

Clyde rarely experienced embarrassment, yet he hesitated, "They don't wanta hear that."

The Brothers encouraged him. "I heard someone bangin' on the kitchen door, right under our bedroom, in the middle of the blame night. Pulled on my pants and went to see what in the world. I knew whoever was there, must be in a heap of trouble to be out that late askin' for help. We'd all bedded down hours ago. I didn't turn the light on, but opened the door and saw the outline of two tall shadows standin' there. Both of 'em lifted buckets from behind their backs, and threw ice-cold spring water on me, drenched me to the bone. They screeched and howled like wild animals and took off running, jumped off the porch and across the field 'fore I could tell who they wuz. If'n I'd got my hands on 'em, I reckon I'd have beat 'em near to death. I was so mad, I saw stars!"

Turner had the floor and resurrected a memory from elementary school that Clyde would rather have forgotten. "Clydie, remember that middle girl of the Perkins' family, Sarah Perkins? She came askin' Cousin Margie how come her hair was so wavy, and do ya recall what you and Margie told her to do?" Clyde's belly shook as he chuckled, remembering the mischief.

It didn't take any coaxing from Guthrie for Turner to finish the story. "Clyde and Margie made up what they's a gonna tell her. Back then, one of 'em would lie and the other swear to it. Well, Clydie told Sarah that the only way to get hair purty as Cousin Margie's, wuz to wash it in molasses allowing it to set up so it'd take real good. That Perkins girl didn't believe Clyde at first and went straight to Margie. Of course, Cousin Margie was full of her devilin' fun too, and vowed and declared that wuz how she got them soft, natural waves."

"Aww, that's a tall tale, and ya know it. They ain't nobody that dumb witted to believe the likes of that," Mrs. Spike was in the store shopping and chimed in.

Clyde slapped his knee and laughed, "Nope, there was one dumb enough to believe it. Sarah went directly home and got into her Maw's molasses and scrubbed it in just as we told her. She couldn't get that sticky mess outta her hair. Her Mother came to school with her the next day. Sarah wuz pert nigh ruined. She coulda been a scarecrow, I never saw the likes of such a mess. The teacher tanned my butt good for tellin' such a thing to Sarah," he continued. "I wuz already in trouble with her Maw for dipping Sarah's braid into the inkwell that sat on my desk, cuz she sat right in front me." She never let me forget that!

They looked to Arville to see if these tales brought a smile to his face. Sure enough, he had a broad smile, but he didn't move. A long sigh escaped his lungs as the pocketknife slid from his hand onto the wooden floor. The angels paid a visit to Guthrie's General Store and quietly escorted Arville across the Jordan River through the Pearly Gates.

SIMMERIN' APPLE BUTTER

The chill to the mountain air marked the arrival of the most picturesque season. It was a miracle transformation from the spring's tiny buds to leaves displaying a parade of color marking the official climax of autumn. Old folks dreaded the harsh winters, particularly March. They'd say, 'if March don't get me, then by snort, I reckon I'll make it another year.'

The men in the general store hunkered closer to the potbelly stove. Guthrie joined the group, rubbing his hands together briskly and stretching his fingers toward the stove. "Have ya noticed the chill in the mornin' air? We had a frost yesterday, we can count our days til the first snowfall now." The men nodded. "I hate to see winter comin', seems I'm never ready to let go of summer, although, I look forward to someone bringin' me fresh bacon when you butcher hogs. Lawrence, when you butchering?" As surely as the leaves turned brilliant colors, the farmers butchered in late fall for the meat to cure in the smokehouse during the winter.

Lawrence studied on that for a moment, "I don't rightly know. It's gotta get colder than this. Don't worry, I won't forget to save ya' bacon. Don't I always? Lord knows, ya' remind us often enough." They snickered, recalling the frequency with which Guthrie mentioned the bacon.

Clyde brought a bushel of apples for Guthrie to sell or give away. All the men in the general store selected an apple and began spinning tall tales as they perfected peeled the apples, creating a long, twirling skin that danced just above the floor. Guthrie examined the dark red apples, "Clyde, I believe these are the prettiest apples you ever grew. What did ya' do different?"

Clyde smiled, "Held my mouth diff'rent, I suppose. I've got more apples than ... Willie's got brains." The Brothers enjoyed the jibe, Clyde continued, "there's no way we can use half of what those trees produced this year. Still, I suppose I'd make more money selling apples than Willie made pawnin' off the walkin' sticks. Willie, how 'bout ya' call that city slicker to come back here onct more." Willie grumbled; he didn't want to rehash that endeavor. Clyde proudly held up the entire apple peel in one long strand, "Lookie here! I do it ever' time."

He bit into the apple and the ample sweet juice slid down his growth of whisker stubbles. "Mmmm—the Good Lord blessed us this year with the juiciest apples ever grew in that orchard."

"Clydie, what are ya gonna do with all of them?"

"I can't even pick 'em fast enough, they all come ripe at the same time. Emma's got all she wants. She made pies, dumplins, fried apples, applesauce, and baked apples every day for a month of Sundays. She plans to make a mess of apple butter. Other than that, if I can't sell 'em or give 'em away, they'll rot on the ground and make the soil good and rich for next year. I hate to see 'em go to waste though."

A far away look possessed Guthrie's face, "Apple butter. Nothing much better than fresh, homemade apple butter loaded with cinnamon, makes my mouth water."

Darrell agreed and turned to Guthrie, "Hush your mouth wide open! You're makin' me hungry for apple butter and hot biscuits. Doggone, Guthrie, that's all I'll think about for days."

As much for himself as for the community, Guthrie suggested, "We could plan an Apple Butter Celebration before old man winter comes sniffing 'round our doors. What do ya' say? I'll furnish the sugar and cinnamon. Have it right out front here."

Darrell nodded, "That's a good idea. The womenfolk can make the apple butter and the men can pitch horseshoes and wait for the tastin'. Maybe get Jotham's boys to do some fancy banjo pickin' and whatnot?"

"How many cauldrons do you reckon we need?" Guthrie started calculating.

The men agreed that three cauldrons going should make more than enough for the mountain community to feast upon.

They chose Saturday after next. Plans formulated quickly. The womenfolk amended the idea slightly to include a hefty assignment for the men—they'd peel the apples, not the women. They reluctantly consented.

"Hey, since you fella's will take care of' the peelin', let's make a contest outta that," Guthrie appeared full of notions. "Every man to keep the peels he does, we'll count at the end and see who peeled the most, and only the peels that are one long strand will count."

"What's the prize?" Lawrence wanted to know if it was going to be worth the trouble.

Guthrie looked around the store, "It'll put considerable wear and tear on your knives. I'll give the winner a brand new Old Timer's pocket knife."

No further discussion. The challenge was gladly accepted.

On the given Saturday morning folks began setting up on the grassy noll outside Guthrie's General Store and situated the huge pots. The fires wouldn't be lit until at least half of the apples were peeled. The experienced cooks knew that to accomplish a thick, rich apple butter, simmering needed to be about six hours. Apple butter would cook in four hours simmering time, but everyone frowned upon that thin apple butter as substandard. They wanted the kind that sticks to yer bones on a cold mornin'.

Fourteen men entered the apple peeling competition and placed the chairs in a circle. Due to the seriousness of the prize, the conversation quickly ceased among the contestants. Winning was considered an honor, but a new knife was like Christmas morning. Ephraim Black worked the hardest at the task and accomplished the least. He kept losing his grip on his small inadequate knife. He became obviously frustrated. After peeling the first dozen, the Brothers began to banter among themselves. As expected, Willie made a mess and readily became the target of the taunts. Everyone enjoyed the light-hearted teasing, except Ephraim. He neither laughed nor looked up from the chore.

Several of the men who did not peel apples fashioned the wooden stirrers. Uncle Jim was organizing the men to make the stirrers. The long-handled wooden devices were formed with a "V" shape on the end for stirring.

With the last round of apples completed, Mr. Guthrie inspected and counted the apple peelings, calling out the totals for each man. Reverend Lawson kept the tally. Clyde won handsomely and Guthrie removed the coveted little box from his apron pocket and presented it to Clyde with a congratulatory pat on the back. The womenfolk wore homemade aprons crafted from the patterned feedbags, and the apple butter creations officially began.

The men organized and selected partners for the horseshoe game. Lawrence yelled, "Come on, Clydie, let's beat any of 'em brave enough to take us on."

Clyde waved at Lawrence, "Go on, get another good partner. I'll join in later." He had a more pressing issue to attend. He saw Ephraim holding the rail to the porch of the general store. "Good to see ya here today, Ephraim. Family sure is growin', how old is your boy now?"

"Gonna be eleven come next Tuesday. He's a big help to me on the farm now. Ya oughta see him throw them haybales onto the wagon. He's strong for his age and a good boy. Never no sass talk come out of him."

"Boy like that is a credit to his Father. A boy like that might need a pocketknife for his 'leventh birthday, to be of much use on a farm." Clyde slipped the prize pocketknife out of the side pocket of his coveralls and into Ephraim's free hand then saundered off the porch toward the horseshoe games. He didn't give Ephraim a chance to respond, and he didn't look back. Ephraim slid the treasure into his own pocket and swallowed hard to dislodge the lump in his throat. His gaze went toward the clouds and the blue skies as he whispered, "Thank ya Lord."

As the hours passed, the smells coming from the black kettles filled the air. The cinnamon mingled with the apples to add an intoxicating auroma. Only the cooks were allowed to dip a wooden spoon into the hot mixture for sampling. The children gathered near the kettles impatiently waiting as the smells filled the air. Children poked sticks into the red-hot embers under the kettles to stir the fires pretending they were sending Indian fire signals. The women shooed the children off to play elsewhere. The men soon ceased their games and gravitated toward the bubbling apple butter. The fiddle and banjo players laid down their instruments in anticipation of the treat. The last half hour of cooking to perfection passed the slowest of the entire procedure. Mouths watered as noses inhaled the magical aroma.

Maggie, declared her batch ready to dip. A line immediately formed of those anxious for the first tastes. Maggie looked up from the rich brown contents of the kettle in alarm, "Where's Guthrie? Get Guthrie." Guthrie appeared at Maggie's kettle. "Mr. Guthrie, what are we gonna put the apple butter on? None of us brought biscuits."

Guthrie turned to two of the children wiggling in and out of a lopsided line, "Come with me. We'll fetch every loaf of white bread in the store to feed this hungry mob."

Maggie scolded those crowding her kettle, "Step back and give it breathing room. Besides, Mr. Guthrie gets the first taste. If it weren't for him, you'd be lapping this hot apple butter up out of the palm of yer hand like a dog."

A wisecrack from the group called out, "Ya can put a dab on my hand if'n ya want to right now 'cuz I think I'll die right here on the spot if'n I don't taste that sweet nectar."

The day of simmerin' apple butter was deemed a great success, the mountainfolk declared this needed to be an annual event. Of course, they hoped Clyde's apples produced in abundance next year to make it possible. Now ole Man Winter could bring on his freezing temperatures, gray days, drifting snow, long nights, and harsh sleet storms. The warm memories of the apple butter celebration would fortify them to endure yet another bitter winter.

16

GRANDPAW OUGHT
NOT TO BABYSIT

The womenfolk committed themselves to rally round the Crosby's and help put up applesauce from their ripened apples lest they spoil. Anna Crosby was down with the consumption and not able to do any late-season canning for her family.

"Clyde, we need ya' to stay 'round the house and watch after Nancy Lynne today. Can ya' handle that?" Emma asked of her husband.

"Course I can. Who can't look after a little four year old girl? Anything I do, she can tag along. That blue-eyed darlin' loves stayin' with her Papaw." He looked at Nancy, and winked. "It'll be more fun than stayin' with a bunch of gabbin' women."

Clyde's daughter, Edna, wasn't convinced, "Poppa, are ya' sure?"

"You womenfolk worry too much! I raised my own children. Git on outta here. Anna will be obliged to ya for helpin' in her time of need. Them apples are better made into applesauce for her family to eat this winter than rottin' on the ground. Quicker ya' git there, the quicker ya' git back."

As Edna got behind the steering wheel of the truck, she asked her Mother for reassurance, "Mom, do ya think Nancy will be alright? Will he keep his eyes on her?"

Emma smiled and nodded, "He better, if he knows what's good for him."

As Emma and Edna veered the truck down the long dirt lane, they met Willie heading to Clyde's house. They waved, but Willie glared straight a head, shaking his head and talking to himself. The two trucks barely passed on the narrow lane. Willie still did not acknowledge them. The women joked about what in the world he'd have on his mind to cause him to be that intense about getting to the house. "Mom, should we turn around and see if something's wrong?"

"It's Willie, ya know good and well somethin' is wrong and it won't amount to an iota. He invents trouble, can make a mountain out of a mole hill quicker than anyone." They laughed, realizing the truth to the statement.

"Clydie! Clydie! Come quick! Where in the blazes are ya?" Willie shouted before he got near the house.

Clyde stepped out onto the porch. "Why are ya' lamentin', hootin' and hollerin'?"

"Cuz ya was to be in my barnyard an hour ago. Did ya take sick?"

"What are ya talkin' about, Willie?"

"Hog slaughterin' day! Ya always come shot 'em for me! All the men are standin' around waitin' on ya."

"I thought ya said we'd slaughter tomorrow."

"Clydie, get yer gun and come on with me. I saw the womenfolk headin' down the lane liggitysplit."

Clyde retrieved his gun from the rack and grabbed Nancy's little jacket and bonnet. "Come on, Honey, we're gonna have us some man fun today." Into the truck they piled, Nancy perched on her Papaw's lap, ready for an adventure.

The corralled hogs nervously pranced in the small fenced area of the muddy barnyard. Little Nancy climbed onto the first rung of the fence, peeping through the rails to see all the pigs. She outstretched her little hand to pet them. She felt a sense of pride to be positioned next to her Papaw as he surveyed the situation. He loaded the gun and steadied it on the top rung of the fence as he took aim. Bang. A hog fell squealing to the muddy earth. Nancy screamed. Bang, another, and another. Papaw was too busy trying to finish this task to notice that Nancy screamed each time the gun exploded. Tears streaked down her face. She didn't understand hog slaughtering, but she understood the desperation of the hogs and the ill fate that awaited each one of them. Clyde continued to pick them off, one at a time, and Nancy remained at her Papaw's side as she'd been instructed, paralyzed in fear. Each time one fell into the mud, Nancy screamed hysterically, jumping up and down, attempting to cover her ears with her chilled hands.

After the shooting, the men took one hog at a time and dropped it into the vat of boiling water, then scrapping the tough skin to remove the hair. The hogs were then strung up by their tied hind feet, slit open and the entrails removed. Nancy stopped crying after the loud gunshots ceased, but continued to watch each procedure with horror. At times the little girl couldn't stop herself from jumping and thrashing about, hoping this scene would halt and go away. The busy men paid no attention to the panic-stricken looks on the little girl's innocent face as she observed each phase.

Clyde did notice his Granddaughter's muddy shoes and he made a feeble attempt to clean them before entering his home. The ladies were tired when they got back to Clyde's. Edna threw her arms around the little girl, "Momma missed her girl today! Did you and Papaw have fun?" Nancy's big blue eyes just stared back at her Momma.

Nancy didn't say anything about the day's adventure. She nervously swayed back and forth on the trip home. She felt safe and secure in the loving arms of her gentle Mother and the hog killing seemed far behind.

That night, every time Nancy dozed off to sleep, she endured nightmares about the horrors of the day, and awakened screaming. Her small body shook with fear. Finally, they placed her between her Momma and Daddy where she eventually drifted into a peaceful sleep while clinging to her Mother.

The next morning Edna asked her Father, "Poppa, what did you and Nancy do yesterday?"

Clyde told her they had gone to Willie's for the hog slaughtering.

"I couldn't believe that you took her to such a thing when she described the awful things she saw! Well, I want you to know, Nancy had nightmares all night and the child was scared half to death! You ought to know better than to let a four year old see such a thing as that! What is wrong with you?"

"Ah, she weren't scared. Ya musta fed her somethin' for supper that made her belly ache. I never seen a kid so excited. That little darlin' just jumped up and down!"

THE KILLING TREE

After Reverend Lawson ate a meager dinner, he remained at the small wooden table to accomplish some serious writing for his book. A pounding on his door interrupted his creativity. He offered a quick prayer, "Father, grant me wisdom to handle whatever the situation, to your glory." He opened the door to discover Willie. "Come in out of the night air. What brings you out tonight?"

"Preacher, my wife, Daisy, sent me. Can you help her?"

Reverend Lawson's heartbeat quickened. He had been Miss Daisy's first acquaintance in Greenbed, and he united Willie and Daisy in holy matrimony after the whirlwind courtship. He felt a sense of responsibility for her. He grabbed Willie's arm tightly, "What happened to Miss Daisy?" He realized his concern and apprehension caused his voice to be much louder than necessary. Willie looked down at his feet and shuffled slightly as he gathered his thoughts. "What's wrong with Miss Daisy?"

"Well, Preacher, she's needin' a mighty big favor from ya."

His anxiety caused him to lose patience, "Mr. Willie, quit beatin' around the bush and spit it out!" Occasionally, this laid back mountain mentality tried his patience.

Willie squinted his eye shut tightly, "She's ailin' tonight and needs ya to teach her lessons at the schoolhouse tomorrow. Can ya help her out, Preacher?"

Reverend Lawson still concerned, "Does she need a doctor?"

"No, she's waitin' til mornin' to see how she fairs. She's got a pain in her belly. Can ya teach for her tomorrow?"

Relieved that it didn't sound serious, relief flooded over the Reverend. "Mr. Willie, I worked at a bank before going into the ministry. Granted, I helped what I could here before Miss Daisy arrived, but I'm not a teacher. Miss Daisy knows all of that. I guess if she trusts me with her pupils again, I'll do my best. What does she want me to teach?"

"She didn't tell me none of that. I reckon whatever you feel like. When I left her thrashing around in the bed, holdin' her belly, she weren't in much of a talkin' mood to tell the truth."

This was not something Reverend Lawson felt comfortable doing, but he'd asked God to give him wisdom prior to opening the door. How could he turn his back on such an opportunity? "Mr. Willie, tell her not to worry. Let me know if there's anything I can do for her. Please get word to me tomorrow about her condition. Take care of her tonight and get her to the doctor in the morning if she still feels poorly."

Willie squinted his right eye tighter, shaking his head in agreement. "I'll take care, don't you fret none 'bout that. The Good Lord done gave me the best gift I ever had in that Little Woman. I aim to see to it that she gits well," he turned and disappeared into the night. Reverend Lawson heard the old truck sputter, rattle, and eventually start.

The Reverend began searching through a box of packed books for a text book. As he rooted through the dusty books, he resumed his conversation with the Lord. "Father, you continue to shower varying opportunities upon me. I pray that I will bless these children tomorrow and teach them valuable lessons while increasing their faith. I'll be calling on you throughtout the day, and listening. And please be swift with answers."

Miss Daisy worsened during the night and complained to William 'it felt like a huge boulder pressing on her stomach.' Willie packed her into the 1925 Model T truck and headed down the mountain into town. She agonized with every pothole the old vehicle encountered. Willie's one eye attempted to dodge the deeper ruts in the dirt road and navigate safely down the mountain. The faster he tried to go, the more excruciating the pain became. By the time they reached town and found a doctor, the pain localized in her right side. She was transported to a hospital 17 miles away for an appendectomy. The doctor pulled Willie aside and confided that he would do his best, but it may be too late.

A slight chill to the morning air helped awaken the Reverend's senses as he walked toward the one-room schoolhouse. He hoped to find lessons on Miss Daisy's desk to offer him guidance. The community had grown accustomed to seeing him walk practically everywhere he went, but it took some doing. The first few months after he arrived, everyone stopped to offer him a ride on tractors, hay wagons, or the rumble seat of their cars. They finally accepted that he always appeared to be talking to himself as he strolled along. He prayed for Miss Daisy, for the children whose lives he would touch today, for wisdom, and above all, patience.

The children straggled in over the first two hours of school. This was acceptable since many of the boys helped with the farming chores. Amused, he watched the surprised expressions as the pupils entered to find what some had heard their parents refer to as the Jack Leg Preacher in Miss Daisy's chair. Their faces revealed disappointment, with the exception of fourteen year old Clair Evans who smiled and shyly waved at him as she twisted like a pretzel into her seat. Clair was, by far, the most matured girl, or woman, in the classroom.

The morning passed without an incident. The biggest challenge for him was discerning if Clair's actions were innocent or flirtatious. She wore a disturbing smile plastered on her face and found excuses to stand uncomfortably close to him. He gave her the benefit of the doubt until he removed his pocket watch to check the time, and she slid her hand over his and drew it to her to also view the timepiece. Her small fingers lingered around his hand. He rapidly withdrew his hand, astonishing Clair. She gave him a silly smile. He made a mental note to exhibit caution not to send any mixed messages to this young lady.

He taught reading and called upon volunteers to read from their textbooks, and transitioned into arithmetic. He noted that every child demonstrated a different level of capabilities with their number work. How in the world did Miss Daisy accomplish anything? He felt he'd lost control of the situation and opted for a change in the schedule. "It's a sunny day, let's take our lunches down the hill behind the schoolhouse and picnic under the big sprawling tree. I'll take a book and read a story to you after lunch."

He expected this announcement to bring welcomed expressions. Instead, he saw horror creep over their innocent faces. Not one child communicated the slightest joy. Puzzled, he asked, "Did I say something wrong? You want a picnic don't you?"

Silence. Reverend Lawson saw them exchanging looks, yet no one uttered a peep. Alarm was clearly demonstrated.

"Gather your lunches, we'll march together." No one moved. Wide eyes stared at him. Confused, he sat on the edge of Miss Daisy's desk and crossed his arms. "We aren't eating our lunches until someone explains to me what is going on."

Silence. He realized, for whatever reason, the children were not going to voluntarily enlighten him about this unwarranted reaction. He looked into frozen expressions and contemplated who might be his best choice to pry information from if asked. "Stanley Thomas, I'm asking you, Son, why did everyone react strangely about this?"

Stanley Thomas stood, as Miss Moretz taught the obedient pupils to do. With a pained look on his face, his eyes locked on the worn planks across the floor. He rubbed the toe of his shoe across the wood as he appeared deep in thought, struggling with a response.

"Stanley, please look at me." Stanley peeped up at the Parson, without moving his head. "I asked you a question and I'd like the respect of a reply."

"Sir, we ain't allowed to go down yonder. Them grounds is off limits."

The Parson was intrigued, "Why?"

Stanley Thomas slid down into his seat, hoping to be unnoticed. "Stanley, why is that off limits?"

Stanley Thomas struggled to his feet slowly. "Sir, my Paw sure to thrash me real good for goin' down there." He paused. "But he'd tan my hide something powerful if'n I didn't show you respect. I don't rightly know what to say." Reverend Lawson felt the lad's apparent struggle.

"Thank you, Stanley. I don't want to make you uncomfortable. Is there anyone in here that would explain to me what you all know, and I don't know." He should have expected this, Clair stood to her feet. Rather than remaining at her desk, she sashayed toward the front of the classroom and stood close, very close, to Reverend Lawson. She leaned over to whisper in his ear. He quickly stood and turned away from her and faced the class. "Clair, please share this with everyone." A disappointed look claimed her face.

She spoke just above a whisper, "Everybody 'round these parts knows that ground is filled with blood dirt. Them trees is killin' trees. It ain't fittin' for live humans to go near."

"Killing trees? What are killing trees?"

Reluctant to go any further, she slinked back to her seat, not without first turning with a silly grin that lasted all the way to her seat.

"Well, how about we get our lunches and sit on the front steps. I'll read there." Instant relief washed over every face, from the first graders to the older pupils. They grabbed their small lunches and scrambled for the door. The killing tree matter dropped and not mentioned again.

Reverend Lawson, Teacher Lawson, gathered his books and papers to make the trek home. This trip seemed much longer than it had in the early morning light. He promised himself that his assignment would be to solve the mystery of that killing tree.

Upon settling in at his home, he heard a knock at the door. There stood a distressed Willie. "Come in. And tell me, how is Miss Daisy?"

"Preacher, I got some bad news." Reverend Lawson's heart sank as he braced for bad news. "The Doc put her under the knife this mornin'. It was touch 'n go, but she's out of the woods now." Reverend Lawson exhaled the breath he unconsciously held. "She's got to stay in that hospital a week, maybe more. Then he wants her to rest at home for a couple weeks. She's worried sick 'bout them youngins' and who's a gonna see to their learnin." Willie paused and squinted the one eye shut as he studied the Preacher.

"Tell her I'll teach the children and not to worry. My writing will still be there waiting for me to pick up again when Miss Daisy gets better."

Spontaneously, Willie gave the Preacher a bear hug. "I thank ya. That right yonder is the best medicine she needed." The day had been long and stressful for Willie. After tending to the livestock, he wanted nothing other than to crawl in his bed and let his troubles melt into the feather mattress. After the passing of his first wife, he assumed he'd never experience love for another woman, yet he passionately loved Daisy with his whole being and couldn't imagine life without her. Willie shut the door softly behind him.

Reverend Lawson turned and ran out the door, leaving it open to the night air, "Mr. Willie! Hold Up." Willie cranked the Model T truck and prepared to leave. "Mr. Willie, could you answer a burning question for me?" The old truck rolled to a halt and Willie leaned toward the window. "What is the killing tree, down the hill from the schoolhouse?"

The one eye focused on the Preacher, "Ya didn't go down there, did ya?"

"No, but I was going to. What is it?"

Willie stopped the sputtering truck. In a low voice he explained, "We ain't none proud of it. All the mountain people's kin tell the same tale. I reckon it must be the gospel truth. Long time back, families of freed slaves settled in the mountains. I heard tell a group of white men didn't intend to tolerate blacks livin' amongst them. They'd go to their shanties, drag 'em out and down to that tree, throw a rope over a limb and string 'em up. Always used the same tree."

Reverend Lawson covered his mouth with his hand. "I had no idea! How awful! Why would they build a schoolhouse near such a horrible place?"

"Simple. Cuz' there weren't nobody else that wanted that land with that curse on it. And it made a good plot of land for the school. Them children know not to dare go close the tree. They learned that at home so it ain't a problem to nobody."

Processing this information aloud, "It is a problem. Those poor children are scared to death of that back field. It terrorizes them every single day."

"We learned to live with it. I didn't say nary one of us is proud of it. It was a different time back then, Preacher. We can't be 'spected to understand it, but we accept it. Them children heard the tales from the time they wuz wee little. They don't want to dabble in superstitions or go near it, and that's the way it ought to be. I don't know for sure, but I heard 'em say that their spirits dwell in that tree. Ain't no bird that will light on a branch of it, much less build a nest. I'll tell ya, it made the tree bloodthirsty and it still has a hankerin' for fresh blood and souls, same as other trees crave rain and sunshine. Them souls are trapped there, they cain't go onto heaven, or that tother place down yonder. It's over and done with and we cain't none help it now. Best you stay a fir piece away and don't go messin' with the likes of it. Cain't nobody guarantee what might become of ya' if'n ya git too close. Heard tell all my life, that them trapped souls might jump into a person and curse 'em forever."

The Parson did not believe the superstitions, but vowed, "With God as my witness, if it's the last thing I do in Greenbed, I will rid this mountain of that killing tree once and for all."

HELP THE PREACHER
WITH HIS COURTIN'

It all started innocently enough with two of the Brothers, Lawrence and Darrell bent over the checkerboard studying the next move while the other Brothers scrutinized and critiqued every move. Unrelated to checkers, Lawrence looked up and said, "Willie, or do we need to call ya William now? I'm still stumped that Miss Daisy would marry up with a man that is as useless as a bucket with no bottom."

Before retaliating Willie huffed and puffed, accustomed to the jabs served up by his Brothers. He knew they didn't tease people of which they weren't fond, and in a weird way, he felt honored. "Here's a thought for ya to smoke in yer corncob pipe. She's smart, educated like, and knows true value when she sees it, unlike you ruffians. I'm just plum tickled pink the hospital let her come home."

If they couldn't make Willie lose his temper it wasn't any fun. Darrell whittled on a small stick to use for driving the stubborn Holstein cow into the barn. "Laying all joking aside, if Willie can find a woman, I'd say there's hope for blamed near ever' man in the world. So, what's wrong with Preacher Lawson? Why ain't he found him a woman? From time-to-time there's eligible women passin' through visiting relatives. I say we best be on the lookout to help him."

Clyde snorted, "Lord knows, he's a heap better lookin' than the likes of William."

"Ya don't always have to be so insultin' about it. Did ya ever think maybe he ain't never dreamed of no woman whilst he slept under a new quilt?"

Guthrie looked up in astonishment, "Willie, I've heard your lip flap many a time with foolishness, but what in the sam hill does that mean?"

"Don't ya know nothin'? I heared tell when ya' sleep under a new quilt, ya' marry the one ya dream about, fair and square. Ever'body knows that to be a fact. It's tried and true."

"Who? Tell me," Guthrie demanded.

"I don't know no names, but I knowed it happens all the same."

"Well, give me one name, Willie. Just one," Guthrie pressed.

Clyde laughed, "I don't know where ya ever heard such a tall tale. I'm surprised ya didn't also say that 'if'n somebody sweeps under your feet with a broom, you'll never marry'. I heard that old wives tale. But ain't nobody who believes that foolish stuff."

Willie squinted the one eye shut and in all seriousness admitted, "Speak for yourself. Those tales are known to have the proof in the puddin'. Trouble with ya'll, ya don't believe in nothin' no how."

Guthrie felt compelled to come to the absent Preacher's defense. "I'm not married, not to a woman, but I reckon I consider myself married to this ole general store and the only thing I've ever missed is that I always wanted a plot of land to plow with a John Deere tractor. Did ya ever think that maybe the Preacher feels the same, married to the Church, same as I'm married to the store? I've heard the Reverend tell y'all that the time will come for him to take a wife, by and by."

They didn't even consider that. Lawrence didn't let it pass. "That's different. Maybe the Preacher is too shy 'bout making acquaintances with the womenfolk. I say we help him out. He'll be powerful grateful to us when it's all said and done." It was agreed that the Brothers, along with the other men congregated there, would be on the lookout for possible prospects for the Jack Leg Preacher. The specifications were basic. She needed to be strong, fit as a fiddle since the Preacher walked everywhere; needed to attend church on a fairly regular basis; and she couldn't have red hair, 'cuz everyone knew that red headed women possessed quick tempers, and that wouldn't do for a Preacher's wife. The word spread throughout the mountain, the challenge was readily accepted by one and all.

Later in the week, the unsuspecting Reverend Lawson accepted an invitation to dine at David Lee Mabry's home. Homemade stew and cornbread was the menu. The Preacher welcomed the opportunity to get better acquainted with David Lee and Sarah, sporadic members of his congregation.

Reverend Lawson walked along the rocky road to the Mabry's small mountain home. An unfamiliar woman opened the door. "Is this the Mabry home?"

In the background he heard David Lee, "Preacher, come in." He opened the ripped screen door, excusing himself as he stepped past this stranger. Sarah arranged the three boys on the wooden bench at the table. David Lee came toward him with an outstretched hand, "Good to see ya, Preacher. This here is Sarah's cousin, Rosie, from down the holler. That side of the family don't go to no church." He quickly added, "but they believe all the same. Go a head, Preacher, ask her a question."

Embarrassed for the young lady, he spoke up, "How do you do, Miss Rosie? How nice you can visit with Sarah and help with these three fine boys." He gave a wave to the boys seated at the table and headed in their direction. The three lads attended school as irregularly as they all attended church.

David Lee jumped in front of him and guided him to the other side of the table. "Preacher, sit over here. Them boys are like as not to spill their supper all over ya." He almost pushed the Preacher onto the opposite bench then turned to Rosie. "Rosie, you sit here by the Preacher. Me and Sarah will sit on the stools at the ends." Sarah placed the large black kettle in the center of the table and began dipping the stew and cut chunks of cornbread for each.

"Would ya pray over the food for us, Preacher?"

He bowed his head, "Father, thank you for this home. Bless each member. Bless this food to our bodies, and our bodies to your use. Amen." He learned the hard way to keep the prayers simple. He recalled one of his first prayers over a meal here in the mountains, when he completed the prayer and opened his eyes, the meal was half consumed.

"Sarah, the stew smells delicious. It is a treat to have a home cooked meal. I'm not much of a cook," he said as he passed the homemade butter to Rosie.

David Lee cut him off, "Rosie is a dang good cook. Ya oughta see that girl skin a rabbit. Why, she can have it in the kettle cookin' before ya can get your gun put away. What is your favorite thing to eat, Preacher? I'll bet ya a sal's silk ear Rosie can cook it good."

"I'm not a picky eater. My Mother taught me that beggars can't be choosers, and I was to eat whatever she set before us."

David reiterated, "Rosie can cook anything she puts her mind to, and it'll taste right where you put it."

Reverend Lawson saw a pinkish twinge appearing on Rosie's young cheeks. He guessed her age to be about seventeen. She was a plain girl and kept her eyes cast downward toward her bowl of stew. She giggled while David Lee continued to sing her praises. Reverend Lawson realized the purpose of this dinner had the makings of matchmaking. David Lee's job was the high-pressured salesman, and unsuspecting Rosie was the merchandise. He shuttered to think of his role as the purchaser. He attempted to keep the mood light and nonspecific. He wanted to engage the children in the conversation. His experience with children taught him if you open the door, they have the capability of filling every awkward silence. David Lee steered the conversation, and the opportunity to engage the boys wasn't occurring.

"Rosie, recite the books of the Bible for the Preacher. Listen to this, Preacher. Ya won't believe yer ears. She knows 'em all."

"Oh, that won't be necessary. I'm sure Miss Rosie does a fine job of that." His attempt to spare Rosie proved useless.

"Go on, Rosie. Show him. Like we practiced, go on, jump on in."

Reverend Lawson was equally as determined not to hear the books of the Bible. "I'll bet the boys love to splash in the cold creek and catch tadpoles. That reminds me, I saw the biggest light colored frog, almost white, down the lane by the side of the creek." The Preacher held his hands out to measure, "He must've been this big."

The middle boy, Dellburt, excitedly seized this opportunity, "That's ole Slipper. He sits there most all the time. Reckon he thinks he's a guard frog." The boys giggled at the thought.

The Preacher smiled, "Slipper. That's a great frog name. How did he get it?"

Dellburt, Lawrence, and Samuel all told the story, each one adding a little to the account of trying to capture the frog. David Lee attempted to navigate the subject back to Rosie's fishing abilities, but the frog successfully derailed the main theme and these three lads gladly continued sharing their own fishing tales. Reverend Lawson breathed a sigh of relief as he thought 'thank God for frogs.'

Reverend Lawson slid around from the bench, "It's a long walk home and I best head in that direction. David Lee and Sarah, thank you for dinner.

Miss Rosie, it was a pleasure to meet you. And, boys, you will never know how much I enjoyed hearing about your adventures of Ole Slipper."

Without missing a beat David Lee made a final effort, "Preacher, Rosie can walk ya home and keep ya company. She ain't the least bit a feared of the dark, and can find her way back here in the pitch black of night, like a wildcat." If David Lee thought that offered comfort to Reverend Lawson, he was sorely mistaken. It struck a note of fear in the Preacher.

"No problem. Actually, I rather enjoy the quiet time to meditate as I walk, especially at night. There's something calming about being out under the stars," he paused before adding "alone." He hadn't lied; he needed calming tonight. Besides, he felt the presence of God stronger during his night walks than any other time. Tonight he desired waling home with his Heavenly Father. Something about the evening evoked a strange loneliness and sadness.

The next time he entered the general store he was taken off guard when Darrell asked him how he enjoyed his date with Rosie. Reverend Lawson informed him it was not a date. He merely visited with the family and she happened to be there.

"What was wrong with her?"

"Mr. Darrell, not a thing was wrong with her? She was there to see her cousin. That's all." Reverend Lawson didn't think much more about it until he deflected other inquiries about the 'alleged' date. Each time he patiently responded, never expressing frustration in hopes that would put an end to this line of questioning.

During the next two weeks he met more sisters, cousins, widows, acquainances, and distant relatives than he imagined existed. Each introduction was followed by a brief history of the woman. He began watching out for such happenstances and when suspected, he would turn around as though he forgot something and quickly disappear. He sought cover and concealment behind rhododendron bushes, parked trucks, trees, anything. He dreaded seeing a woman. Any woman. Every woman.

The next major entrapment transpired on his own turf, the church. Dinner on the grounds followed the morning service. Blankets had been spread on the thick grasses, overlooking the valley some 3,000 ft. below. He always marveled at this view and recalled the appropriateness of the name 'Greenbed.' The thick, lush grasses did, indeed, form an inviting bed. From the east side of the property, six mountain ranges stood boldly reaching toward the skies. Reverend Lawson visited each family, resembling a bee gathering nectar from honeysuckle vines. Before he realized what happened, he was ushered to the Stamper's quilt and instructed by Edward Stamper to sit a spell. Edward launched into his discourse, "We got us a serious matter to talk over." Reverend Lawson settled himself in the midst of the throng of Stampers. The faces of the three adult brothers and three adult sisters, and a gaggle of cousins portrayed a serious matter requiring attention. Edward Stamper, the patriarch of the clan, passed the fried chicken, immediately followed by potato salad, pole beans with an ample slab of fatback laying across the top. Reverend Lawson refused the food, trying to save a cavity in his stomach to allow other's to share with him. Mr. Stamper scowled and barked, "Our food not good enough for the likes of a Preacher?" He accepted the plate and began mounding the food.

"It's come to my attention that ya need a wife. I 'spect ya ain't much in the courtin' way, bein' a Preacher 'n all. No offense. It's jest that there's a heap more to life than wearin' out the knees of yer britches down a prayin'. Winter's comin' on, ya need someone to keep ya warm at night, to put yer cold feet on. I aim to help ya out in these matters."

Reverend Lawson nearly choked on his first bite of chicken. "No, no, you've been misled. I . . ."

"Now don't go contradictin' me. I know what I heared, and I see the half of a man sittin' here afore my eyeballs. Ya need ya a wife."

"Mr. Stamper, thank you for your concern. Believe me, I am NOT searching for a wife. In God's good timing, when and if it is meant to be, then by and by He will provide that person for me. It is not now though."

"There ya go agin', contradictin' me! I done warned ya onct. See these here boys? They don't take kindly to nobody sass mouthin' their Paw. Now listen up, I've brought my three daughters for ya to take yer pick of. They're all in the marryin' up way and good men are scarcer than hen's teeth. The black haired one is Annabel, she works like a man, does field work with my sons all the time. Tell ya somethin' else 'bout her, she ain't one to complain. The one with freckles and brown hair is Maribel. She runs the house with Maw. She's got a heart of gold and she's a good worker too, but even if she is a trite bit moody at times and powerful trifflin'. But if ya scold her right sharp like, she'll snap out of it and won't hold no grudge agin ya for hollerin' or slappin' her. And this here short, stout one is Loulabelle, and she is the songbird of the Stamper family. Don't let Loulabelle's ample size bother ya none." He turned his attention to his daughter and commanded, "Strike up a tune, Loulabelle."

Obediently, Loulabelle poised herself, and sat up straighter in preparation of her serenade. When she looked at Reverend Lawson and smiled, Loulabelle was missing one of her front teeth. Mr. Stamper quickly commented. "That missin' tooth don't stop her from bein' the best singer ya ever heard. I've told them youngins not to rough neck like a bunch of heathens, but they didn't heed my warnin'. First thing ya knowed, her tooth done been knocked smack out. We reckon she swallered it down. Never saw hair nor hide of it. Well, which one will it be?"

"Fine ladies for sure." Mr. Stamper wore a proud grin as he surveyed his offspring. Reverend Lawson continued, "Talented ladies. That much talent in one family is hard to come by. You are a lucky man, Edward Stamper. I'll tell you the truth, I guess I'm not ready to make a decision that important."

"I could pick one for ya."

"Oh no! When the time comes, I insist on making my own selection. By and by, the right time and the right person will come together." Having sounded more final in his decision, he quickly bolted in the name of having other obligations. He felt the beads of sweat trickling down his spine. Thankful to survive the hot seat, he escaped on shaky knees.

The final blow came when he had been summoned to pay a visit to one of his parishioners, Velma Wiggins. The request relayed said 'it was critical'. Velma being up in years and of poor health, the Reverend assumed the worst. He left his teaching duties early and went straightway to the Wiggins' home. Joseph Wiggins was working in the field and dropped his shovel where he stood and hightailed it to ambush the Preacher. "Preacher, come over here before ya go into the house. I gotta talk to ya, man to man. Reverend Lawson thought Joseph needed to prepare him.

"I thank ya for comin' right quick like."

"I heard it was urgent. What's the problem?"

Joseph looked down and shifted his weight from foot to foot. "It ain't so urgent fer us as yer well being, Preacher."

"I don't understand. I heard it was Velma?"

Joseph was obviously having difficulty getting started. "Well, no, it tain't Velma. But Velma's cousins' granddaughter is here for a spell and . . ."

Reverend Lawson threw up his hand, "Stop right there! Are you telling me you called me out here under the false pretenses of an emergency just to meet some relative of yours?" Joseph shook his head. Reverend Lawson continued, "And, let me guess, you want me to meet her?" Again Joseph nodded in agreement. "Joseph, I don't mean any disrespect, but I'm not even going in that house!"

Joseph looked up in shock, "Ya've heard 'bout her, ain't ya?"

Now Reverend Lawson was confused, "I haven't heard about anybody, but I can guess what you are up to, and I'm plenty tired of it. I just want people to mind their own business as far as my finding me a woman. Are we clear on that?"

"I reckon. She's gonna be powerful disappointed. She'll think for sure ya heard about her bein' a soiled woman and all. She couldn't help it none. It weren't her fault. She'll have that baby in a month, then the two of ya's can get right onto the bizness of makin' a youngin' of yer own."

Reverend Lawson didn't bother to respond to Joseph's proposition, turned on his heels and practically ran. The time was at hand. This must end and end immediately.

He would search for the source behind this plot. He felt, more than likely, the situation would trace back to the Brothers as the instigators. They'd meant no harm, but if he didn't squelch this, his happy and contended life was doomed.

19

WHAT'S IN A NAME?

Reverend Lawson could not have been more jubilant when the campaign to find him a wife ceased. The explanation was that 'he was too hard to suit, that there ain't a woman alive that could please him.' His philosophy remained unchanged, and it didn't matter what they thought, just so this matchmaking ceased. He'd learned that sticks and stones may break his bones, but matchmaking would surely kill him. Finally, normalcy was restored. He had the luxury of greeting females without the worry of an ulterior motive or misinterpretation.

Winter knocked at Greenbed's door with the long shadows of autumn replaced by gray skies, suffocating the shadows. Mountaineers scurried with the squirrels to make the final preparations for the lurking Old Man Winter. The long and quiet evenings grew tedious for the Parson. Loneliness always existed just below the surface. And most certainly, he never wanted the horrifying matchmaking experience to reemerge should the residents suspect a glimmer of the degree of his loneliness.

Miss Daisy experienced frequent bouts of illnesses after the appendectomy. Reverend Lawson continued teaching for her. He'd managed to cool Clair Evans' advances toward him by ignoring her flirtatious attitude while keeping a wide berth between them at all times. Currently, she expressed an interest in one of the Hess boys. This innocent lad didn't have a clue about her intentions. The Preacher finally relaxed and let down his guard in her presence. He continued to be aware of her, but the uncomfortable feeling slowly faded. He thanked God for puppy love and fickle girls.

He grabbed a small blanket to wrap around his shoulders as he gathered the worn Bible in his hands for the peaceful time of day that never failed to fill his cup. "Lord, what will we share today? I'm thinking the Father of the Jewish Nation, Abraham. You showered blessings onto Abraham and promised him more descendants than stars in the sky. Lord, you continually bless me. Life is richer when we spend these times together. I hunger for your Word to be the light unto my path in these dark and lonely nights." He turned to Genesis 24 and read aloud how the Lord led Abraham's servant to the future wife for his son, Isaac to distract him from mourning the death of his mother, Sarah.

"Rebekah and her maids got ready and mounted their camels and went back with the servant. The servant took Rebekah and left. He went out to the field one evening to meditate, and as he looked up, he saw camels approaching. Rebekah also looked up and saw Isaac. She got down from her camel and asked the servant, 'Who is that man in the field coming to meet us?' 'He is my master,' the servant answered. So she took her veil and covered herself. Then the servant told Isaac all he had done. Isaac brought her into the tent of his mother, Sarah, and he married Rebekah. So she became his wife, and he loved her; and Isaac was comforted after his mother's death."

With his Bible open to this passage, he reflected 'filled with love at first sight.' He bowed his head and committed this loneliness to His Lord.

The following day he taught in the one-room schoolhouse with the same enthusiasm as if he taught at Harvard University. He read aloud about the Revolutionary War. He paused frequently to bring the history to life for them. "Do you understand what happened? Here these people left their homes and all things familiar, made a dangerous trip across the ocean, their rights were being taken away, and now taxed unnecessarily with no choice other than pay the King's taxes. We might compare it to some stranger coming in the schoolhouse and demanding that we all give them our shoes because the children in England needed them." He saw their eyes widen as they realized the unfairness. Suddenly, it became a war worth fighting.

As he packed up his books at the end of the day, he knew this lesson would not be forgotten. He smiled as he recalled the uproar of laughter when he described the Boston Tea Party. They accused him of making it up until he referred them to the page in the history book to verify this amusing account. Educating these young, hungering mountain spirits rewarded his sense of accomplishments. As he walked home, he reflected. 'If only I could make arithmetic appealing.'

His mind quickly transitioned to his ministerial responsibilities. He must stop by Mrs. Daisy's and check on her. Besides caring deeply for her, he selfishly wished for her improved health so she could resume her teaching duties and he could devote more time to writing.

He tapped lightly on the door. The door swung open and the Reverend lost his breath and stumbled a step backward. Before him stood the most beautiful, perfect woman he'd ever seen. For one of the first times in his life, he stood speechlessly. "I, I'm Preacher Lawson ... Is Miss ... a ... Mrs.," for the life of him, he could not think of her name. "Is Mr. Willie's wife up for a visit?" He felt ridiculous, but gave himself credit for stammering through at least one name.

The lady, as gracious as she was gorgeous, smiled sweetly and extended her hand. "How do you do, Reverend. How kind of you to teach for Auntie Daisy." Her dainty hand slid naturally into his. His mind went to the scripture he read the previous night, 'Isaac loved her and was comforted.' She gave a small tug at her hand to withdraw it from his grasp. How he wished he could hold that hand longer. Her coiffured auburn hair swept upward on the sides and pinned into delicate ringlets with stray pieces loosely framing her face on each side. He felt certain that nothing was an accident with this woman, and she purposely withdrew the hairs to cascade to accent her charm. Her eyes were neither brown nor blue, but a unique shade of gray that he'd never witnessed, and they sparkled like the north star. How could such a beautiful creature possibly be under Mr. Willie's roof? It didn't add up, even if she were Miss Daisy's niece and not Willie's blood relative, she seemed grossly out of place here. He wanted and needed to stare at her beauty to absorb every feature, the defined cheek bones, the slant of her eyes, the smooth and clear complexion. His thoughts were interrupted by her melodic voice.

"May I take your books? I'll get Auntie Daisy. Oh, where are my manners! Please have a seat and make yourself comfortable. She'll be here in a jiffy," and she winked at him. His heart fluttered in his muscular chest. Suddenly, he felt light headed and steadied himself on the wall. She mysteriously floated out of the room with the poise of royalty.

He was disappointed when only Miss Daisy entered the room. He closed his eyes and refocused. Mrs. Daisy looked frail, more now than his last visit. He was startled to see her slowly moving toward him. He stood to exchange greetings. "Mrs. Daisy, how are you?"

"I've been better, but on the brighter side, I've been worse." At least her attitude was not dampened by the lengthy recuperation. "Tell me, how are my students?" Before he answered, she interjected, "You met my niece?"

"Yes! I did, indeed!" Immediately, he realized he'd responded with more enthusiasm than he should, a flush crept onto his face. Mrs. Daisy did not miss his obvious reaction.

"She came to help me for a while. Willie means well, but he's like a buffalo maneuvering around the house when I'm trying to rest. And the man can't boil water. I don't know how in the world he didn't starve to death before we married."

Her niece entered the room with a tray of lemonade. She handed the first one to Mrs. Daisy and moved over to stand before the Reverend and bent slightly from the waist and made direct eye contact, "Sweet lemonade, Reverend?"

As Reverend Lawson reached for the tall glass, Mrs. Daisy broke the trance, "Rebecca makes the best sweet lemonade you ever tasted." Hearing her name, 'Rebecca', the glass slid from his hand. Had he not just moments ago recollected of the love of Isaac and Rebekah? Luckily, the glass landed back onto the tray, miraculously without spilling a drop.

"Rebecca. I guess we met each other, but we never officially exchanged names." He felt sick to his stomach. Before attempting to remove the lemonade again, he steadied his hand by allowing it to rest on his leg before carefully cupping the glass with both hands. He did not trust himself with the simplest of tasks.

"I apologize, how rude of me. I didn't think to introduce myself."

"No apology needed. By process of elimination, we figured out which one of us was the Preacher and which one the visiting niece." She laughed, and he wanted to roll his eyes at his own stupidity. What had come over him? He continued to make a complete fool of himself. Nothing came out right.

Mrs. Daisy to the rescue, "Rebecca is my youngest sisters' daughter, and from a little girl she refused to be tagged as Becky or Becka. We thought her terribly stubborn, but now, I'm rather glad she adamantly held out for Rebecca. I think Rebecca fits her well, don't you? It's more sophisticated, it fits her." Pride flowed from Mrs. Daisy as she looked adoringly at her beautiful niece.

"Now Auntie Daisy, don't you turn into a doting aunt on me. I don't deserve such flattery. Truth be told, I probably tried to be stubborn and unbending about the name. I remember pitching my share of Mississippi Hissie Fits over that very thing."

"The more dignified name fits nicely. Miss Rebecca, where is home for you?" Reverend Lawson managed to ask.

"Finishing school taught us to respond eloquently, like 'home is anywhere loved ones are.' For now, that's Greenbed, as well as Cambridge, Massachusetts."

"You're a long way from home. I imagine you notice quite a difference between Greenbed and Cambridge. How do you like the mountain life?"

"In the three days I've been here, I'm not sure that's long enough to make a fair assessment. I've never experienced such beauty and peacefulness. The mornings are incredibly crisp. I'm enjoying the experience."

He relished the softness of her voice. She spoke as though she were reciting poetry. He hesitated to ask yet felt compelled to know, "How long will you be able to stay, to help Mrs. Daisy?"

She glanced affectionately at her aunt, "I didn't purchase a return train ticket. We want to nourish her back to good health first."

Mrs. Daisy looked uncomfortable and straightened her back, preparing for her announcement. "I asked my niece to help me with the teaching duties while she's here. I've imposed on your good nature too long. Who knows? She may be content to stay on as a teacher. I've been pondering how taxing it is to have all the grades together. It may be beneficial for the students to divide into two separate classes. It would make teaching a lot easier. It's challenging to teach a little one the alphabet next to a twelve year old. Don't you agree?"

He nodded, "Absolutely. Yes, I share your frustrations. It ends up being wasted time for half the pupils." He rejoiced at the possibility of Miss Rebecca becoming a permanent member of the community.

"Mrs. Daisy, I must be heading home now. I don't want to over tire you, or I may not be welcomed the next time."

Rebecca gave him a sheepish smile, "No chance of that. You come back any and every opportunity." She stood to walk him to the door. "And it is a pleasure to finally meet you. Aunt Daisy and Mr. Willie speak very fondly of you." She momentarily shifted her gaze downward, slowly raising her eyes to meet and lock with his, "I understand why after meeting you for myself."

His knees buckled and he corrected himself quickly, "Ut oh, if Mr. Willie told tales about me, you definitely need to consider the source." She nodded in agreement. "No, Miss Rebecca, it has been my pleasure."

Rebecca lightly touched his arm, "Reverend Lawson would you do me a favor, providing you are comfortable with it?"

Without hearing the request, he immediately responded, "Anything."

"Just call me Rebecca."

His manners faltered, and he turned to leave. Again, he found himself speechless. He replayed this visit over and over in his head for the remainder of the evening. He desperately needed to think of a legitimate reason to visit Mrs. Daisy again, the sooner the better. The best excuse he could summon, besides checking on Mrs. Daisy, which was admittedly regarded as secondary, was to invite Rebecca to attend classes and observe the school firsthand. He should wait a week. Somehow.

Two days later, Reverend Lawson found himself tapping on Mrs. Daisy's door. He shifted his weight in anticipation. He rehearsed his speech each step of the journey from the school to this humble wooden door. He heard heavy footsteps coming toward the door. The door swung open, as he prepared to look upon the perfect face of Rebecca. Unkempt wild hair, eye squinted, right coverall strap unhooked and drooping off his shoulder, Mr. Willie motioned him to enter. Disappointment washed over the Parson like a bucket of stagnant pond water.

"How are you, Mr. Willie? I didn't expect to see you in the house."

"I don't know why ya'd be so all-fired surprised to see me in my own house." He stepped aside. "Who'd ya expect to see?" Willie smiled sadistically. "Git on in here. You're lettin' the flies swarm in by the droves. She's 'round here somewhere." He turned and yelled, "Becka, the Preacher's here to see ya. Don't keep him awaitin', he's a busy man." Willie nudged Reverend Lawson as he left the room.

Mrs. Daisy and Rebecca slowly came in. "How nice of you to call, Reverend Lawson," Mrs. Daisy smiled at him, "and so soon," she jovially added. He knew the wise old bird knew the true purpose of his return visit.

He prepared to launch directly into the scheme. "I wondered if it would be helpful to Miss Rebecca, sorry, I mean Rebecca, to join me teaching. That may help her decision-making process about assisting you when you are able to return to your teaching duties."

"That's a splendid idea. Rebecca, what do you think, Dear?"

"I couldn't possibly be away from Auntie Daisy all day." Reverend Lawson felt disappointment wash across his face. She continued, "Unless... I came to the schoolhouse in the afternoons while she rests." She turned to face her Aunt with a stern admonishment, "Auntie Daisy, I absolutely will not agree to this unless you solemnly promise to rest during that time."

"Honey, I think that can be arranged without any problem. I'm dead dog tuckered out by noon."

"I'm so glad!" He was embarrassed for responding with that degree of enthusiasm. He felt like a two year old. Rebecca sweetly smiled at him. "Should we start tomorrow?" He did not attempt to conceal his excitement.

"Hold onto your wild horses, Preacher," Mr. Willie entered the room to join the conversation. "Don't come prancin' in here gommin up the works. Becka came here to help Daisy git back on her feet. I'm powerful juberous of her leavin' Daisy just yet."

"William! I know what I'm capable of, and if I tell Rebecca that I'll rest, then that is precisely what I'll do. Rebecca brought me several books to read and the quiet time to do that will be a blessing." Mr. Willie knew he'd best drop the issue. Ultimately, he worried about Rebecca preparing his dinner. But, when Daisy spoke, he knew to sit up and take notice and keep his mouth shut. Reverend Lawson admired her spunk, and he could've kissed Mrs. Daisy for assisting him in his desperate plot to gain time with Rebecca!

"Reverend Lawson, I suppose I'll be seeing you tomorrow after lunch then, unless that is too soon."

"One more item," he paused. "Please call me Gerhart."

"That won't sound unprofession in front of the students?"

"Of course, I meant all the other times. In fact, those children would never respect me again if they heard that old family name." He left with butterflies waging war within his stomach. As he walked away, it dawned on him, Rebecca was the only person in the mountain community he'd requested to use his given name. Why didn't he want to be just her Preacher? As a matter of fact, he didn't know what exactly it was that he wanted to be to her. He knew that he was drawn to her in a way he'd never experienced.

20

BY AND BY ARRIVES

Sleep would not come for Gerhart Lawson—the Minister, the Teacher—Dreamer. He tossed and turned for hours before surrendering and getting up to review his lessons. He focused primarily on the times after lunch when Rebecca would be there. He wanted to be proficient, and at ease as he instructed, if that were remotely possible. The thought of her scrutinizing his teaching abilities caused more anxieties. He reached for his Bible and turned to Philippians 4:13 and read aloud for reassurance, "I can do all things through Christ who strengthens me."

"Lord, I never doubt your involvement in my life. How foolish of me. I know You care about my successes and happiness. I commit tomorrow into Your hands." Before he finished his prayer, peacefulness washed over his stressed body. He straightened the disheveled covers and enjoyed an hour of restful sleep.

Reverend Lawson greeted the morning with a renewed confidence. The morning hours passed slowly. He informed the students Miss Moretz needed further recuperation and her niece would assist with teaching duties. The children moaned. Linnie wanted to know, "What's she like? Is she as good as Miss Moretz?" The children never used Mrs. Daisy's married name, few in Greenbed did.

"She's energetic and fun like Miss Moretz, and she is . . . ," he thought better of giving his heart-felt description. "You can form your own opinion." He saw Rebecca coming toward the school. "Here she comes." She opened the door and glided into the small schoolhouse. The children gasped at her beauty and stared open mouthed as she brushed her fitted skirt with her hand to smooth superficial wrinkles. The children sat mesmerized, waiting to hear her first words. When she spoke, her eyes twinkled as she surveyed the classroom, "Hello. I believe you know who I am." Some nodded, most kept the blank stare. "Reverend Lawson, I am at a disadvantage. I have not had the privilege of meeting these young people. With your permission, Sir, could they tell me their names and one thing about their lives?" He nodded, captivated under her magical spell the same as the students.

The children recited their names, as Rebecca drifted around the room, absorbing every detail. The students sensed her genuine interest and they seized the opportunity to hold the attentions of such an unusually lovely woman. The 'one fact about their lives' grew bolder and more personal. Clair Evans, the only student that felt the necessity to stand as she shared her one detail. "I used to be in love with Preacher Lawson, but it's all done and over now." Snickers erupted in the room. Clair didn't appear embarrassed in the least. She plopped unceremoniously into her seat, smugly glanced at the Reverend, crossed her arms over her ample chest, proud that she'd shared an intriguing and mature fact.

Reverend Lawson felt his face immediately turn beet red, not believing what he'd heard. Rebecca did not acknowledge this any differently than she did James Hoagg telling that 'he had a new liter of puppies and witnessed their births.' Reverend Lawson breathed a sigh of relief that James spared the details of the birthing. He imagined how the younger children might have interpreted this depiction.

After Miss Wentworth heard each child's contribution, she turned to the Preacher, "Thank you, Children. Now, we're friends, not strangers." She sat down to observe.

"Let's take a fifteen minute recess in the school yard." Surprised by this stroke of good luck, the children jumped to their feet and noisily crowded for the door.

As soon as the last child exited, the flustered Parson turned to Rebecca, "I am genuinely embarrassed, but obliged to tell you, I have no earthly idea where that came from. I assure you, I view Clair only as a student, a young lady here to learn, the same as every other student. And I certainly did not intentionally encourage . . ."

She put her hand up to stop him, "Give me some credit! I know that, and her statement had nothing to do with you. That effort was to even the imbalance between girl and woman. I know young girls. I'll tell you something in confidence about me." He leaned closer to hear the whispered secret. "I used to be one too. Trust me, there's nothing unusual about having feelings for your teacher, especially one like . . . ," she stopped midsentence. "Besides, if you'd been my teacher . . . . ," now it was her turn to blush.

He took two steps forward, closing the gap between the two of them. "Thank you for believing in me." He resisted the urge to put his arms around her and draw her to him. As much as he desperately wanted to, he dared not. He inhaled her sweet perfume and longed to stop time as he drank in the wonder of this moment.

"What would you like to do now?" her soft voice searched and broke the enchanted moment.

He immediately reacted, "Come with me this evening to Fred Boggs' to the barnyard banjo pickin'. It's always amazing, with incredibly talented musicians."

She stammered, "Thank you. I meant, what do you intend to do when the students return from recess."

He shook his head laughing at himself. "Yes, well, would you be up to reading them the next chapter of the book we've been reading?" He really wanted an excuse to openly glare at her.

She read the book and led a marvelous discussion as she taught them the importance of listening skills. At the conclusion of the day, the students reluctantly left Miss Wentworth. She helped ready the room for the morning session and prepared to leave. "Want to join me as I walk home? I'll pass on the barnyard banjo this time, since it's my first day away from Auntie Daisy. Please ask me again another time." He wasted no time slamming the book closed, leaving everything in a haphazard pile on the desk to escort Rebecca.

As they walked, she utilized those keen listening skills and finishing school knowledge of conducting an engaging conversation. "What accomplishments would you like to see at the school?"

"It is my belief that the classes could be more challenging, particularly for the older students, and that is no reflection on Mrs. Daisy, or her fine teaching. She's right, it is impossible to teach the wide age ranges without one end of the spectrum being left out. That's when I notice wandering minds and the invitation for mischief."

She pondered, "I'm inclined to agree. Other than Clair, which students do you find you relate to the best?" she gave a playful chuckle.

"Not a fair question! And I thought you said you understood that!"

"I'm only teasing. I, personally, relate better to younger children, perhaps I might focus on them. How have you been able to balance your ministerial duties with teaching, plus, I understand that you're also a writer?"

They talked every step of the way to Mr. Willie and Mrs.Daisy's. His opinion confirmed that she was intelligent and interesting. He'd never had the opportunity to converse with such a woman. She spoke with an exceptional ease on every subject. He regretted reaching the porch, "Rebecca, will you come back to school tomorrow?"

"It depends."

Fearfully he asked, "Depends on what?"

She angled her head slightly and smiled broadly, "Whether or not I'm invited."

He laughed at the sheer absurdity, "Oh, make no mistake! You're invited for every day and all day, as much as you can endure. The children would be sorely disappointed if you did not come tomorrow."

"Oh, I don't want to disappoint the children," she said sarcastically. "Thank you for an informative afternoon. I enjoyed the conversation. I shouldn't invite you in, she should be resting." She opened the door and disappeared inside, gently closing the door. He felt an immediate void. One minute his world had been beautiful and exciting, and suddenly it was empty. Confusion consumed him. Was his prediction coming true? Had 'by and by' arrived? What was happening? His heart pounded at the thought of Rebecca.

He lingered at the door looking at the wooden panels, but not seeing them. He turned, looking toward the heavens. "My heart overflows! Thank you, Lord."

HEARTS

From the time the bell announced school in session until the noon hour, when Rebecca would arrive, felt more like twenty hours than four. When he saw the auburn hair top the ridge, he stopped talking and focused his complete attention on her, the flow of her skirt in the breeze, her right hand securing the hat on her head, dainty yet determined steps. The best reward of all, when she saw him at the window and waved with her free arm. Her entire countenance smiled back at him. Unconciously, he moistened his lips with the tip of his tongue as he watched her drawing nearer. His heart rate accelerated.

"Children, welcome Miss Wentworth." Practically in unison they responded, "Good Afternoon, Miss Wentworth." He noticed how her presence radiated happiness to every corner of the room. Even Clair Evans curiously peeped from behind other children to peruse the guest. The light blue paisley printed blouse accentuated the depth of her gray eyes. She wore a white A-lined skirt, accented with a wide blue belt.

"Clair, I brought something for you."

Clair's face was unable to conceal the joy of a surprise for her. "I had this comb for my hair. I seldom wear it. I thought it would look stunningly in your raven black hair." She retrieved the hair comb from her purse, and slowly unwrapped the tissue paper surrounding it. Clair pushed her way through the others. "What do you think? If we swoop the side up, your pretty face will be more visible. May I?" Miss Wentworth ran her soft fingers through Clair's hair, gently lifting the hair on the left side. The silver hair comb adorned with small decorative pearls created a striking contrast to Clair's dark hair.

Unconsciously, Reverend Lawson turned his head slightly to admire the transformation, "That looks very nice." The rest of the school day proved equally as successful. Rebecca effortlessly won every student with her charm. He knew she was capable of handling this responsibility without his assistance, but he wasn't willing to give up the opportunity of spending time with her. He wondered when, or if, Rebecca might be comfortable leaving Mrs. Daisy for longer periods.

The third day Rebecca treated everyone, including Reverend Lawson to a surprise. Rebecca arrived an hour early and brought a picnic lunch for Gerhart and her to share. She'd baked and iced sugar cookies for the class. He was treated to a genuine picnic, complete with a tablecloth spred on the ground and fried chicken. The class, as well as the teachers, totally engrossed in the picnic atmosphere, enjoyed the leisure lunch together. They kept sitting on the front steps and lawn of the schoolhouse after lunch. She told them of the charm and woes of being raised in the northeast and described city living. Her life sounded, to their untraveled ears, like a storybook. Reverend Lawson allowed this to continue, after all, this imaginary journey served to educate the pupils and afforded him the opportunity to hear her soft voice and gaze into those gray-green eyes.

After three weeks of having the able assistance of Miss Wentworth, Reverend Lawson enjoyed each day more than the last. Rebecca consistently proved to be a brilliant, vibrant, and fascinating woman. Each day he witnessed more similarities between Mrs. Daisy and her niece.

As he walked Rebecca home, she stumbled on a root crossing the dirt path. Instinctively, he reached for her hand to steady her. Cupping her silken hand into his muscular hand was not only comfortable, but natural, as he expected. They stopped walking and stood looking at each other. When they continued walking, he held the small hand the remainder of the journey. Her fingers wrapped tightly around his strong hand, returning the warmth. Neither spoke until they were at Mrs. Daisy's. "Rebecca, may I call on you?"

A shy look came over her, "I thought you were."

"Well, yes, maybe, but officially call on you?"

"Oh Gerhart," she rested her hand on his arm and gave it a slight squeeze. "I would like that very much. Thank you. You make my stay here most enjoyable. It hasn't been easy being away from the city. Don't get me wrong, the mountains are beautiful. Life is just ... different here. There's very little to do and I'm accustomed to going and doing. If I weren't caring for Auntie

Daisy and having school to look forward to each day, I'm not sure I could handle this without feeling stale, or unchallenged." She laughed, "Oh you know what I mean. I'm not expressing it very well. You do remember how you felt when you first arrived from the east?" She leaned into him close enough to take his breath away, "Don't listen to me, I'm being more fickle than Clair." She laughed at herself.

"Perhaps you'd join me on a walk this evening to Big Belly Rock and watch the sunset."

"What is Big Belly Rock? I admit, the name doesn't do much for me, but the company will." She gave him a coy wink.

"It's about half a mile, the rock is formed with a little hump, which if we use our imagination we call the belly, then becomes flat and hangs out over the mountain and you look all the way down to the valley. The view is spectacular at 3,255 ft. elevation." Reluctantly, he released her hand after she agreed.

He arrived ten minutes early. The evening unfolded better than he envisioned. They laughed about childhood experiences and shared the heartbreaks of losing loved ones. She made herself vulnerable by sharing her fears and failures. She wanted to hear about his call into the ministry, specifically, how he knew. They talked nonstop, forgetting to witness the sunset. He regretted not attempting to kiss her in the moonlight more than not watching the sunset. He felt a huge let down that the following day was Saturday and there would be no school, which equaled no Rebecca.

Saturday morning he headed to Guthrie's. The Brothers already at their usual places—hunched over the checkerboard. Studying the next move did not deter Clyde from engaging the Preacher with an onslaught of inquiries.

"Preacher, are ya gonna marry up with that little filly? I'm tellin' ya, we got to have us a warnin' if you do. That'd be some serenade!"

Mr. Willie sat with his Brothers, most interested in not missing any of these answers. His bad eye tightly closed, he turned his head perpendicular to the floor.

"You asked so many questions I don't know where to begin."

Willie couldn't stand the suspense, "Don't matter none. Pick one, any one of 'em, and run to town on it."

"That's easy. I don't have any answers yet."

That was not the response for Willie. "Ya better dadblame find some answers. Ya been courtin' her, and cuttin' a shine with that girl. I won't have her made a fool of, don't matter if ya are the Preacher. Daisy'll have your hide. Make no mistake."

"Mr. Willie, no need being upset with me. I assure you, I've been a gentleman, and Rebecca is a proper lady. You shouldn't feel it necessary to have concerns, if that's where this questioning is headed. Goodness gracious, we are not two fourteen year olds! However, I suspect the real purpose of this inquisition is for you to get something to gossip about, so you'll have the glory of spreading it first." Reverend Lawson left his items sitting on the counter and walked out of the store allowing the screen door to slam shut.

Before he cleared the bottom step he'd decided not to share this conversation with Rebecca, no need embarrassing her with such nonsense.

The Brothers exchanged stupefied looks. Clyde broke the silence, "What do ya reckon got his dander in an uproar, ain't never seen him act like that before. He seems a mite touchy."

Throughout the next month, no one mentioned his relationship with Rebecca again. He continued to see her every day at school and call on her as often as possible. He exhibited great willpower to refrain from grabbing her in his arms and kissing her long and hard, as he longed to do. He'd never dealt with such passion for a woman.

Occasionally, Rebecca accompanied him on visitations. She always added that special woman's touch to the conversation. The women, in particular, related and bonded with her. Some of the men appeared intimidated by either her beauty or intelligence—or both.

Walking her home in the moonlight he complimented her, "Rebecca, I appreciate your joining me on these visits. It's a special time and I relish sharing the experiences with you."

"It's my pleasure. Since living here in Greenbed, I've become aware that everyone—whether man, woman, or child—has a story unique to only their life. How fascinating to me to hear those stories. We all become a product of how we handle what life dishes out."

"Somewhat. I believe that one's faith plays a major part. I've had church members that absolutely fall apart when the slightest thing disrupts their life, and others cope with monumental problems and keep a smile on their face. Over and over again I've witnessed the ones that allow God to carry most of the burden, fair better in the long run."

"Easier said than done, Sir. I'm living proof of that. I trust God up to a certain point and then the "I" in me takes over."

He slipped his arm around her trim waist, giving her a slight squeeze, "I'd say you're more the norm, than the exception. It's hard for all of us to have that faith and trust."

"But why is it difficult? Why are we stubborn by nature?"

"I fall into this trap, same as everyone. We get impatient and don't realize God's perfect timing is not the same as our timing. His pocket watch doesn't have just twelve numbers. Time is limitless."

They walked in silence along the path, savoring the comfortable closeness of one another.

"Look," she said, startling him with the broken silence. "On the branch of the tree, a huge owl is watching us. I've heard that's good luck."

"The owl is late then. I've been showered with good fortune ever since you arrived! I feel like I lived life in black and white before I met you."

He had given considerable thought to his life since she arrived. It occupied his waking thoughts, and many of his dreams. "Rebecca, I've known you a short time, but I've known you my entire life. You're radiant and the most magnificent woman! You compliment my life in wonderful ways I never imagined." He drew her closer and she lifted her head to face him. Time stood still. The owl watched as he lowered his lips to meet hers. The kiss felt exactly as he'd dreamed—warm and inviting. His lips slid to her cheek as he whispered her name over and over against her soft skin. He tightened his arms around her as he drank in her closeness. Her left hand slid down from his neck to rest on his muscular shoulder while her right hand playfully ran through his dark hair. Returning his affection seemed the most natural thing she'd ever experienced. He felt her press closer to him and his heart nearly leapt from his chest. She caressed his back and a low moan escaped her lips as she softly uttered, "Gerhart. Oh, Gerhart."

Suddenly, she withdrew and stiffened her body, "Don't!" She held her hand up, "Please, don't say another word."

"What? Why?" he almost shouted. "I must. I've thought of nothing else but you for weeks. Rebecca, I long to share my life, my love, my all with you, I love you with all that I am. I've never experienced such feelings. I knew from the first instant I saw you that we were destined to have this exact conversation."

"Please stop, Gerhart." Tears clouded her eyes.

"Why? I can't stop telling you any more than I can stop loving you. I believe God brought you into my life at this particular time for a reason, not just a season. I also know you feel the same way. I see it in your eyes, in your smile, and in your general countenance. I felt it in your kiss. You can't deny it! I don't know why you'd even want to deny it. We enjoy one another's company." He paused and dropped to one knee and held both of her hands tightly in his. "Rebecca Wentworth, my heart no longer belongs to me. Next to my salvation through Jesus Christ, you are the most precious part of life. Would you walk with me, love with me, be my helpmate, and my wife?"

In the clearing the full moon streamed down upon them as though they were positioned in the spotlight on center stage. His face glowed with anticipation as he looked up at her exquisite features. Tears flowed down her cheeks. Her face bore a pained expression where he'd hoped to see joy.

"Rebecca, do you feel the same?" he finally managed to ask after she stood in silence.

"Yes! Oh yes, I do. I do. I truly do. You are the kindest, most compassionate man. I admire everything about you. You are handsome beyond my wildest dreams, you're intelligent. And I agree, we've shared wonderful times together." She paused.

His heart pounded harder than if he'd raced up the entire height of the mountain. He'd never felt it beat with such force. "But what? Rebecca, what are you not able to say to me? Tell me."

"This will sound selfish and horrible."

"Rebecca, I must know your true feelings. It's essential that we talk about this, and right now. I can't bear waiting."

She looked toward the owl and released a long, labored sigh. "The only way I see this working would be something that I cannot bring myself to utter."

"Oh, but you must! This is the most important conversation either of us has ever had in our entire lives. It requires an honest response from you."

Rebecca sniffed and looked into his searching eyes, "You are a respected minister. I see how the mountainfolk revere you, and rightfully so, even the ones that are not believers look to you with respect. You could not be more admired or loved. We all see God in and through you. And, believe me, that speaks volumes about you, and the man you are. I wouldn't, I couldn't ask you to give that up."

"What do you mean by give it up? You've been with me and you related to everyone and seemed at ease accompanying me. Rebecca, you are comforting, compassionate, and concerned about these people as well. God never created a more perfect wife for a minister."

"But, Gerhart, the mountains have a genuine, quiet beauty and I've loved every minute of soaking in the uniqueness . . . but not for a lifetime. In Cambridge, for instance, there's much to do and getting around is easy. I can't fathom how these mountains might be in the treacherous winter conditions. Surely, one would be stuck inside from virtually November to April. I don't think I want to endure or experience that isolated feeling, almost like a disease requiring one to be quarantined. That life must be extremely confining. You are at peace here. I see that your soul found its perfect resting place. Calmness exudes from your whole being, and anyone in your presence appreciates that."

"Yes, I love it here, the simplistic life, and the people are genuine. It would be difficult for me to turn my back on this mountain ministry. But, Rebecca, make no mistake, I would leave here for you, only for you; and never regret it. The Lord's harvest can be found anywhere. Remember, you know that I've lived in the city and I'm very capable and willing to do that again. With you by my side, I can minister anywhere and be the happiest man on the face of the earth."

The sounds of the night surrounded them. The owl made his first timid attempt at hooting. The tree leaves faintly rustled in the soft breeze. It should've been a glorious moment, but turmoil brewed. The Parson rose from his kneeling position, desperately clasping Rebecca's hands.

Finally, Rebecca found her voice. "Gerhart, you see, being a parson's wife isn't the life I want. That probably makes me a horrible person. I didn't intend to fall in love with you. I always thought I'd marry a president of a bank or college professor. I never envisioned myself the wife of a minister. I wouldn't be contented." She turned her head from him as if she could not say anything further while facing him, "Now you know, that makes me a shallow person. But honestly, I thought we would be friends and before I knew it, my heart made room for you. But I won't do this, I know myself and my goals for life. I simply don't know what else to say."

After several minutes of awkward silence he finally found enough voice to respond, "That makes two of us."

"Two of us?"

"Two of us that doesn't know what to say. I cannot leave the ministry. I have a higher calling that I must fulfill. Make me a promise." She nodded in agreement before hearing the request. "Promise that we will both pray and wrestle with this and we'll allow God to work through us for a resolution. I have faith that love is more powerful than obstacles."

They walked in silence. No words adequately expressed the feelings and confusion they both struggled with in the moonlight. They used the quiet of the night to explore thoughts. They continued walking hand-in-hand. He lightly kissed her on the cheek at Daisy and Willie's front porch. "It will seem an eternity until I see you tomorrow at school." She held firmly to his hand and pulled him toward her. She wrapped her arms tightly around his neck, gently kissing along the side of his neck until he faced her. Tears streamed down her cheeks. He turned to leave and glanced back over his shoulder. She remained on the front porch watching him as he walked away. He glanced back several times and as far as he could see, she remained standing there on the porch. His heart was troubled. He resisted the urge to run back to her arms. He hadn't intended to propose marriage to her tonight. Yet, when the moment presented itself, professing his love for her and the proposal felt totally right.

Thankfully, the children behaved well the following day. Concentrating proved a difficult challenge. He found himself doodling aimlessly as he sat at the desk and watched the pupils work. He looked toward the ridge many times, hoping Rebecca might arrive early to announce her change of heart. The suspense was maddening. Throughout the morning, he offered many prayers for guidance and peacefulness. At 11:00 A.M., rather than seeing Rebecca topping the ridge, as she had faithfully done for these months, he saw Mr. Willie's old truck rattling down the dirt road toward the school. Mr. Willie, leaving the door open, sluggishly made his way to the schoolhouse, talking to himself every step, waving his arms, shaking his head. Reverend Lawson met him in the school yard, "Mr. Willie, what's wrong? What brings you?" The Preacher's heart sank before Willie opened his mouth.

"Who can figure 'em? Danged if I know what to make of womenfolk. This mornin' that fickle-brained Becka got up at the crack of dawn, I reckon. She done had her steamer trunk packed when I rolled outta bed. Soon as I opened the bedroom door, in she dashed, almost knocked me flat as a pancake. She rushed in like the house was a fire! Woke Daisy out of a sound sleep, and stayed in yonder jawin' and hoopin' for over an hour. When she come out, she'd been bawlin' her eyes out. She commenced to begin to beggin' me to take her down the valley to the train station. And, jest like that, with no 'fare-thee-well,' she was off 'n gone. Dogged woman, cried ever' inch of the way to the dad blame train station. It liked to drove me mad, lucky I didn't run my truck off the side of the mountain. I hate to hear a woman carryin' on with that nonsense. It makes my brain hurt clear to my toenails."

Reverend Lawson struggled to keep his composure. "Thank you for bringing the news. I would've been worried when she didn't show up." He fought to remain calm while his entire world fell apart, here on the school yard.

Willie withdrew an envelope from his overall pocket. "She asked me to give ya this, made me promise to bring it directly to ya,' soon as I got back."

Reverend Lawson took the envelope and returned to the classroom. Immediately, he decided to dismiss early today. The envelope burned in his pocket. When the last child left, he tore the envelope open. Rebecca regretfully closed this chapter of her life, but not without also professing her own broken heart.

He remained at the school house until dusk reading the letter over and over, committing every word to memory. Still, he didn't understand or accept the reasoning behind her decision.

Facing the sunrise tomorrow would test the faith about which he preached. Could he do it? Right now, he honestly didn't see how that would be possible. A night on his knees.

CHANGING TIMES

Mr. Guthrie knew nothing else of life for the past 62 years other than Guthrie's General Store, born in the back bedroom to Esther and Ezekiel Guthrie. Esther died in childbirth delivering Lucy, her second child. His Grandfather, Elli Guthrie, carved out his legend here on the mountain by establishing Guthrie's General Store, and passed the store to his son, Ezekiel.

Darrell teasingly pried, "Guthrie, why didn't ya never settle down?"

Without a moment of hesitation, "I did. I reckon I been hitched to this store since I was knee-high to a grasshopper. I stocked these same old shelves when I was no more than five years old. Yep, she's the love of my life. What's more, she don't fuss at me, nor suffer with hot flashes and mood changes, or any of the other aggravatin' tendencies of a woman."

His younger sister, Lucy, wanted no part of the store, the Greenbed community, or the mountain. She married and relocated to a town a smidgen more than three hours northeast. Ezekiel swore that Lucy had loved the idea of the 'move,' not the 'man'. This attitude drove an ugly wedge between daughter and father. Lucy's discontentment sprang from being raised in a general store, without a mother. After all, women came and went as customers, but there was not a female role model. Hard feelings surfaced when she 'pulled up stakes' and ran off with Geoffrey Snodgrass in the middle of the night. Over the years, the visits grew less frequent, especially after the birth of her only child, Tobias. Days prior to her 43rd birthday, Lucy slipped and fell on the icy city sidewalks that she cherished, hit her head and died. Guthrie always thought Lucy's demise ironic—the thing that meant the most ultimately would be responsible for her death. City life!

Guthrie reflected on the day he timidly knocked at Lucy's door before the funeral and a stranger greeted him, his own nephew, at least a half foot taller than he.

"Hello. I'm Lucy's brother."

The youthful arms encircled him, "I know. You're my Uncle, I'm Tobias, or Toby. Come in out of the cold." It seemed impossible that time transformed the spoiled brat who terrorized the general store on the rare visits into a well-mannered young man.

After the burial, Guthrie returned to the general store. That marked the last communication with the Snodgrass family, although each expressed good intentions to keep in touch.

Lately, Guthrie felt more than his age. He lay in bed struggling to get an ample breath. As most of the mountain men, Guthrie's pride made going to see Doc Hess a last resort. "Doc, I'll tell ya, I can't do what I used to. It takes me forever to get the simplest job done. Everything wears me out. And for the past two months, many a night, I fall asleep sittin' propped up to keep from choking to death. It's aggravatin' to me."

The good doctor, no spring chicken himself, spoke sympathetically, "Guthrie, everything about our old bodies is bound to slow down, including our tickers." Doc Hess lightly patted his own heart.

"Come on, give it to me straight. I don't know why I wasted my time to come see ya."

"Listen to me, Guthrie, when ya commence to feelin' weak and breathin' becomes labored, for Sam Hill's sake, quit and rest." The old doctor walked to an upright cabinet painted white stretching from floor to ceiling. He opened the glass door, displaying large bottles of pills. He retrieved and replaced four bottles before pouring some into a small envelope and licked the flap shut. "Try two of these a day, it's a startin' place. But, to tell the truth, which you seem to not want to hear no way, we wear out and there's nothing we can do to remedy that, short of dying. I'll do my best to keep ya on this side of the grass. Take better care of yerself, don't be such a stubborn ole coot."

Guthrie slowly shook his head as he thought that advice was easier said than done with no one to help him in the store. He couldn't quit and rest when he felt that familiar pressure in his chest. The next couple of weeks created even more of a challenge for Mr. Guthrie. He continued the same hours in the store, and went about his routine as consistently as possible. Each evening as he put the tattered "Closed" sign in the window and locked the door, he beat a path straightway to his bed. By the time he stretched out on his bed, he felt like someone plopped a pot-bellied stove smack dab in the center of his chest.

He prayed, "Dear Lord, I beg ya' to jes' grant me the time to get my matters in order. I won't be greedy and ask for no more than that." He felt an urgency to admit his condition to someone. The decision came easy.

The next day he saw Reverend Lawson walking past the store. Guthrie stepped out onto the front porch and waved him over. Guthrie envied the spry spring in the Parson's step. Guthrie seized this opportunity while no one else was in the store. "Preacher, could ya spare a minute? I need to talk to ya private like." The pleasant smile on Reverend Lawson's face quickly vanished when he detected the seriousness in the beloved Guthrie's voice.

"I been meanin' to ask ya, how ya gettin' on since Rebecca took her leave? I'm obliged to say, I'm sorry that happened to ya."

"I appreciate that. I admit, this has been the hardest two months of my entire life. I've had to force a smile on my face." He looked lost in deep thought, "and the long nights, they seem to never end. I can't stop thinking about her, no matter what I do. I haven't been able to write a word in my book. I trust it will come with time. I'm still trying to sort the whole confusing thing out. It baffles me."

Guthrie gritted his teeth and charged full-steam ahead, relaying how poorly he felt and Doc's assessment and warnings. "I 'spect the end is drawin' nigh."

The Parson's eyes moistened as he looked into the earnest eyes of this respected gentlemen. "Mr. Guthrie, let's go down into town and consult another doctor. I know Doc Hess has been the faithful doctor to Greenbed all of these years; but perhaps a younger doctor with more recent knowledge could help. We best act fast. This is very serious."

Guthrie shook his head, "That's mighty kind of ya, but it ain't no use. I feel it in my bones. What I do need ya to do for me is to put your mark as my witness to these papers. It says what I want to become of my things and . . . and . . ." he could scarcely utter the words, "and my store when I'm no longer runnin' her." He had precisely written every distribution he wished to occur. After the Preacher signed it, Guthrie tucked it in an envelope, sealed it, and it became the only item on top of his chest of drawers; so that it would be easily located when that time arrived. "Preacher, you see where I'm puttin' it, don't ya?" Reverend Lawson nodded. "I want ya to promise me when ya hear that I passed over into glory, come straightway and get this, and make the arrangements I put down. Are we clear on that? And don't tell nobody what it says. I trust ya with all I got and that ain't much." Reverend Lawson assured his dear friend.

The document labeled 'Last Will and Testament' looked out of place in this room among the living.

After Guthrie attended to that vital business, he noticed more energy and that weight on his chest was somewhat alleviated. He chuckled to himself, that he'd prematurely cried wolf. Whatever the reason, he felt encouraged and thankful.

Reverend Lawson made it a point to stop by Guthrie's General Store at every opportunity and was pleased to witness the improvement in Mr. Guthrie's energy and attitude. The Parson patiently waited for the secret nod from Guthrie indicating he felt well today. A wealth of information was silently passed between the two men.

The Brothers held their post by the front window, enjoying the view from the store, one of them commented, "Lookie yonder a comin', if it ain't Bertha Tyson waddlin' down the street. Look at those three little tackers trailin' along behind like baby ducks in a row, followin' the mother. Say what ya' may, they may be dirt poor, but those little girls are always clean."

Bertha held the wooden handrail and half hoisted herself up the steps, her fourth baby due any day and she'd come for the last minute supplies knowing she might be confined for a spell.

Guthrie stood behind the glass-top counter and watched Bertha slowly make her way to him. A troubled look plastered on her face, she wasted no time fretfully inquiring, "I must ask ya' a mighty big favor."

Guthrie nodded, putting her at ease. He always exhibited a keen insight to his customers' needs. "Go right ahead, Bertha, get anything ya need. We'll worry about settlin' up later."

The deep furrows in her brow slowly disappeared. Her expression relaxed into the hint of a smile, "I'm beholdin' to ya'." She gathered only the bare necessities.

Guthrie watched her as she timidly selected the few items, he silently offered a prayer. "Lord, be her anchor to hold onto to get through birthing this baby."

Bertha dipped her head in gratitude at Guthrie as she assembled her little flock and painstakingly trudged across the wooden floor. Guthrie always enjoyed the familiar squeaks of the hardwood floor. These were the sounds that served as his companion all through the years. Of late, they were as beautiful and soothing as music to his hungering ears.

Turner looked the full-term mother-to-be up and down before speaking, "Bertha, looks to me that ya' best be gettin' the Midwife. You'll be havin' that lit' one any minute."

"Ain't no need botherin' her. My Momma was there for the first two." She looked toward Mr. Guthrie and smiled, "If ya remember, Mr. Guthrie helped me with the third, right here in the General Store. It ought to be tolerable easy this time. Besides, I heard Granny Cheeks left to be with her daughter who is sickly. She's the only person 'round these parts that'll come to do midwiving."

"You be careful. And tell that No Account Homer Tyson, Jr. not to go runnin' off leavin' ya' now or he'll answer to us. I mean it! Onct we finish with him, he wouldn't be fit fer nothin'. Be sure to tell him that soon as ya' see the whites of his eyes. He best take heed."

Guthrie stopped stocking and sorting the recent delivery of spices and joined Clyde, Turner and Willie. It was one of those delightful days of teasing Willie about his new wife. Even Guthrie, the bachelor, relished these attacks on the more than deserving Willie.

Adjusting the checkerboard squarely between his legs and motioning for Turner to sit across from him, Clyde winked at Guthrie. "Sweet William here can't stay long enough for a checkie game. His Little Woman wants him home to help with fixin' supper. He can't boil water and it come out fit to use and she thinks she needs him home." Guthrie, Clyde and Turner enjoyed the joke. Willie waved them off.

Guthrie had noticed Willie's absence from the general store, "Willie, ya haven't been about for a month of Sundays. What's been keeping ya' busy?"

Clyde clearly not ready to let it drop, "Ya' know, fellas, ain't it just the dog gonest mystery how a little woman, no bigger than a minute, can boss a man and have him tiptoe 'round like he's dodging a floor lined with goose eggs."

"Ya think you're so dadblamed funny. Well, ya ain't nary a bit funny! Yer jealous. Daisy's still gainin' her strength back. Since that fickle Rebecca done run off, Daisy needs me for a lot of things." The gathering of men roared at that admission. "Aw, you shut up. Ya' don't know nothin' about how to treat a woman." Willie dug the hole deeper each time he attempted a retaliation. Willie became more flustered by the minute.

Willie's agitation caused him to start fidgeting. "Sweet William, I'll give ya this about that little heifer that ya married, she's pretty as a speckled pup under a red wagon, that's for sure." The proud smile on Willie's face was like fuel for Clyde. "I've got a mean ole bull pinned up in my barn. He's got a big brass ring in his nose and that's the only way I can do anything with him. By golly, let me look at yer snoot and see if'n I see a ring there. Come to think, William is better behaved than my bull. She has done a good job. Think she'd come over and give that bull some lessons?"

The expressions on Willie's face proved more entertaining than the jibes Clyde dished out. The outbursts of laughter flustered Willie until he sputtered unintelligible sounds. Guthrie hadn't laughed so hard in months. Willie stood and headed for the door, without looking back, mumbling under his breath with every short stride. Bang. He slammed the door and disappeared down the steps. Guthrie held his ribs with crisscrossed arms.

After the last of the men left, Guthrie reluctantly pulled the shade and locked the door. He went about the daily task of sweeping the rough wooden floors with his straggly broom. He chuckled as he relived the fun they enjoyed at Willie's expense. Today offered the best amusement in weeks. As he swept behind the glass counter, a sudden pain gripped his chest. He dropped the broom and grabbed for the counter for support. Perhaps if he rested here for a minute until the pain subsided, then he could make it to his bed. He felt the tightness moving up his chest into his neck and down his arm. His jawbones didn't feel right. A cold sweat broke out on his forehead which was different than previous attacks. The pain was relentless. Mr. Guthrie slumped to the floor. Just before losing conscientiousness, he heard knocking on the door and the familiar voice of the Preacher yelling his name. The sound of the breaking glass was the last he remembered hearing.

Reverend Lawson wasted no time putting his fist through the glass panel on the door to gain entry. Effortlessly, he lifted Guthrie into his arms and carried him to the bedroom. He placed a cold cloth on Guthrie's head and patted his hand. Guthrie's eyes fluttered open and a faint smile pulled at the corner of his mouth.

"I'll go call for help. You hang on. Stay with me." Guthrie shook his head 'no' and held tight to the Preacher's hand. "Let's pray. You know, I never recall hearing your first name."

Guthrie uttered, "O."

"Is the pain worse?"

Guthrie barely shook his head from side to side, "No!"

"You said, 'Oh!' I don't understand?"

"O for Obadiah. Momma and Poppa called me O."

Under different circumstances both men would have seen the humor in the misunderstanding. "Lord, I'm calling on You, from the bedside of your faithful servant, O. Help him now." Guthrie tightened his grip on the Preacher's hand. Reverend Lawson looked into his hurting eyes and read the silent message, revising his prayer he continued. "Your servant is ready to come home. Tenderly guide him safely into the kingdom. Amen."

After the prayer, Reverend Lawson glanced around Obadiah Guthrie's room, at his personal artifacts. Simple, but neat, like the man. His eyes froze on an unsightly bundle in the corner—the walking sticks the Entrepreneur Willie carved for sell to Lance Thurston. "You never sold any of them, did you? You bought them all!"

Guthrie clutched his chest tighter, "Don't never breathe a word of it. When I'm gone, bury them sticks out back of yer place." He rested before adding, "These are proud people, even Willie."

"You didn't attempt to sell them?"

"Nobody'd want 'em. Ever' man makes his own. I removed 'em one at a time. Willie was none the wiser."

Reverend Lawson retrieved his well-worn Bible from his coat pocket. He read from John 14, "Let not your heart be troubled, ye believe in God, believe also in me. In my Father's house are many mansions. If it were not so, I would have told you. I go to prepare a place for you. And if I go and prepare a place for you, I will come again . . . ." Guthrie motioned him to stop.

"Preacher, the 23rd Psalm, please."

Reverend Lawson spoke from his heart, "Lord, You are Obadiah's Shepherd caring so lovingly and tenderly. We want for nothing. You allow us, Your sheep, to be comfortable and to find the softest, most delectable grasses to nibble in the green pastures." Guthrie closed his eyes and smiled, enjoying the words of comfort. "You lead us to calm, safe waters because You know we fear those swiftly moving waters of life knowing if we get our heavy wool wet, we'll drown. You continually restore us, over and over again. It is Your desire for us to travel down the path of righteousness. You are holy. Even though we walk through the valley of the shadow of death, we needn't fear, You promise to be with us, be with Obadiah now, protect him with Your mighty rod. You created all sorts of delicious, nourishing foods and placed it on a table before us. Just as You anointed King David and King Solomon, anoint us for that which we are called to do. You pour so much of life out for us that our cups overflow with blessings and mercies. May goodness and mercy be with Obadiah as he dwells in your house—forever."

"Amen." Guthrie smiled, "Preacher, I gotta tell ya something." He paused, catching his next breath, "You've shown up at the most unexpected times and done the most surprising things." He gasped for breath and frowned from the pain. "You're good for these people. Keep 'em guessing." He let out a groan and quieted. "Thank ya for being a breath of fresh air."

He held Guthrie's hand tightly with misty eyes. "Well, my dear friend, Obadiah Guthrie, the next time you see me, you will not be surprised to see me there!"

Guthrie smiled and nodded. His grip loosened in the Preacher's hand, his eyes looked toward the ceiling of the room. A radiant glow consumed his joyful face. Obadiah attempted to raise both arms toward the ceiling as he kept his gaze intently focused upward. His arms dropped onto his chest as a long sigh escaped his body. He did not struggle for the next breath, nor grimace from pain. Reverend Lawson lowered his head to the side of the bed and wept. "Father God, Alpha and Omega into Your hands, we commit our friend and Saint."

Commotion on the porch interrupted his grief. Someone pounded on the door of Guthrie's General Store. He heard the desperate cries of a child.

THE CIRCLE OF LIFE

"Help! Help! Somebody help me!"

Reverend Lawson hurried through the store and swung the door open. He recognized this little girl as the oldest of Bertha and Homer Tyson, Jr.'s. Panic consumed the child. She shook all over. "Poppa said for me to fetch Mr. Guthrie and be quick about it."

"Mr. Guthrie can't come."

The child covered her face and wailed, "He got to! Momma's gonna be dead." Reverend Lawson saw the distressed look on her tear-streaked face. Hand-in-hand they leapt down the steps and headed toward the Tyson home. He silently prayed as they jogged along, 'Lord, not two deaths in the same day! Grant us Your peace. Help me to help them, and be with Bertha right now.'

The child sobbed as they ran through tall weeds, her small fingers digging into his hand, gripping his strong hand with all her might. The terrain was frozen and the dried bushes reached out to scratch them as they passed. He attempted to calm the hysterical child. "What's your name?" He knew Beatrice was the oldest daughter of Bertha and Homer's.

She didn't acknowledge his question for several seconds, without slowing her pace one iota, "Beatrice. I'm Beatrice."

"Beatrice, you're a fine runner and an obedient daughter. Your Poppa will be proud." She didn't respond, but her cries quieted.

Before they reached the clearing where the small house sat, Reverend Lawson heard the piercing scream. A sick feeling formed in the pit of his stomach. Beatrice stopped running, but her small fingers did not loosen the grip on the Reverend's hand. He wanted to swoop her up in his arms and comfort her, maybe tell her everything would be all right, but the chills on his spine cautioned him not to make idle promises. Solemnly, Beatrice and Reverend Lawson crept across the frozen tundra to the front steps. For the first time since leaving Guthrie's, he noticed the cold. His nose and ears were numb. He shook, uncertain whether to blame the freezing temperatures or the screams he heard. He stood outside the door praying for wisdom and composure.

Little Beatrice tugged at his sleeve as she turned the doorknob. The door squeaked as it opened. The house was eerily quiet now. The young Parson felt a rock forming in his stomach.

The silence quickly broken by Homer's voice from another room, "Beatrice, that you? Send in Guthrie! Ya best git to yer room and take care of the tother youngins."

The child started to speak. Reverend Lawson squatted down eye level with the terrified girl, "Beatrice, you did a very important job. I'm proud of you." He patted her back and she threw her thin arms around his neck and squeezed the Preacher with all her strength. Unprepared, he almost toppled to the floor. "Now you go hug your little sisters and stay with them." Obediently, Beatrice disappeared down the darkened hallway, shutting the door.

Reverend Lawson made his way in the direction of Homer's voice. He prayed every step. Before reaching the closed door, another scream, followed by a deep, mournful moan erupted from behind the wooden door. Reverend Lawson gripped the doorknob with a trembling hand.

He'd never witnessed a face revealing more agony than Bertha's. Homer stood helplessly by her side wringing his hands. "How long has she been like this?"

"Pert nigh all afternoon. She commenced to feel poorly right before lunch. She took to the bed about 1 o'clock. It's been gittin' worser and worser."

The Preacher moved closer to the ailing Mother. "Bertha, can you hear me?" Judging from the look on her face, he wasn't certain she was conscious. He noticed the pains griped her every thirty seconds. She grunted and mumbled an unintelligible response. "Miss Bertha, we're going to do this together, but I need your help."

She half screamed, half screeched, "I can't! I can't do nothin'! No more!"

"Bertha, you *can*, and you *will* do this! Come on, we're going to birth a baby—you, Homer and me." He quickly added, "and God." He thought, if only they knew, it is mainly going to be God, and God alone, at work here. "Bertha, do you feel pressure?"

For the first time she opened her eyes and shot an angry glare right through Reverend Lawson, "Pressure! Ya crazy fool preacher! I'm 'bout to die from this awful pressure. I can't stand it any longer. Oh Lordie, take me, take me now." She screamed and beat the bed with clinched fists, "I wanta die right now. Lord, God, take me out of this misery!"

The young Parson stepped up to take control. In the firmest manner he could muster, he grabbed her hands from thrashing wildly, "Bertha! Stop! Don't waste your energy. You're going to need every ounce of strength. Now get hold of yourself." She calmed and the most pitiful look seized her face as she peered deep into his eyes and whispered, "Help me, Preacher! It's powerful bad. Please help me. Me and this youngin' are knockin' on death's door."

"Miss Bertha, I'm going to remove the covers from you and look at you . . . to . . . help you." He slowly began pulling the frayed homemade quilts from her. He was greeted by a pooling of bright red blood on the bed. He struggled to conceal his shock. The sight of blood always made him sick. Silently, he prayed for knowledge and calmness. "Homer, fetch hot water, towels, and a knife or scissors." Homer started for the door in his usual lackadaisical pace. "NOW, Homer! Hurry! Move, man! Get the lead out of your . . ." he caught himself, "the seat of your pants, or I'll kick your butt all the way to the door! This is your baby and your wife!" Homer looked stunned that the Preacher dared raise his voice at him and speak to him in such a manner. Reverend Lawson returned a threatening glare until Homer grasped the urgency of the situation and ran from the room.

Reverend Lawson placed his hand on Bertha's creased brow and stroked her hair. "You're a brave woman. Your family needs you." Bertha only groaned. The pained expression remained. Her severe pain persisted continually now.

When Homer returned with the water and towels, the Preacher grappled with his next action. "Homer, I'm going to have to look at your wife." He pointed, "Down there." He couldn't bring himself to say the words.

"Preacher, it ain't' fittin' for ya' to do that."

"What ain't' fittin' is to let this woman and baby die in your own bed! What kind of man would stand by and let his wife suffer like this?" He didn't expect an answer. Homer nodded in consent and stepped aside. Reverend Lawson already decided he was forging ahead with, or without, Homer's approval. "You're never here for this woman and those little girls, but by golly, you will be there today. And since this is all your doin', you better be here for them from now on! Do you hear me, Man? Shut up and act like a husband and a Father!" Gerhart Lawson shocked himself at what spilled forth from his lips, but he'd held these words in since arriving on the mountain. Homer's mouth gaped open, but he did not strike back.

Bertha was obviously ready to birth this baby. He gasped as he saw grayish skin, not hair. He couldn't be certain, but the skin looked smooth, like a back or leg, not the head of a baby. Without meaning to voice his suspicion, the word "Breech" escaped from him. Although Bertha continued with the most forlorn moans, intermittent with ear piercing screams, she was no longer totally coherent. The front door slammed and a man's voice interrupted his contemplation.

"Hey, where in the tarnation is ever'body?" Mr. Clyde called out. "I brought some eggs and a slab of bacon. I'll leave it here on the kitchen table."

Reverend Lawson quickly thanked God and yelled out, "Mr. Clyde, hurry! Back here." Clyde didn't miss the urgency in the Preacher's voice.

They heard the heavy steps crossing the bare wooden floors nearing the bedroom, and a deep chuckle. "What's the Jack Leg Preacher doin' in the bedroom?"

He swung the door open and one look at the grim faces in the room told the story. He did not hesitate to approach the bed and scrutinize the situation. "That baby needs to be turned, or it'll die and take Bertha too. She's ready and it's gotta be birthed."

"We have towels and water ready." Reverend Lawson indicated the large pan.

Clyde laughed. "Yes, I see. Were you gonna wait for the towels to do this job for ya? Preacher, pick up her right leg and press it up agin' her chest, but not tight. Homer, grab the other one and bend it there at the knee and do the same thing. And both of ya be gentle about it. She's spent and can't take much more. She may not make it now." Homer looked up horrified, finally realizing the seriousness.

Clyde reached into his pocket and pulled out the Old Timers knife and lay it on the bed. The Preacher's face drained of the small amount of remaining color, "Mr. Clyde?"

Clyde shook his head, "It ain't what ya think'. I'm not that dogged crazy! It's for cutting the cord if we manage to bring that youngin' into the world."

In earnest the Preacher asked, "Miss Bertha is sweating heavily, should I wipe her brow, or try to revive her?"

Tossing his coat onto the floor, Clyde roughly pushed up his sleeves. "No! Let's hope she stays unconscious until this is over. She don't need no more pain. She's got bigger problems than a trickle of sweat in her eyes. The tears of a dead baby would sting a heap more. Let's get to work. We got us a baby to meet."

Clyde began gently manipulating the unborn child into a position that the baby could pass through the birth canal. Bertha screamed throughout the process without fully regaining consciousness.

"There. That's the best I can do. It's in our Maker's hands now." Clyde pressed and massaged the upper part of Bertha's tummy, pushing hard in a downward motion. Bertha had another strong contraction and the head of the baby crowned. "Wake her up. We need her help now." Bertha did not respond. The Reverend's heart ached. He feared the worst.

Clyde dipped his hand in the pail of water and threw water on Bertha's face. "Wake up, Woman. It's time to birth a youngin', your work ain't done. Let's see what kind of a baby these Tysons' is gonna have today." She sputtered and spit and her piercing brown eyes opened wide and wild. She was fighting mad. "Good, Girl. We got her. Push Bertha! Push for all yer worth."

The dark tuft of hair, accompanied by a baby's head appeared. Clyde gently held the baby's misshaped, lumpy head in his large hands. "Again, Bertha! Do it again! Give 'er all ya got this time! That'll finish her off." Bertha gritted her teeth and grunted until her face passed from scarlet red to nigh onto purple, expelling all the air from her tired lungs. It was enough to thrust the baby into the world. A perfect baby. Clyde quickly cut and tied the cord and burst out laughing. He held the baby up for all to see. "Would you lookie here! Shut my mouth wide open! Homer, ya sly ole devil, ya finally figured out how to get a son!"

Clyde lightly slapped the baby on the back. The beautiful sound of a squallin' baby filled the room. He held the baby out for Bertha and Homer to see. At the sight of the wet baby, Homer fainted, hitting the floor with a hard thump. "Preacher, make yourself useful. Wrap this boy in one of them towels. Poor little feller is wondering what happened to him."

"What about Homer? Should we revive him"?

Clyde snickered a mischievous chuckle, "I'll take care of him. He'll come 'round." Clyde visited the water pail and emptied the remainder onto Homer's face. Indeed, Homer responded when the water hit his face. He sat up, grinning like a small child on Christmas morning. "Homer, whatcha gonna call this boy?"

"I've knowed that since we wuz expectin' the first one. His name is Obadiah. I been a wantin' a youngin' named Obadiah, but the Lord only gave me girls. I said ever' time, if'n this one's a boy, he'll be Obadiah; and three times the Lord laughed and gived me girls."

Reverend Lawson had to turn away from the happy parents as he relived the earlier part of the evening, bidding a farewell to another Obadiah. How fitting to witness the birth of an Obadiah on this day. The Lord, indeed, moves in mysterious ways, His wonders to perform.

Reverend Lawson and Clyde stepped out onto the rickety porch. Clyde retrieved the stub of a cigar and relit it. "Preacher, one thing botherin' me."

Reverend Lawson was still in awe at witnessing the miracle of birth. A death and a birth all in the same day! "What's that, Mr. Clyde?"

"What in the sam hill were ya fixin' to do with that pail of water and bunch of ragged towels? Did ya know where to start? Ya did know where that baby was comin' from, didn't ya? I don't know much about what Preachers know about womenfolk."

"Let me put it this way, Mr. Clyde, I've never been so glad to see anyone in my life as when I heard your voice! You were truly a God sent angel. I'm still amazed that such pain could bring about such a joy."

Clyde beamed with pride. "I reckon I never pictured myself as much of an angel." He took a draw of the cigar and slowly let the smoke escape, enjoying the weightless circles he produced with the little puffs. "Preacher, how come ya ended up with this job anyhow?"

He told Clyde the sad news. Clyde shook his head in disbelief. He dabbed at the tears with the back of his hand. "That blamed ole fool. He never told none of us. We'd a been right there to help him with the store, if we'd only knowed."

Clearing his throat in an attempt to dislodge the huge lump, Reverend Lawson responded, "He wanted it this way. He didn't want any special treatment or sympathy. Mr. Guthrie's customers were his family. We all know how he cared for that store. There's much to be said for being that satisfied with one's circumstances in this life. Guthrie knew and lived contentment, as much as any man I ever met. The Good Lord granted him his last wishes.

Oh, Mr. Clyde, for any of us to be that blessed." Reverend Lawson's thoughts turned to Rebecca. He longed for contentment and that involved her love. Often he wondered if life would ever be the same without her, knowing how much he'd loved her. He felt incomplete as a person without her by his side.

Clyde snubbed out the fire in the cigar on the rail of the porch. "Let's go send them little girls down to meet their brother. It's been a scary day for them little darlins." He slapped the Preacher affectionately on the back, "Ya' done good today, Parson. I'm mighty proud of ya'. I think ya had that situation under control. If'n I hadn't come by, ya would've done just fine. But if Homer Tyson, Jr. had been here alone with Bertha, I fear ya'd been a plannin' two more funerals."

24

A MOUNTAIN MOURNS

Word spread throughout the tight-knit community that the Jack Leg Preacher delivered Bertha a baby boy. The Parson was given full credit for the Tyson's finally getting a son. Clyde found humor in the situation. Each time the account was retold, the circumstances changed until it was nothing short of a downright miracle that the Preacher single-handedly performed. Clyde imagined the Parson's embarrassment by the time he'd heard this embellished account, not to mention if he would be called on to perform this courageous feat again.

The Brothers met out front of the general store. Oddly, no one wanted to even sit on the porch, or steps, without Guthrie. Reverend Lawson had secured the broken window he'd crashed into, pulled the shades and locked the store. Curiosity and speculation about the future of the general store ran rampant. Darrell looked to Clyde for an answer. "What's to be the fate of Guthrie's now?"

Clyde didn't want to be the source of any rumors. He chose his words selectively, even with his Brothers. "I heard tell that Guthrie had a Will. That's all I know."

Only one person in Greenbed knew the future of Guthrie's General Store, and he held the confidence of Mr. Guthrie in high regard. Reverend Lawson did not discuss this privileged knowledge with anyone.

Everyone could rely on Willie to engage his mouth prior to his brain. "What did his Will say? What's to become of it?"

"Ain't nobody heard, it's none of our business no how."

Of course, Willie continued prying, "Is to our business! Don't we all trade at the general store? It's just as much my business as anyone else's."

Darrell knew Clydie would never divulge any additional information if Willie continued selfishly questioning. "Shut yer mouth, Willie, it ain't about you nor yer tight little wad of money. It's about losing a good friend. He was the backbone of Greenbed. I don't know what we're gonna do without him. Long ago, Guthrie could've moved on like his sister did, he might've even owned that John Deere tractor he longed for, but he stayed here, know why?"

"Yep. He stayed put cuz he only knowed how to take money off of us. He didn't know nothin' 'bout how to work the fields, milk cows, grow crops or raise cattle."

"Willie, sometimes I'm ashamed to call ya my brother. Guthrie stayed on at the store to do all us'ns a great service. He was plenty smart with book learning. It wouldn't a been no problem for him to find another trade. We best mind our own business and put our thoughts to how to give Guthrie the most respected send off possible. I need to find Reverend Lawson and see what he's planning. One idea keeps rollin' around my noggin." With that, Clyde turned and left the bewildered Brothers. He hurt. He missed his friend already and also questioned how life would go on without Guthrie at the helm.

Clyde drove straight to the Baptist Church and found Reverend Lawson preparing Guthrie's funeral service. The Preacher welcomed the interruption. "Come in, Mr. Clyde. Again, I'm glad to see you, but not as thankful as last time! You saved the life of Bertha, her baby's, and probably mine as well." Both men welcomed the levity on this solemn day and task.

"Why, Preacher? Ya got another baby for us to deliver?" They laughed appreciating the reprieve.

"No, not today, if I find myself in that situation, I'll be sure to include you. We're a great team." The seriousness returned to the Parson's face. "No, truth be told, I'm struggling with this memorial sermon. Nothing seems adequate. How does one prepare a service for the likes of a man like Guthrie? The words won't come. I don't know where to start."

"What ya got so far?"

The Reverend held up his paper and turned it toward Clyde. "It says, 'We've gathered here today to honor our friend and brother in Christ. He lived his religion everyday.' That's it. I stared at this sheet of paper for the past two hours and that's all. Pitiful. I should be able to write volumes about a man like Guthrie, what he meant to every single person here, how he concerned himself with his customer's well being, his giving spirit, how much he sacrificed."

"Preacher, the the rest of the sermon is in your head. Ya already told it to me, standing on Homer Tyson, Jr.'s front porch."

"What was that, Mr. Clyde?"

"Promises. Clinging to the right thing, the thing that don't change and leave us a hurtin'. We need to hear that now. We're all missin' that ole coot powerful bad, and scared about what his death means to us. Are we gonna have to travel down this mountain to get a sack of sugar? We're needin' a message of hope and you're the Messenger."

"Do you really think that's what the people need to hear? Will that bring any sort of comfort and honor Guthrie?"

"Preacher, you'll do him proud. I got faith in ya. I ain't even worried 'bout it so long as ya don't take advice again from Willie." They both chuckled at that. "I've got an idea for honorin' him and want to run it by ya first." For the next hour and a half Clyde and Reverend Lawson laughed and wept together as they reflected on Obadiah Guthrie and planned a 'send off' to honor their friend, like nothing the small community of Greenbed had ever witnessed.

"Preacher, I'm not meanin' to pry none, but do ya think there will be anyone in Guthrie's family to take care of layin' 'im out? I 'member hearin' Guthrie talk about his sister, Lucy, havin' a youngin' somewhere in the big city."

"Mr. Clyde, I wouldn't count on that. They won't be here in time to handle any of the details. Who could we get to look after that?"

"I was fixin' to go down to the saw mill and plead our case to J.C. He's been known to help out in times like this and, I believe, he'd consider it an honor to do it for Guthrie. Ain't nobody that wouldn't jump at the chance to pay respects to that man. I suspect Guthrie helped more people than we'll ever know. During the Depression, he let every family buy on credit, and never got paid back by many of 'em, he never complained. Me and the Brothers could help J.C. make the coffin, if he don't have one stored away. When he ain't busy at the saw mill, he makes coffins and stores 'em in the loft. I'll speak to Emma, she'd be willing to help make a fine lining to fit inside. She thought the world of Guthrie too. Lawrence or Turner can stain the outside of it. If ever a man I knew would make it to heaven, I know Guthrie did. He's probably up there laughin' at us right now."

"That would be helpful, thanks for offering. Mr. Guthrie was blessed with a lot of good friends. He never lacked in that department."

Clyde picked up his wide-brimmed white felt hat and adjusted it on his head. "Well, Preacher, we've done went and done it again."

"What's that?"

"We put our heads together and come up with a plan."

"Mr. Clyde, we make a good team."

"Now, Preacher, don't ya be tellin' that 'round the mountain. I wouldn't want to ruin my reputation by teamin' up with the likes of you. Them folks at the Primitive Church might run me outta town." Clyde turned back and extended his hand to Reverend Lawson. "I'll see ya day after tomorrow at the funeral. I know ya'll do fine honoring Guthrie."

The next day both men busily made the contacts and plans necessary to orchestrate the most respectful, memorable service the mountainfolk of Greenbed ever witnessed. This funeral needed to be special, because Guthrie lived a most unique life.

The gloomy weather matched the moods. Lawrence dug into his bureau to find gloves. "Wouldn't ya 'jest know it? It'd rain on the day of his funeral."

His wife, Minnie, shook her head and agreed. "Maybe the rains will slack up atter while. I always heard tell that the heavens shed tears right along side us when a saint dies."

"A saint for sure, I'll give ya that; but I don't know 'bout the heavens sheddin' no tears. Seems to me the party would be there, cuz they're the ones that's gonna get to enjoy Guthrie from here on." He opted to hush, as that lump in his throat increased.

At the funeral every man, woman, and child that entered the Baptist Church draped themselves in black. The women respectfully covered their heads with black cloths or knitted scarves. People stood in the aisles, and along the back of the small church. It seemed imperative to pay their last respects. The mourning was as sincere as it was evident. Guthrie touched the lives of every resident in a personal way; and it seemed only fitting that each person grieved in his or her own way. Some openly sobbed, others fought succumbing to tears. The elder women wept and called out during the service. Reverend Lawson was startled when one of the women shouted, "Ya know it to be the truth!" He continued on with his eulogy, and again she called aloud, "Tell it, Preacher. Come, Holy Comforter." Reverend Lawson paused to regain focus. He looked over the congregation and his eyes locked with Mr. Clyde who nodded to the Preacher, as if to confirm 'yep, she's one of ours at Primitive Baptist.'

Reverend Lawson read from the 14th Chapter of the book of John. During the reading of the scripture, the Parson heard the rains turn to light sleet gently tapping on the glass panes of the small church. The comforting symphony increased in intensity.

"Obadiah Guthrie will be missed by everyone. He will never be replaced in our community, or in our hearts. Life is for the living, and we're the ones forced to keep surviving. Guthrie's memory remains with us." The Preacher launched into the sermon that Mr. Clyde suggested. It became the sermon of hope. Life would go on and they would endure the hardships of adjusting to Guthrie's absence, it would be difficult. "Obadiah Guthrie lived a life fitting to be an example to all. The best way to make his life count is to remember the things important to him; like respecting every one of his customers, compassion and caring, living a life in the shadow of the cross."

Reverend Lawson asked the congregation to recite the Lord's Prayer with him. Mr. Clyde gave him a nod of approval and the Brothers quietly slipped out the back door.

Word spread throughout the congregation during the service that the young man and woman, dressed like movie stars, on the front row was Guthrie's nephew and his wife from the city. The couple sat stoically throughout the service. Reverend Lawson motioned for them to follow the wooden casket from the church. The congregation strained to get a better look at the young man. Some of the older mountain residents whispered, "That's bound to be Toby, I 'member his Mother. She run off and didn't want nothin' to do with the mountain." Her decision to leave was viewed as her deserting not only the mountain, but of all of them, as individuals. They took the rejection personally. Whispered murmurings could be heard throughout the small church.

The pallbearers solemnly exited the church carrying Obadiah Guthrie to his final resting place. The revving of tractors disturbed the solemnness of the procession. Questioning looks dashed from one to the next. Three John Deere tractors were positioned with three of the Brothers sitting tall in the seats, gripping the steering wheels. Lawrence motioned for the pallbearers to bring Guthrie to them. Dutifully, the pallbearers slowly made their way toward the first tractor and gently slid the coffin bearing Guthrie onto the bed of the wagon. They quickly secured the ropes across the wooden coffin to guard against the slightest jolt. Slowly, the curious mourners filed out of the Baptist Church and walked behind the roaring tractors to the burial grounds. They hummed Amazing Grace as they trailed along behind the tractors. Not one person broke the line. They walked two abreast over the rough frozen grounds, enduring the inclimate elements without a complaint to the graveyard a quarter of a mile down the mountain road. Guthrie was escorted in proper style, by the John Deeres he dreamed of owning.

The Preacher kept the graveside service brief. The sleet became treacherous and the faithful friends shivered in the freezing temperatures. "Friends, neighbors, there's nothing left to say about or for Obadiah Guthrie. He will be sorely missed as he was deeply loved. Dust to dust, ashes to ashes . . . . Now, go and live your life and celebrate the living."

Immediately, the questions began anew about the general store. The heavy green shades to the store remained pulled, while every light in the store irreverently glowed the evening of his funeral. The few outside speculated, "What do you reckon is goin' on in there?"

"I don't know, but I don't think it's fittin' for nobody to be in there prawling 'round, particularly tonight. It ain't respectful to the dead." The door to the store opened and the Preacher came out, closing the door behind him. "Lookie yonder! What in the blue blazes? If that ain't the Jack Leg Preacher, I'll eat my hat."

"I'll be cow licked by a mule, you're right, it is the Preacher! What business do ya reckon he has in Guthrie's store tonight? And look at him, he's hightailing it."

25

FORMERLY KNOWN AS GUTHRIE'S

The mountainfolk thought of excuses to head in the direction of the general store for the purpose of keeping a close watch over the store. The shades remained drawn and no activity could be discerned. Never had they seen such a car as the nephew drove into the mountains for Guthrie's funeral. The shiny green 1938 Hudson came adorned with white-wall tires containing all the bells and whistles the mountaineers had only heard existed. "I believe that vehicle costs over $600! Can you beat that with a stick? Paying that kind of money, what a sin." Most of the farmers not coming close to the national yearly income of $1,729, a car costing that amount was obscene! The majority of the mountainfolks owned aging trucks or vehicles that struggled to climb the steep grades.

They feared this closed out an era, and their lives would never be the same. Guthrie's nephew, Tobias Snodgrass, along with his wife, Bethany, loaded up the big Hudson and headed down the mountain without a hint of their plan for the store. The community had no answers about the future of Guthrie's General Store. As the long, green vehicle departed, the mountaineers hearts sank, and they experienced the grief of losing Guthrie all over again.

Ten days later, the mighty Hudson, driven by Bethany peering over the steering wheel with a determined look on her face, headed up the dirt roads of the mountain, loaded to the ceiling. Close behind followed Toby in a pickup truck, also completely loaded. Curiosity caused the residents to ache for answers. The flurry of activity created wild speculation.

The following day, the tattered "OPEN" sign appeared in the window of the general store. Little was sold, but at times the store buzzed with a flurry. Toby told everyone that he and his wife, Bethany, planned to sell their home in the city and re-open the general store. A new endeavor for them, and they welcomed the challenges and opportunities. He smiled, shook hands, and introduced himself to each potential customer. Bethany stayed out of sight busying herself in the living quarters, preparing a home.

One of the customers asked Tobias, "I reckon you're still callin' the store Guthries?"

Toby scratched his head, seriously pondering, "I don't think so. My wife and I considered other names for a fresh start." Toby noted the frowns and the conversations ceased.

Three days later the old sign unceremoniously replaced by a new sign with bright colors declared: "Snodgrasses' Groceries and Gadgets." Puzzled, the mountainfolk studied the sign. They didn't like the change, and they certainly didn't approve of this new sign or what it represented to them. Few people ventured into the general store that day. Along with the name revision, unwelcomed internal changes occurred. The checkerboard and the seats at the front were removed to make room for more shelving, even though the new shelving remained empty. Sadness washed over the shocked customers as they ventured into the general store. Again, it proved another day without transactions.

Toward the end of the day, Brothers Darrell and Clyde stopped by the store. Bethany Snodgrass stood refolding bolts of previously folded fabric. She didn't speak to them as she continued to smooth the fabric with her hand. She wondered why anyone would waste their time making clothes when mail order had the latest fashions. Clyde attempted to engage her in conversation. He remembered the first day Guthrie introduced the line of material for sale and the fuss the womenfolk made over it, and the proud look on Guthrie's face as he watched the women excitedly sort through the material. He'd beamed like a proud new Poppa. "I remember the time when your uncle . . ."

"Stop, right there," she interrupted shooting her right hand into the air, "not my uncle, my husband's uncle. I don't care to live in the past of how the store previously ran."

"Listen here, Missy, you and them high filutin' ways. If you live to celebrate your hundredth birthday, ya couldn't hold a candle to the likes of Guthrie. Ya ought to take some 'mannering' lessons from a dead man!"

154

Her eyes shot daggers, "I'll have you know, we're the new owners now and I won't be disrespected in this manner. You can just get out of here if you don't like it."

Clyde and Darrell promptly left the store, purely out of respect for the store, not out of respect for Bethany. This little city gal could never have been prepared for what Clyde almost spat back at her.

The mountainfolk spread the word that they needed to boycott the general store. The nerve of this stranger, even if he was blood related to Guthrie, to come to their mountain and insult them—first the sign and then Clyde.

Reverend Lawson stopped by to pay a visit to the Snodgrasses. He heard the plot and hoped he could derail the conflict before it was set firmly into motion.

"Not so good, Reverend. I don't know how my Uncle made enough money to exist here. I don't get it. Sooner or later, I guess these folks will need supplies and come here."

Reverend Lawson had been in the mountain long enough to know exactly why the store remained idle and he realized the mountain pride threatened to keep the store empty. He opted not to offer advice unless Toby asked for it.

Days later things still had not improved. The mountaineers did without, borrowed from one another, or made the trek down the mountain to the valley store, if absolutely necessary. Not only was he not selling anything, rotten eggs splattered the new sign late one evening to send a clear message.

Toby went to his only acquaintance, Reverend Lawson. "We're forced to leave here. I can't afford to do this for another week. We can't abide the isolation of the mountain, besides lose the shirt right off our back."

Reverend Lawson weighed the consequences and decided the time came to offer some unsolicited advice. "Toby, mountain life and the families that have lived here, on the same plots of land for generations are different. They don't embrace change in any manner, for any reason. They see no need for change." He paused. "Your Uncle was one of the most, if not the most respected member of this community. He didn't have his own family living here, but became a member of everyone's family. People came into his store to socialize, not necessarily to transact business." He prepared to step out into shaky territory. If Toby wanted to survive someone needed to enlighten him before he threw up his hands in defeat and headed back to the safety of the city. "Guthrie's store served a vital part of their lives from an early age. They don't have a lot to look forward to, except hard work. The times they spent at your Uncle's store offered an escape, lightened their loads." He paused to let that much settle with Toby. "I might suggest you try this as a start. Put the chairs back in the front of the store. It would say that you welcome them into a comfortable, familiar surrounding. They may've interpretted the chair removal as a direct insult."

"I didn't intend to send that message. My Uncle willed this store to me and, surely, I can run it the way I see fit. Anything new is a change at first. Then we get used to it, and eventually even forget how it was before the change." Reverend Lawson knew Toby was correct, indeed, the new owner could make any changes he desired. However, the Preacher realized the community's refusal to accept changes, and this line of reasoning did not guarantee success of the general store.

No changes were made, and no customers came. At the end of the week, Clyde and Turner made a trip to the lumber yard, they glanced toward the general store and smiled when they saw the old sign hanging in its original position with three words crudely painted above the sign to make the original sign now read,

"Formerly Known as
Guthrie's General Store."

Clyde and Turner walked over to further inspect. Once inside they noted the chairs and stools reinstated, along with the checkerboard on top a keg of nails.

Without making any comment to Toby, they straddled the keg of nails and began setting up the checkers. They occasionally waved at people out the window as they passed by, some drizzled in, no one shopped . . . yet. But the promise of a new beginning filled the general store. As Clyde and Turner completed their game and stood to leave, Clyde turned back to Toby and tipped his hat at him and said, "Good job." Toby saw a glimmer of hope that a little acceptance from both sides may bring about a slow recovery.

TOO MANY UDDERS—
TOO FEW HANDS

Toby, the new proprietor of the general store became keenly aware that the community continued to make small gestures of acceptance. He had no delusions of replacing his uncle. This small, tight-knit mountain community loved Obadiah Guthrie with a deep abiding love. Toby also feared his wife, Bethany, may never experience acceptance. Bethany was as inflexible as the mountaineers.

"Hey there, Toby, how are you?" the familiar voice of Reverend Lawson derailed this troubling thought. "You look like a man with the weight of the world on his shoulders. I noticed activity, that's a good sign. Anything wrong?"

"Life," Toby solemnly answered.

"That's a broad and deep subject. What specifically about life?"

"You know, I made concessions since moving here, I'm trying in my own way, to be a friend to these people, but it seems that I get so far and then I run head-on into a wall. What's wrong?"

"Rest assured, my friend, it takes a spell for them to warm up to accept you. Want to know how I finally got the nod of approval when I was new, although, I'm not recommending it!"

"I'm all ears. I'm fresh out of ideas, nothing seems to get me over that last hurdle. You know, living in the city, you don't have these battles to conquer. I guess I want to be genuinely considered a friend, not simply tolerated."

"Well, when I first moved here from the city, like you, I wanted to be considered a friend. I thought if I understood their struggles, and listened to their dreams as well as problems, I'd have the church filled and busting at the seams in a month's time. Let me tell you, it didn't happen like that! First of all, they're proud people, but they don't wear their problems on their sleeves. They're private about hardships, particularly to an outsider. Sorry, Toby, you're still considered an outsider."

"But you overcame that, because they respect you and your position and that's not confined to just your church members, even those who dare not darken the door of a church. How did you manage that?"

"You sure you want the nitty gritty details? I was doing visitation at a farm and my stomach cramped and I needed a bathroom in a hurry; and used the outhouse. It collapsed and I fell into the pile of . . . a . . . . waste. I came into your uncle's store to get soap to clean myself. At the time I thought, 'just my luck—the store was filled with men'. Looking back, that was God's plan. When I told the story, they saw my humanity. I stank as though I spent the afternoon rolling around the barnyard, which come to think of it, that's pretty much excactly what I'd done. From that day on, everything smoothed out and I no longer felt like 'the' outsider. When I could see the humor of the awful fix and share it with them, we shared a good laugh at my happenstance."

"You're sure right, Preacher. I don't want to have to take that drastic of an approach." He laughed at the thought of Reverend Lawson falling into a dung heap.

"What I'm suggesting, Toby, let's pray for an opportunity to come along for you to seize. I don't know what that would be, but I know God can provide it. He is faithful to hear and answer prayers, according to His Will. You need to be on the alert and watch for it. I'll let you know if I think of anything."

"That sounds reasonable and simple enough. I'll give it a try and the first chance I hear of something, I'll jump on it like stink on poop." Toby snickered, "But you've already done that!" They enjoyed a good chuckle at the Preacher's expense.

Two weeks passed, and Toby dedicated himself to eavesdropping on the conversations in the store, waiting for an opportunity. Then it happened. As he stocked the shelves, Maddie Wagner came in the store. The gathering of men greeted her and asked about her husband, Josiah.

"Law Mercy Sakes! He's laid up in the worst way. He fell off the barn roof this mornin', and hurt his back tolerable bad. He ain't even able to turn over in the bed, let alone get out of it. I reckon that's where he'll stay for a few days. We're in a fix. Don't know how we're gonna get them cows milked tonight. I came here to see if any of you'ns know where Doc Hess might be. He ain't in his office, nobody seems to know his whereabouts. He probably took off to some fishin' hole out yonder. I just as well get a sack of flour while I'm here to make the trip worth it."

Toby's heart skipped a beat as this presented an opportunity for him to step up and win respect. "I'll help with the milking." Toby meant precisely what he said—that he could help. Mrs. Maddie heard and interpreted that offer as he would handle it.

"Them ole cows need to be milked, and soon."

"I'll ask my wife to fill in for me. I could leave now and follow you." Toby glanced at the checker players in the store to be certain they heard his generous offer. He needed them to spread the word throughout. He saw the exchange of looks and smirks. No one commented, yet he knew they heard.

Maddie's wrinkled face displayed relief, "We're beholdin' to ya', that's mighty sure."

Toby disappeared into the living quarters of the store and returned, steering a scowling Bethany toward the front counter.

The long shiny green Hudson with its white-wall tires looked out of place delving in and out of potholes along the dirt roads, down the long and bumpy lane to the Wagner barn. Maddie slowly crawled from behind the steering wheel of their old truck. "Well Sir, the cows are yonder in the barn waitin' for ya. The buckets hang on nails inside the door. I thank ya, Josiah thanks ya', and them cows thank ya' for helpin' them out." She turned and headed toward the house, with the sack of flour gripped tightly in her clutches.

For the first time, Toby's excitement waned as he thought, 'what on earth did I get myself into? I don't have the faintest idea what to do now.' He recalled the Reverend's words and trusted that since God sent this his way, somehow he'd manage. He opened the door to the barn. Sure enough, there stood 20 cows in their stanchions. His heart sank. Suddenly, the task at hand seemed immense. Dazed, he strolled through the barn to assess this job. The cows restlessly shifted their mighty weights from hoof to hoof, vocalizing complaints.

"All right, Ladies, looks like I'm all you got." He retrieved a couple of buckets from the nails on the wall and squatted next to cow number one. Timidly, he reached in toward her udder. He squeezed, gently at first, then with more force. He saw a single drop of milk appear. The cow swished her tail at his head, landing right across his face. Trial and error soon taught him he needed a downward motion with a gentle squeezing. A small stream of milk sounded like beautiful music to him as it hit the metal bucket. Toby immediately felt encouraged. He realized, at this pace, it would still be a monumental job, he'd be lucky to finish before the morning milking rolled around.

The slight measure of progress occurred through an excruciating effort. The second cow expressed her opposition to the amateur gripping her udders. After the first pressure he exerted, she kicked at him and moved in his general direction to knock him off balance. Toby concerned himself more about guarding the precious milk already in the bucket than getting kicked. He made several more attempts before opting to skip this gal and move on to a more deserving-natured lady. He'd return to her after gaining valuable experience. He hoped cow number three might be more predisposed to cooperate with him. After a slow process, he completed cow number three and headed for the fourth. This cow, while not cantankerous, seemed a constant complainer and influenced her immediate neighbors by her foul mood. They began mooing and getting more and more restless. He patted her back and told her he understood her mood, that he married a similarly natured woman.

Progress came painstakingly slowly. He pulled out his watch to check the time. The expensive, gold watch, engraved with his name also felt foreign in the dairy barn. He sighed in defeat and wondered how in the world he would complete this task. He squatted beside the next cow and she immediately shifted at precisely the right moment to land her right back hoof squarely on his left foot.

He firmly placed his shoulder into her mammoth side and pushed with all his might. She stood her ground, on his foot. Toby attempted to twist his foot to freedom from under the firmly planted hoof. Out of desperation, he began pushing, slapping, and swearing at the cow. He heard a chorus of laughter erupt from behind him. There stood three of the Brothers. "Don't hurt her feelins or she'll never let ya go. Sounds to me like the two of you already bonded." Clyde gently, yet firmly, laid his hand on the cow's back and slid it down her leg and lightly tapped her. Immediately, she transferred the weight to another hoof. Toby quickly retrieved his throbbing foot.

Toby let fly a few more choice words for the cow before turning his attention to the Brothers. "What brings you fellows all the way out here?"

"Came to check on ya. There's a lot of milkin' here for just two uncalloused city hands. Besides, we figured ya probably had enough fun by now and a few more hands might speed things up," Turner chuckled, "unless you plan on stayin' here surrounded by all these bags full of milk the rest of the night. Must be real temptin' for a man like you to handle such female delicacies."

"I've never been happier to see you Brothers!"

Clyde readjusted his felt hat, "Have ya fed 'em yet? They seem perturbed, might be hungry."

A startled expression crossed Toby's face, "Fed them? No. I came to milk them. Nobody mentioned feeding these critters."

"Hadn't ya noticed they're gettin' jittery? Lawrence, get the feedin' scoop going. Toby, the first thing ya need to do is turn one of them empty buckets upside down and put yer skinny city butt on it and save yer achin' knees. I dare say ya won't last more than fifteen more minutes in that squat. Next thing we know, you'll be bellowin' bigger than them cows with the pain in yer knees. And introduce yerself to the cow before ya grab her tit, afterall, that's only the gentlemanly thing to do." They all laughed. Toby didn't know if he was serious about that or not. "If ya take a minute first, ya figure out quick like, her disposition—if she's a kicker, tail swatter, or yer person favorite, a toe tromper."

Toby watched how the Brothers tenderly, yet firmly, manipulated the cows. He witnessed brotherly love, jovial good-natured taunting, and compassion for a fellow struggler—himself. The remainder of the task passed far more entertaining than the first three cows he attempted to milk. The time passed quickly with the Brothers bantering back and forth. He learned more during the next two hours about mountain living than all the books he'd ever read.

The milkhands left Wagner's farm with the promise of being back for the 5:00 A.M. milking. Without a thought of his soiled clothes or weary bones, Toby slid behind the wheel of his classy Hudson to return to the general store, to 'home'. Now, it felt like home. The feelings of alienation, replaced with acceptance. He wondered if his wife might ever gain acceptance. A smile tugged at the corners of his mouth as he traversed the bumpy roads.

He decided some bridges take a long time to build, before one is able to cross. He knew for certain, her acceptance would not come about by milking cows. But, as Reverend Lawson assured him . . . God is still in the miracle business.

WARS AND RUMORS OF WARS

These days, the majority of the time a gathering of men occupied the general store. The radio broadcasted at all times. A hot topic of conversation always centered on the war abroad. Although the fighting occurred an ocean away, they were troubled.

"Toby, do ya think, we're gonna get involved in this here war? Seems they talk more about it each day."

Toby was pleased that Jeremiah asked his opinion, and desired to respond in such a manner that the men might continue to include him in discussions. After the milking experience, he made every effort to be accepted.

"I listen to the President's Fireside Chats every night, without fail. It seems more grim every week. That Hitler is gaining more power all the time. He's to be feared."

Willie joined in, only after squinting his bad eye completely closed and turning his head sideways, "Why do ya reckon they're messin' in everybody's business? Reckon they've run out of land and needin' more?"

Toby assumed they looked to him to respond, "I don't think that's it. Maybe it's more about power and control and greed. He wants to be a dictator over the people, more and more people. The man is power hungry. And even more frightening is the way the Germans blindly follow him. Now, that worries me plenty. I don't know where it stops."

Jeremiah pushed the brim of his felt hat back slightly, "It's sure to end bad."

No one dared respond. The suffering of the Great Depression was a harsh reality; the bitter tales of World War I still present in their minds.

Reverend Lawson leapt up the steps to the general store, whistling as he entered with a wave of his hand and a broad smile. "What on earth did I stumble upon? You fellows look too serious for such a beautiful day. What's going on? Maybe I shouldn't ask."

Toby shrugged his shoulders and rounded the end of the counter to complete sweeping the floor. "Trying to solve the world problems, it's a bigger task each passing day."

"Yes, the world does seem more complicated. President Roosevelt sounded grave during the last "Fireside Chat." Imagine the weight on that man's shoulders during this critical time. Makes me glad I'm a humble preacher."

"Preacher, I thought after that last war, there weren't to be no more wars. It was the war to end all wars. Don't ya' think this ole world is ready for a long season of peace"? Jeremiah was serious, as he presented an excellent point.

"One would think there'd been enough bloodshed to last a lifetime and here we go, looking right down the barrel of a cannon. The Bible doesn't say we're promised peace. In fact, just the opposite, only in heaven is there peace, and that peace lasts for eternity. The Bible speaks of wars and rumors of war. The old sinful nature of mankind is always present, whether in our community or across the Atlantic Ocean."

"Preacher, what if them Germans come here after us? What do ya reckon will happen?"

"Well, Mr. Darrell, it would be a long trip for them to transport troops across the Ocean. I'm not saying they won't, it seems unlikely. I pray to God they never do that. It's awful enough being an ocean away." Each man searched his soul in this fervent thought. "I know I've said this before, if our country goes to war, I'm packing my bags the same day." Reverend Lawson often made that declaration, and each time he stated it with more conviction and determination. They couldn't fathom this young, man of God proclaiming war on anyone or anything. However, he'd surprised them many times in the brief time he lived among them. Therefore, no one dared question or challenge him. "We must commit to pray for our country every day, in fact, pray as Saint Paul taught us 'pray without ceasing.' Pray like your very life depends on it, because, Dear Friends, it does."

Silence filled the room. "Freedom is not free. We must never, ever, ever forget that. It comes with a huge price tag."

28

PAY NO MIND TO CRAZY IKE

Toby immediately stopped his work in the general store and tuned his ear toward the panic shriek from his wife, "Tobias, I saw a man at our back door, peeping in through the screen door at me! Come here." Toby headed toward the living quarters of the store to investigate. When his wife made a demand, she was not one to be reasoned with, or ignored. "There he is, walking away now! He rummaged through those boxes out back and put something in a bag. Go see what he wants."

Lawrence turned from his seat by the front window to see what man caused such a commotion, "Oh, pay no mind to him. That's Crazy Ike. He don't mean no harm."

"No harm?" Bethany screamed, "He spied on me! And he scared me half to death."

Clyde couldn't restrain his laughter, "Spying on ya'? Why, what was ya doin' that ya wouldn't want Crazy Ike to see?"

"Dusting furniture is what I was doing," Bethany snapped angrily. She resented being the brunt of the jibe. Not only did the gathering of men in the store chuckle, the lone woman shopper covered her mouth and turned her head to conceal the smile. "Don't you make fun of me! This is none of your business anyhow, Mister." Unlike Toby, Bethany didn't bother to make the acquaintance of any of the mountain residents, except Reverend Lawson. She could care less that she knew few residents by name, and was baffled that Toby liked it here with these uneducated, crude heathens, as she referred to them.

The spark of her flared temper delighted the men. "Next time Crazy Ike comes 'round, we'll be happy to introduce ya to him. Shoot fire, if ya got an extra dust rag, ya might persuade him to come in and help ya with yer womanly chores."

"I'll have you know, first of all I don't need any help keeping this little crackerbox of a house clean and, secondly, I wouldn't have the likes of that man enter my home. I want him to stay away from here, the further the better."

"Little Lady, ya' could do a whole lot worse than Crazy Ike. He didn't mean to scare ya none. Better get used to the likes of him. He ain't gonna change one iota," Clyde grinned, "I bet ya' scared him a heap more than he did you. He ain't used to women cuttin' such a shine as that."

Bethany stomped out of the general store retreating to the living quarters, feeling she'd been bested—again. "This whole place is dreadfully savage."

"I do declare, Son, that woman of yers could talk the ears off a field of corn," Clyde jokingly quipped.

"Mr. Clyde, I agree with you. That's my Bethany. No one ever referred to her as timid." Toby seemed to admire her vim and vigor. "Seriously, where does Ike live? I've never seen him around, or heard anyone mention him."

"Crazy Ike lives ever'where, anywhere, and no where. He claims the world as his home. I reckon that's the truth. He don't hardly have a care. He roams all 'round. He's got a little lean-to hut, way back in the woods up at Cricket Grove. He keeps to hisself most all the time. From time to time he roots through people's discarded stuff and garbage heaps, lookin' for a treasure of some sort. He don't talk to none of us much. He and Guthrie did some tradin' and were friendly like with each other. I swear, Guthrie would befriend a grizzly bear."

"How does he live?" Toby was intrigued with this strange little figure of a man.

"Well, Sir," Darrell began, "ya might not believe it. He makes and sells a magic potion."

"You're right, Mr. Darrell, I can't believe that. But, tell me, this gets better all the time."

"Ain't no tall tale 'bout it, your Uncle bought the salve from him and sold it in the store. He could hardly keep it stocked. Ever'body wants it. Fact of the matter, he probably don't know Guthrie's gone."

"I'm afraid to ask . . . what is the potion?"

"Crazy Ike makes somethin' that works on achin' bones and if'n ya got rheumatism, it's the only thing that'll give the slightest bit of relief. Best make sure to keep a hefty supply, cuz when folks need it, ain't nothin' else will do."

The following days, Bethany managed to forget about Crazy Ike. One evening in mid-August Toby and Bethany sat in their living quarters, listening to the radio when Toby saw a shadow pass a side window. His heartbeat quickened, his first thoughts envisioned a wild animal. He went to the front of the store to check the locks. Crazy Ike peered into the storefront window, his rounded nose pressed flat as a pancake, and hands cupped around his eyes, as though he were holding binoculars.

Toby waved and forced a smile. He shared Bethany's apprehension of this unpredictable character. He opened the store's door, "Ike, hello. Come in. Let's get acquainted."

Timidly, Crazy Ike entered the general store. "Whar's Guthrie?"

"Guthrie was my uncle and he's gone. The store is mine now."

"Gone? Ya tellin' me a lie, boy? When's he a comin' back?" Ike was a man of few words. Toby surmised the shorter he kept his answers, the better.

"He died. Do you have your potion? I need some."

Ike reached into the burlap sack and retrieved six small bottles and placed them on the checkerboard.

"How much did my Uncle pay you for each bottle?" he asked as he walked toward the old cash register.

"Didn't never pay me none. We traded."

Toby's first experience at bartering, but he somehow knew it wouldn't be the last. "What do you need, Mr. Ike?"

Ike quickly snatched items from the shelves and stuffed them into the worn burlap bag, gathered the opening of the bag and shuffled back to the door. He turned around to face the new proprietor and shook his finger as a warning, "Ya best bring them plants on your porch in tomorrow night," slamming the door behind him. He disappeared.

Toby recounted the weird encounter with Harl. "Don't pay no mind to Crazy Ike. He's as daffy as a June Bug in the month of September."

The following night Toby and Bethany were awakened at 11:00 P.M. to howling winds and rains beating against the windows. Bethany lay in bed with her hands tightly covering her ears to muffle the daunting sounds. After the storm passed, they heard several loud crashes. Toby immediately recognized the source as the two planters filled with geraniums posted by the front door of the general store which Bethany insisted on having to add color to the entryway. He recalled the warning from Crazy Ike and a chill ran down his spine.

Ike didn't venture back into civilization for another five weeks. This time he came directly to the front door, during regular business hours. The men in the store greeted him, Ike tilted his head and glared at each one, never returning the greeting.

"Ike, did you bring more jars of rheumatism medicine? My shelf better never be without it. Everyone says it's the only thing that works on aches and pains." Ike retrieved four bottles from the burlap sack. Without any coaxing or conversation he gathered items from the shelves. "Ike, you were right about the wind storm, how did you know."

"Same as I know the river's gonna flood next rain. Best be on guard for it 'cuz it'll be a gullywasher. Best ya dig out yer high-top boots." He left.

"Reckon it will?" Turner seemed concerned since he lived the closest to the river. The river had never posed a serious threat to his home.

Nathaniel reminded them, "Tell me, ya ain't worried 'bout a prediction that comes from Crazy Ike? He's likely to say most anything to hear his own voice talkin' and tellin'. Pay him no mind."

"Ike knows these things. He's betterna' any of them Farmer's Almanacs sittin' yonder on the shelf for sale." Clyde relit his short cigar and took a draw before continuing, "I've heard he watches the animals, the wooly worms in the summer and the squirrels gatherin' hickory nuts to judge how severe winter'll be. He never misses. His best forecasting comes from his bones. He says, when the weather's due to change, his bones ache somethin' tolerable. Ike ain't no spring chicken. He's been 'round long enough to know what makes things tick. Don't never belittle his predictions."

As Ike predicted, August 15th, the peaceful river and streams did flash flood and spilled over the banks and devoured everything in its path. Normally, most portions of the river remained shallow enough to wade across. Turner looked out the window and moaned as he witnessed his early corn left in ruins as the rain saturated the ground. He watched in horror as the muddy waters crept up and over the bank, across his yard, into his home, claiming the entire first floor.

After the storm engulfed the area and dwindled to nothing more than sparse drizzles, all the conversations centered on the havoc the storm delivered. Streams overflowed the banks, widespread reports of hail damage, including a tornado on the outskirts of town touching down briefly and claiming one life.

Crazy Ike wasn't spotted for two months. Rumors spread that he died in the flood. Toby's shelf sat empty of the potion, and customers demanded the potion. Mrs. Sadie ordered Mr. Burl to make a special trek to the general store twice for the medicine. He dreaded returning home empty handed. "Toby, ya got to git more of that blame stuff. Ain't ya got a spare tucked away? My wife'll be as mad as a wet hen if'n I return empty handed agin."

Reverend Lawson visited with Toby in the store when Crazy Ike walked in. "Where've you been? People need the potion. You can't disappear like that! It's your responsibility to bring this to me in a timely manner. We had a deal." Reverend arched an eyebrow at Toby and shook his head slight enough to check Toby's frustration and bring him back to the reality. Talking to Crazy Ike about responsibility wouldn't amount to a hill of beans.

Crazy Ike stared at him as if to say, 'wanta bet!' Ike just stood there and a slow smirk gradually consumed his face.

Toby attempted to describe how many people relied on the medicine and appeal to his sense of power and importance. Ike responded, "Ya can't rush the potion. It takes as much time as it takes. Some batches are ready sooner than other's."

"Well, why not?"

Reverend Lawson sensed Toby's desperation and attempted to lighten the mood, "How do you make that anyway, Mr. Ike?"

"Can't tell ya' with him here a listen'." Crazy Ike jerked his head in Toby's direction. "Come to my shanty in the mornin' and see. I'm startin' another batch directly."

"Mr. Ike, I will do just that. I'm real curious now."

"Preacher, it's a secret. We can't tell nobody. I got somethin' else to show ya'. Somethin' real purty."

As Crazy Ike left, he called back over his shoulder, "Preacher, watch out for the bad dog chained out behind my place. He'll gnaw yer whole dadburn leg off 'fore ya know it. Onct he chomps down, he ain't lettin' go 'til the cows come home."

Reverend Lawson headed toward Cricket Grove the following morning. A chill captured the clear air, causing the walk to be invigorating. Clyde had given him general directions to Crazy Ike's. Reverend Lawson knew this would be an experience of some sort. He pondered the warning of the dog several times during the walk. He prayed that chain was strong enough to hold the savage beast.

He saw Crazy Ike down on his hands and knees five feet to the side of his small abode. Right on cue, the deep growl of monster dog exploded. Reverend Lawson halted in his tracks until he surmised the dog's chain was secured. Ike patted the ground. As the Preacher stepped closer and saw Ike gently rubbing potato peels, leaves, and corn shucks into dampened soil.

"Preacher, I done started without ya. I got out here at first light. I feared ya might not show."

"Started what? What are you doing?"

"I'm startin' the next batch of the potion. Ain't that what ya was comin' to see?"

"You make the potion out of scraps?"

"No silly! Don't ya know nothin'?"

"I guess I don't know much about whatever you're doing there. What are you doing?"

"Preacher, the first step to makin' the potion, ya' gotta make a worm bed. That's why it takes a right smart time to make the potion. First, ya gotta grow them worms. They 'bout eat a man outta house and home. Sometimes I gotta do a heap of scratchin' and scavengin' through people's garbage to find enough to feed them slimy little boogers."

"How much do worms eat? I don't see how it could be much, considering what a worm looks like."

"Well, if ya is tryin' to grow 2 lbs of worms, you need 1 lb. of garbage ever' day. It's powerful 'portant to keep the dirt warm. It can't git below freezin' or them pesky critters die dead as door nails. That's why I can't make nigh as much in the winter months, cuz I gotta grow my little batch in the corner of the kitchen, to keep them worms warm enough. It ain't much worth messin' with in the cold of winter."

Reverend Lawson straightened up from the worm bed, amazed. "You use all your garbage on the worm bed and then make the potion from what?"

"No, Preacher. Ya oughtn't to never use no meat on it. Meat'll make ever' dog and rat from 'round these parts come hightailin' it here and they'll dig it up and yer worms'll be ruint."

Reverend Lawson hesitated before inquiring, "After you have the worms, what's next?"

"Ever how much ya feed them worms, is how fast ya harvest 'em. I take 'em out of the dirt, and wash 'em off real good in the stream. Then I put 'em in a mason jar, screw the lid on real tight like, and set 'em in the sun until they melt altogether. After them little suckers melt, I put a drop or two of grease in to make it easier to apply, and a dab of kerosene or whatever else to make it smell. They be ready to rub on yer' rheumatism. That's it. They're fine for fishin' too."

"Ike, how did you learn that melted worms was good for rheumatism?"

"I'd been puttin' kerosene on my achin' bones and I 'membered hearin' my Grandmaw tell folks 'bout the Cherokee Injuns in these parts usin' melted worms. I tried it onct. Sure as fire is hot, it helped. I got my gumption up and took a jar to Guthrie to see if'n he'd buy 'em. I reckon, he tried it first on hisself. That Guthrie couldn't be beat! Always good to me. He ain't never one to make fun of nobody, never called me Crazy Ike, or nothin. I don't care no more though, it keeps people a far piece away from me. Shucks, Preacher, Guthrie done told me, that we wuz bizness partners." Ike ran the worn toe of his shoe through the dirt. "It ain't the same a'thout him."

"Well, I've learned something today."

"Smear some on ya and see if'n it helps?"

Reverend Lawson quickly responded, "No! No thank you. I thank God that I don't have aches and pains—yet. I'm sure I will and that will be a sad day because it may mean I'll ride rather than walk to get around." Being a walker himself, Ike fully appreciated that. He nodded his head in agreement.

"Preacher, I got somethin' else to show ya." Ike reached deep down in his coverall pocket and pulled out a sparkly stone. "Lookie here, what I done found. Ain't' she purtier than a speckled pup?"

Preplexed, Reverend Lawson held the gold nugget in his hand and turned it from side to side. "Where did you find it?"

"I was down prowlin' 'round the creek bed by the mouth of that ole cave over yonder mountain and there she laid just a smilin' up at me, a beggin' me to pick her up."

"Have you shown this to anyone else?"

"Nope. Nobody but you, Preacher."

"Ike, this is a very important rock, worth a lot of money. If you want me to help you to take it down the valley to town, I will. But understand, when people see this, they will be all over this land, and they will never leave. Never."

"I don't want no one up here, 'cept maybe you onct in a while, if ya don't make a nuisance of yerself."

Reverend Lawson placed the gold back in Ike's hand and closed his fingers tightly around it. "Ike, now listen to me, this needs to be our secret unless you want strangers tearing through these mountains. You must never, never, never tell anybody, or show the shiny rock to anyone else. Do you understand? This is very, very important, Ike. Your life and your home would never be the same if anyone else sees the shiny stone. You best look over your shoulder to see if anyone is watching before you take it from your pocket to look at again."

Ike shook his head that he understood. As Reverend Lawson moved away from the isolated settlement of Ike's, Ike called out, "Preacher, it'll be a secret, just like the worm potion. Right?"

Reverend Lawson waved goodbye, "Absolutely. Our secret. You have my word."

He was out of sight of Ike's tiny homestead, the worm bed, and that treasured gold nugget when he heard echoing down the pathway, "Two! Two! Me and the Preacher's got two secrets. Preacher! One, Two. Two Good Secrets." Then he heard Ike turning the information into a song that floated into the air, "Yep, Sirs, Ike and Preacher's got two. None for you. One. Two. We got us two, and you won't never know."

HIGH FASHION AT
THE BAPTIST CHURCH

"Toby, it's high time you and Bethany came to church. Actually, I'm surprised you haven't attended yet. What's keeping you?" It wasn't Reverend Lawson's intention to pressure the new owner of the general store, but to cordially invite him. He felt their relationship secure enough to inquire.

Shaking his head Toby slowly, deliberately spoke, "To tell the truth, Bethany isn't keen on doing that."

"What? Bethany is very hospitable to me. Is there a problem? I'd like to know what I could do to encourage her. I believe the mountainfolk might warm up to you both faster if they saw you as part of them."

"I'm embarrassed to admit this, but I'm sure you already know; Bethany is not accepted here. I'm not laying the blame entirely on her. The few times she attempted to reach out, she was met with rejection. She brings most of it on herself. Occasionally, she genuinely tries to put forth the slightest effort only to be shot down."

"Well then, Toby, don't you think coming to God's house might put everyone on the same level? I've always maintained that the ground was level at the foot of the cross. It would be the ideal place for her to intermingle with the mountain families."

Reverend Lawson left Formerly Known as Guthrie's General Store satisfied that Toby would broach the subject with Bethany. He desired to see Toby and Bethany succeed here in the mountains, afterall, their presence presented a groundbreaking adjustment. The mountainfolk needed them as much as they needed the mountainfolk to make a 'go' of the general store. He still hungered for the conversations he'd enjoyed with his darling Rebecca. The pain had not diminished in his aching heart.

Sunday morning Reverend Lawson stood at the front of the church to welcome the worshipers as they arrived. The young boys with their slicked down hair and girls with tight braids ushered in by faithful parents slid into the pews. The mountain women wore simple, loosely fitted homemade dresses of calico prints that touched the calves of their legs, or below. Some of the dresses were of similar prints since they'd been crafted from the printed feedbag material. Being dressed in one's Sunday best sometimes meant nothing more than removing the apron.

Reverend Lawson felt a disappointment that Bethany and Toby were missing again. He took his place behind the wooden pulpit and led the gathering in 'The Old Rugged Cross.' The congregation sat and routinely bowed to pray. Reverend Lawson began his prayer when the door opened and Bethany and Toby appeared. Her heels on the wooden floor caused every man, woman, and child to peer at the commotion. Reverend Lawson knew before looking up who would be credited with this disruption. Bethany paraded to the front of the church to claim the empty second row on the right. The Preacher momentarily lost his train of thought when he saw Mrs. Bethany Snodgrass dressed in a fashionable deep maroon dress barely covering her knees, with an angular-lined skirt tapered at the waist, accented with a thin belt with the accessories of a matching maroon veiled hat and gloves to complete the ensemble. He forced a smile as warmly as he could muster in his state of shock.

Reverend Lawson realized regardless of what his sermon contained, he couldn't recapture the attention of the parishoners. He mused if even jumping the pulpit would win the attention back today. Every eye in the church locked on Bethany Snodgrass and remained there throughout the service. These mountaineers had never been exposed to such high fashion.

After the service Reverend Lawson greeted the Snodgrasses and felt embarrassment for them because of the open whispering and stares directed at them. Toby and Bethany left in their shiny green Hudson with Reverend Lawson being the only one that had spoken to them. As the white wall tires rolled onto the dirt road back to the general store, the comments flew '... did you ever see such a show as that before in all your live long days,' and 'she was dressed to kill,' 'it wuz awful to behold,' or 'what on earth was that woman a thinkin' to enter the Lord's House lookin' like that', and 'well, I ain't never!' 'law mercy sakes alive, the nerve to leave her house dressed like that.'

By Wednesday, practically everyone throughout the mountain had heard of the spectacle Bethany Snodgrass presented at the Baptist Church. Reverend Lawson spent the days 'putting out the fires' doing his best at damage control. Since what was being said was the truth, it was not considered gossip; but he encouraged 'acceptance' of all persons. He felt strongly that his mission for the week should focus on preaching the characteristics of Jesus. He was prepared to deliver that sermon to everyone who'd listen—in hopes the witness of Their Lord, Himself, might sway a few opinions.

Bethany and Toby continued to come back to the Baptist Church. Bethany proved unrelenting in her dress code. She wore the stylish wide-shouldered dresses with the short hem lines and hats of various styles and colors. This was simply who she was and she wasn't changing for the sake of 'fitting in'. The Reverend dared not argue that point, because in essence, she was justified. After all, acceptance needed to go both ways.

Bethany was true to her promise, she, indeed, kept up with the latest colors and fashions. Her parents faithfully mailed catalogs with the newest trends; enabling her to sport the popular chartreuse and fuchsia items. The first time Bethany wore the Parisian new red lipstick, happened to be the same Sunday she chose to introduce the wedge sole shoe she'd received by mail order. The perplexed congregation didn't know whether to stare at her mouth or feet, they'd never seen the likes of either. The actual gasps in church were audible. She knew she was chic, and that was all that mattered, even if these bumpkins weren't aware of trendy fashion.

The talk of her high fashion decreased with each successive week. Both the men and the women at the Baptist Church began to look forward to the show to which they were treated each Sunday. With her head held high, Bethany strolled down the aisle to claim their second row seat, as necks craned to see what outfit she sported. The congregation almost in unison peered around any heads obscuring a clear line of vision to openly gawk. The observers started at her hat and hoped to get the opportunity to check out each article all the way to her shoes before she sat.

Reverend Lawson smiled to himself after the service as he overheard Clem Bartlett, dressed in his faded denim, bibbed coveralls lean close to his wife and whisper, 'She's done wore that yeller pokie-dot dress before.' And

Clem looked proud that he remembered the yellow dress. Reverend Lawson felt the community would comfortably settle now, the contempt replaced by interest. It would only be a matter of time until Greenbed accepted the Snodgrasses.

SILENT NIGHT,
HOLY NIGHT

Throughout the month of December, Reverend Lawson posted messages at the general store, all three churches, and mill informing the residents there would be no morning service on Sunday, December 24th, but a special service at 6:00 P.M.

Speculation at the general store centered on this highly unusual announcement. Nathaniel and Uncle Jim pried Toby to see if he knew what the Preacher planned. Toby professed ignorance, the same as every other resident. No one knew what unusual service the Preacher intended as a surprise. Nathaniel shook his head in disbelief, "I never heared tell of a Preacher shuttin' down the church on a Sunday mornin'; but particularly on Christmas Eve. It's plum hard to believe he'd do such a thing."

The reoccurring theme on everyone's tongue for the two weeks prior to Christmas, "We've never done nothing like this before."

Reverend Lawson smiled, refusing to offer any further explanation. His only response was the standard, "Wait and see."

Sunday, the 17th of December, practically every parishioner that left the church after the service inquired about the next week. "If I told you, it wouldn't be a surprise, only one more week to wait. Christmas and surprises naturally go together."

Throughout the following week, the Preacher knew the community scrutinized his every move. He was spotted going in and out of the schoolhouse to see Mrs. Daisy. That wasn't deemed as unusual since he periodically continued to help her with teaching duties. He'd been spotted at the lumber yard asking for scrap pieces of lumber and getting the lumber cut to specific dimensions. Greenbed inhabitants felt like a child anticipating Christmas morning.

"Come on, Toby, you must know what the Preacher is up to. He's been doin' a powerful lot of whisperin' to your wife," Blane and Hettie Franklin came into town for feed from the mill and stopped by the general store for a 10 lb. sack of sugar to make the seasonal iced molasses cookies and quizzed Toby.

"Honestly, I don't know! And, I haven't noticed Reverend Lawson whispering in Bethany's ear. He comes into the store frequently, as much to visit the patrons of the store as to see us."

"Are ya blind or just stupid?" Blane retorted. "Right this minute, they're standin' out back talkin' and tellin' in mighty hushed tones. Ya think that ain't got to do with the surprise?"

Heretofore, Toby never experienced the slightest twinge of jealousy. He whirled his head to catch a glimpse of his wife talking to the Preacher outside in the freezing temperatures as she wrote something down on a small pad of paper. The fact that Blane crudely questioned him caused embarrassment and he squirmed uncomfortably. Yet he chose not to respond. He shrugged his shoulders as if it meant nothing and pretended not to be concerned. As soon as Blane and Hettie left, Toby grabbed his coat, pulling it tightly together around his neck, and joined Bethany and the Parson. Immediately, they ceased talking in mid-sentence. "What are you two doing out here in the cold?" They made no respond. "At least come inside. Tongues are wagging about you out here in the cold."

"Hi, Toby," Reverend Lawson said, extending his cold hand to shake Toby's. "Thanks, but I must be getting back. Things to do. Good to see you." He patted Toby's shoulder and abruptly left.

"Bethany, what on earth is so important that compels you to stand outside in this cold?"

"Oh, you're too cute, Mr. Nosey." Bethany shivered, and turned to go inside, "Whew, it is nippy out here. I didn't notice." She briskly rubbed her bare arms as she stepped inside.

Bethany made trips in and out of the general store during the afternoon, selecting baking items from the shelves and toting them to the living quarters. Toby watched as she took a bottle of vanilla and baking soda. Her next trip through, she retrieved brown sugar and smiled sweetly at Toby before disappearing into the back. She was happy these days. Toby dreaded the holiday season fearing how Bethany would miss her family and the festivities of the city. Whatever this guarded secret, it helped her cope with Christmas in the mountains.

On Saturday, the 23rd of December, wonderful baking smells floated from the living quarters into the general store. Toby opened the door, "Dear Wife, what're you baking? It smells scrumptious, please bring me a sample."

"I'm baking sugar cookies and no. They are not for you."

Toby shut the door. His feelings slightly injured. He wondered why she wouldn't give him a cookie. He laughed at his own childish behavior. He wasn't going to beg his wife for a cookie. Why the mysterious behavior?

Before the close of the day, Reverend Lawson came into the store and asked Toby to call Bethany to come out. Toby opened the door, "Bethany, Honey," and he over emphasized the word 'honey' strictly for the Parson's benefit. "Reverend Lawson is here to see you . . . again."

Bethany rushed into the store, and handed Reverend Lawson a box. He thanked her and left.

Even though two men were playing checkers, Toby did not conceal his frustration, "What's going on?" The men stopped concentrating on the red and black disks and looked toward the young proprietor and his wife. The checker players exchanged looks as if to say, 'this may be more entertaining than checkies.' They halted their game to watch and listen.

"We'll talk about it tomorrow," she answered in an uncharacteristically sweet voice.

"No, we need to talk about it now. You've been acting peculiar for two weeks and I want to talk about it now. I don't want to have an unpleasant conversation on Christmas Eve. Let's get it out in the open now. You don't want to be the talk of the town, or do you?"

Bethany had no intention of having this conversation, much less explaining herself, in front of these men. She turned back into the living quarters, slamming the door behind her. Toby followed her, "Bethany, stop it."

"Reverend Lawson has . . ."

Toby put his hand up to stop her, "I don't want to hear about Reverend Lawson. I want to know why you have been acting all squirrelly like."

"Squirrelly? Me? You are calling me squirrelly? If I am squirrelly, then you are thick headed and more stubborn than you ever dared to accuse me of being, Mister Snodgrass! What I was trying to tell you, before you rudely cut me off, Reverend Lawson put a great deal of thought and effort into planning a special event for tomorrow night at the church. He asked for my assistance. I was pleased to help. No one else needs me for anything, and that includes you. You run that store like it's your kingdom and you sit on your throne at the cash register. You ignore my wants and desires. I want to be needed. There! I hope you're satisfied. Now, that ruined the surprise for you. Merry Christmas!"

Toby knew he behaved foolishly. He gathered his wife in his arms and kissed the top of her head. "I'm sorry. Maybe I've been putting more effort toward being accepted in Greenbed and ignoring my responsibilities of making certain my wife is happy here. I promise to do better."

"For once, I totally agree with you. I might find it in my heart to forgive you, but only because the season promotes love and forgiveness."

Toby knew he was pushing his luck, "Now, what are you up to exactly?"

She pushed him away jokingly, "You, and every other person, will have to wait. Patience is a virtue, even for kings!"

The 24th dawned and Mrs. Daisy offered Mr. Willie's truck to the Parson for the day and he walked to their farmstead while the darkness still claimed Greenbed. Christmas Eve rapidly transitioned into one of those overcast days with the clouds lightly kissing the mountain tops.

Reverend Lawson was at the church before the sun came up. He still had much to accomplish before the evening service. He made several trips carrying the supplies to the clearing in the back of the church, about 25 feet from the woods. He placed the pieces of scrap lumber at an angle and nailed them to form an X. Next, he sawed the other two pieces to the exact length of the first two boards and made another X, then built the sides of the manger. The straw lay on the ground ready to place in the bottom of the manger. He wrapped the borrowed baby doll in pieces of an old white sheet to form the swaddling clothes and placed it in the manger. He stood back to admire his handiwork. Struck by the scene's humility, the Parson dropped to his knees, holding onto the side of the manger, he rested his head on his hands. "How can I thank you for sending Your Son! Such a gift beyond all comprehension. The Savior of the world placed in such a lowly bed as this. No room for Him. Father, never let our hearts give the message of 'No Room' for Your Son. I ask for wisdom and guidance as we worship tonight."

The Parson stood and began constructing a makeshift stable frame. He dug holes into the hardened ground, and eased the 2 by 4's into place, to secure the sides. He filled the holes and packed the dirt tightly around the wood. To shed a soft light on the scene, he cleared brush and weeds, down to the dirt and constructed a small fire pit. He strolled into the woods in search of suitable burning material. The wind whistled through the pines and a thick carpet of fallen leaves covered the ground, cushioning his every step, as he ventured deeper into the mountain trees and pines. Even with the chill in the air biting at his face, the quiet of the woods created a calming, yet thrilling chore. He carried several armfuls back to the pit. How he wished he could have been sharing this unique experience with Rebecca. He wondered what preparations Rebecca was making for Christmas. Was she shopping in the busy, decorated stores or attending festive concerts? He yearned to share not only this holy season with her but everyday for the rest of his life. All the joys and disappointments for better or worse.

He checked his worn pocket watch to calculate the amount of time he would have to stop by Mrs. Emma and Mr. Clyde's to collect the homemade spiced cinnamon apple juice. He was thankful that he'd gotten the sugar cookies from Bethany the previous day. He chuckled as he recalled the irritated expression on Toby's face. He made a mental note to thank Toby for sharing Bethany and allowing them to keep the secret for everyone's enjoyment.

Mrs. Emma appeared on the porch and waved for him to come in. Who could resist her gentle manner or an opportunity to feel the glow of her love? She wiped her hands on the long, faded apron before offering the soft, warm hand to him. "You're sure busy this week, Preacher. You got the entire mountain in a stir like swarming bees. I never remember Christmas holding such a mystery as you caused this year."

"I hope you meant that as a compliment and not a complaint." They both laughed as she shook her head. "You and Mr. Clyde are coming tonight, aren't you?"

"Well, Preacher, ya know we go to a different church? Clyde always wanted to go where his Poppa and Grandparents went," she lowered her voice to a scant whisper, "truth be told, I want to come see what you're fixin' to do. Primitive Baptists don't never do nothing on Christmas Eve night."

"Oh, yes, Mrs. Emma. You and Mr. Clyde must come tonight. After all, you generously donated all the apple juice that will be heated and served after the service. Christmas isn't just for our church. It's for everyone. Please spread the word, everyone is welcomed."

Clyde yelled in from the other room as he removed his boots, letting the first clunk to the floor, "We wouldn't dare miss your show. I reckon you'll be selling tickets."

"It's only fair to warn you that I will not be jumping the pulpit!" Clyde snickered as the second boot thumped onto the floor. "It really isn't my show though. This night belongs to honoring God's perfect gift to us."

"Hold your horses, Parson. Don't commence to preachin' in the middle of the day!"

"Clyde!" Mrs. Emma chastised him. However, both she and the Reverend knew it useless. Mr. Clyde would always do or say what Mr. Clyde wanted to do or say.

"It's alright, I know Mr. Clyde doesn't mean that. We have an understanding now." He leaned close to her so Clyde wouldn't hear, "He's a good man. He's just full of his fun; that's not a bad thing." He winked at Mrs. Emma as he shook Mr. Clyde's hand and thanked him for the apple juice.

They loaded the jugs of apple juice onto the bed of the truck and secured them for travel. He rechecked the time, and pushed Mr. Willie's old truck to go as fast as possible down the mountain, into the valley to the train station. His cousin, Edmund Lawson, from Richmond, Virginia agreed to play the bagpipes for the service and spend Christmas Day with the Preacher.

Reverend Lawson estimated by the time he returned to the church there'd be just enough time to start the fire, heat the apple juice, adding the cloves and cinnamon sticks to simmer, and make the final preparations. Reverend Lawson proudly showed Edmund the stable area, "Edmund, here's where the after-service celebration will be. Come take a look." They walked in the direction of the stable. "I'm just glad to see it's still standing. I wondered about that. My carpentry skills are at a minimum." They both chuckled, knowing they shared similar shortcomings. "Now, I thought you might come from around the other side of the church so they won't see you until your music starts filling the night air, and . . ." He stopped abruptly as he neared the manger and noticed the Baby Jesus was gone! "Where in the world? Who could possibly have taken the doll? Now what?" He fell silent. He looked around the frozen earth. It was too late to replace the doll. How could it be a Christmas Eve service without the Holy Child!

"This ruins everything!" He kicked at the hard ground and threw his jacket into the empty manger. "Of all the . . . ." He swallowed the last word and focused on Edmund's shocked expression.

Edmund stood looking at his cousin's disappointment not knowing what to say or how to console him. "Ah ha, Cousin, it does my heart good to see that the Parson does indeed still have a little of that famous Lawson temper."

The Reverend placed his arm around his cousin, "Edmund, I'm a sinner saved by grace. I'm no different than the next man. I don't know if I'm angrier or more baffled and totally helpless. There's nothing I can do about it now. It's time to change and get ready. Be sure to wear something warm. When the sun drops, the mountains sing a different song. I'm going to have a small fire lit to give everyone enough light to walk to the stable, then I'll throw more wood on for a better blaze and warmth."

Not a single person was late for the 6:00 PM service. Reverend Lawson took his place at the pulpit and looked into eyes filled with anticipation. There was already a hushed posture, setting the stage for the reverence of the Holy Night. "On this the night we celebrate our Lord's birth, I would ask that you follow me to the clearing out back. Following the brief service, you are invited back inside for hot spiced apple juice and homemade cookies, compliments of Mrs. Emma and Mr. Clyde and Mrs. Bethany." He didn't miss Toby's gratitified expression. He assumed everything had been smoothed over at their house now. He saw the questioning looks exchanged as he stood to exit the church by way of the front door. As he opened the door, a light, dry snow softly fell. The temperature had risen to the point that the snow melted as soon as it landed on the ground. The snow added a further reverence to the solemn night. The group softly muttered as they filed in behind him and headed toward the light of the fire. In the dim light he saw the outline of figures in the stable area. He tried to make out whom or what awaited them. He thought, 'Oh no! What else? No baby Jesus and now I'm going to have to escort someone from the stable. Could these be drunken visitors that staggered out of the woods. This isn't turning out as planned, at all.' He squinted to focus on what the two or three figures were doing within the stable.

Four or five feet from the stable his eyes adjusted to the darkness as he saw Bertha with a sheet draped loosely over her head and shoulders, Homer Tyson, Jr. with a towel over his hair to resemble Bethlehem head gear, and baby Obadiah, wrapped warmly in blankets, lying in the manger. Homer displayed a proud smile plastered on his face as he looked into the innocent face of his son. The baby smiled at his Father, and kicked with glee. Reverend Lawson stood frozen in the moment watching the snow between him and this beautiful nativity scene. He felt a hand on his shoulder administer a slight squeeze. He turned his head enough to see Mr. Clyde's tall frame. Mr. Clyde winked at him and whispered, "We done a good job deliverin' that youngin' into the world. Homer's been a changed man. Ever'body's talkin' about it." The Preacher nodded in agreement, that was all he could manage. The living nativity was as much a surprise and gift to him, as to the group, he was overwhelmed by the authenticity of this humble scene. He didn't want this extraordinary moment to ever end. He burnt the details into his permanent memory bank, to recall for years to come. The congregation formed a semi-circle around the nativity and stood in silence for several minutes. The only faint sounds were the sighs and coos from Little Obadiah portraying baby Jesus. Reverend Lawson recovered his voice enough to read the Christmas version from Saint Luke. As he completed the familiar reading, he noticed every eye focused on the infant. He saw hope in their eyes.

"Please join hands and hearts as we sing an old favorite, Silent Night." The first note of the carol was accompanied by the rich sound of the bagpipe, as Edmund appeared from behind the church and walked toward the worshipful scene. The baby stirred and whined. Homer picked him up and cuddled him closer, rocking him back and forth ever so slightly to comfort the babe. The music flowed throughout the mountain as Greenbed celebrated the most memorable Christmas Eve service they ever experienced. Hope abounded.

EARTHQUAKES AND
THE END OF TIME

"Shhh—listen, what did that radio say? Turn up the radio, Toby," Clyde called across the store. Toby laid his pencil down, and turned the knobs of the famous World's Fair Model Firestone Radio. By the time he made the final adjustments to the dials and the static dissipated, the news report had ended. "What did it say, Toby?"

"I'm afraid I was concentrating on setting down some numbers, and didn't pay attention."

Willie, not to be excluded, chimed in, "Clydie, what did ya hear? There's always so blame many people working their rachett jaws in here, can't nobody hear themselves think." Clyde snickered, knowing Willie was the biggest culprit of all.

"The radio was talkin' and tellin' about a disaster, I believe the man said an earthquake."

That was all Willie needed to hear. He jumped up, grabbed his coat, slipped his arms in the sleeves of his coat as he made for the door. He didn't bother to tell his brother good-bye. He headed straightway for his old pickup, pumping his arms back and forth to gain more speed. He cranked the window down in the truck, stuck his head out into the freezing temperature and warned everyone he saw, "Earthquake! Earthquake a comin'! Git Home!"

Toby knew he missed something, "Mr. Clyde, what happened to your brother? He left abruptly."

"Nobody ever knows what runs through Willie's head. Half the time he don't know hisself," Clyde laughed. "He acted like he got a case of the back door trots. You oughta know by now, Willie don't necessarily stand on anybody's protocol. It's not unlike him to gather up and skedaddle without so much as a fare-thee-well." He relit the cherryblend tobacco in his pipe and took a satisfying puff, "One thing for sure, you can bet your bottom dollar, no good'll come from this. We'll be hearin' about it, I suspect. Lord only knows what the outcome of his story will hold, but it'll be something to behold. Rest assured, he'll involve as many people as possible."

Willie drove home, not making any effort to dodge the potholes as he sped dangerously along the treacherous mountain roads. The small snow from Christmas, two days earlier, lingered in patches, enough that one should take precautions. The only thought on Willie's mind, 'If he was gonna die today in an earthquake, he wanted to be a holdin' Daisy's hand when he saw the death angel comin' for 'em.'

Daisy sat mending a torn quilt when she heard him stumble on the front steps. He rushed into the room, threw her sewing in the floor, and tugged at her hand. "Come with me, Daisy." He pulled her to the bedroom and slammed the door and locked it.

"William, have you lost your mind? What's the meaning of this? Remember your age, old man!"

"It ain't passion I'm a hankerin' for, Woman. I hate to say it, we're gonna die any minute. I figure our chances are best if we're in bed, on a soft feather mattress."

"William, slow down. What are you talking about?"

"I heared it at Guthrie's, on the radio. There's an earthquake a comin' right now. Well, Clydie heared it. Daisy, if'n I'm a goin' today to the Great Beyond, I want us goin' together."

Daisy jerked her hand free from Willie's tight grip, "That's ridiculous. Settle down. You'll have a stroke, or give me one! I'm going out to tune in our radio and see if I can get the news. You must be mistaken. We aren't in an earthquake zone, but I'll see what I can find out." Daisy slowly turned and adjusted the dials until she found a station. She called down the hall to the bedroom to Willie, "The news will be on at the top of the hour, ten minutes."

Her heart rate quickened as she heard the title of the first news story, "Earthquake." Her knees trembled and she pulled the rocking chair closer to the radio. She appeared at the bedroom door, "William, the earthquake was in Erzincan, Turkey! It's all over now. You're safe to get out of bed and go about your business."

Willie wasn't convinced, besides, on this chilly December 27th of 1939, the warmth of the feather mattress as it folded around his body, and the pile of quilts comforted his trembling body. He had feared he might lose the contentment of living here on the small farm with this special woman. He didn't want any of this satisfaction ripped from him by an earthquake or anything else.

Daisy stood in the doorway and watched his frightened expression surrender to relief. He gave her a sly smile, threw the covers back and patted the mattress right next to him. "These covers feel mighty decent on a cold afternoon. Only thing to make it powerful better would be my purty woman snuggled in beside me. Daisy, I love ya so doggone much."

"William, I believe you're dafted in the head."

"I'm dafted over my Woman. Come on. Whatcha waitin' fer? Yer' wastin' good time."

Blushing like a young bride, Daisy joined her husband on the featherbed. She nestled in beside him and kissed his cheek. "William, I pray for those people in Turkey. They've lost their lives, maybe coming home to loved ones missing, or homes devastated. I'm thankful that God brought me here to Greenbed and into your life. And, I'm proud to be invited to lay beside my husband on his featherbed, in the middle of the afternoon."

Back at the General Store, Toby and Clyde heard the full newscast and spent the rest of the day performing damage control. Willie indeed managed to spread panic to everyone that heard his frantic proclamation.

Residents stopped Reverend Lawson numerous times over the next couple of days. Willie was embarrassed about the false alarm and to divert the attention from that, he planted the seed that 'in the Good Book it says that in the end days, there will be earthquakes. This must be the end of time, 'specially since the earthquake came on the heels of Christmas. It was a sign.'

After Reverend Lawson heard the entire account and knew the source of all these questions, he found humor in the situation; but did not respond in any less than a professional manner. He also referred those inquiring to the passage that the Bible: 'no man knows the day or hour that the Second Coming will occur.' It took two weeks to put everyone's mind at ease.

Clyde and Toby were the only two in Greenbed to enjoy all the confusion; they had been present at the conception of this tall tale and witnessed it unravel.

32

A DISASTROUS EASTER PARADE

The dreary, cloudy winter days with the long nights drew to a close as the first promises of spring became visible. All those lackluster days of the winter months made the anticipation of spring more appreciated.

Reverend Lawson attempted to create enthusiasm with a celebration for Easter. He desired for Greenbed to embrace this holy season with an excitement that awakened hope and love from deep within hearts. The Parson posted a sign to the rail in front of the general store announcing the "The Easter Parade," every woman and young girl to decorate a hat with flowers and march in a parade on the Saturday preceding Easter. The highest honor would be awarded for the best depiction of new life.

Bethany Snodgrass seized this as a personal challenge to not only participate in, but win. She insisted on keeping her masterpiece a secret. She wanted the flowers to be fresh, and she spent countless hours driving through the mountains looking for colors and textures of both flowers and foliage. She went for long walks through fields and ventured into the woods behind the general store in search of the perfect plants.

Toby teased her, "Darling, I should've known you would display your competitive side and become excited over something to do with fashion. It's good to see your interest peaked."

"Oh, Toby, I do want you to be proud of my design." Shyly she admitted, "and I really want these people to see that I tried very hard. I believe I have located the most exquisite wildflowers and green vine to weave between the flowers. My lips are sealed. You have to wait for the finished product." She proudly beamed as she spoke of the hat.

He kissed her lightly and held her close. "Bethany, you are an incredible woman. I'm always proud of you. No matter what the judges say, I know yours will be unusual with a true flair of high fashion."

On Friday, Bethany worked tirelessly selecting, gathering, and securing the flowers, vines, and leaves to create her masterpiece. She wrapped it and hid it to be a surprise for Toby.

Saturday arrived and the congregations of the Baptist Church, Primitive Church, and Methodist Church gathered in front of the Baptist Church for the Parade. Little girls with flowers pinned in their hair marched alongside their Mommas, while the Mothers sported various forms and styles of hats. Most were the same straw bonnets they wore in the fields and gardens during the week, transformed into Easter bonnets, adorned with wildflowers or ribbons.

Bethany placed hers in a fancy hat box until the last possible second as she took her place in the line. Carefully, she retrieved the hat from the box and placed it on her head. She noticed the men and women's eyes affixed to her hat. She assumed they admired its unique beauty. After all, she found the most unique green plant of all. The women backed off from her and gave her a wide circumference to pass. As she passed her husband, she expected to see his encouragement, perhaps a knowing wink. He looked directly at her hat, a deep frown creasing his brow. His eyes never left her hat as she passed by. He reached out for her, but she jerked her arm free of his clutch. She was determined to complete the parade.

All eyes focused on her creation, just as she'd hoped. Toby approached her and instead of congratulating her, he firmly gripped her elbow, steering her away from the others, and whispered, "Don't touch the flowers. Carefully, take it off. Now."

"I most certainly will not!" She snapped. "We're wearing our bonnets to the final judging table."

"Bethany, for once, do not argue with me. Remove the hat and put it in the box. We're leaving."

Her frustration caused her voice to be louder and higher than intended, "No! Why are you asking me to do that when everyone else is still wearing theirs?"

Toby lost patience, but whispered stearnly, "Because all of those pretty shiny leaves on your hat are poison ivy!"

Bethany shrieked, threw the hat on the ground and stomped off. She and Toby missed the Easter service. Bethany spent two miserable weeks dabbing lotions on the itching patches covering her face, neck, arms, and hands.

THE DEVIL'S INSTRUMENT
ARRIVES

Bethany Snodgrass wasted no energy endearing herself to the mountain community. Her only form of socializing was with her husband and, occasionally, Reverend Lawson. Other than that, she remained in the living quarters of the general store the majority of the time. Bethany longed for the city life that she and Toby left behind. She did not share Toby's desire to manage this store bequeathed to him by an uncle, an uncle he scarcely knew.

Monday morning, Willie and Mrs. Daisy came into the general store. It was unusual for the 'Open' sign to be hung with no one minding the store. Willie unceremoniously plopped down by the front window, in hopes a man would come in to keep him company while Daisy went about the woman's work of selecting a piece of material.

As Daisy inspected the bolts of fabric, raised voices came from the living quarters, mainly Bethany's high-pitched voice. "We could take the train. We must go see it!" Then an unintelligible mumbling from Toby, followed by Bethany again. "Don't you realize, this is a once in a lifetime opportunity?" More exchanges and Toby slammed the door and entered the general store, shaking his head in total frustration.

"What's wrong?" Willie asked primed and ready, "Woman trouble?"

Daisy attempted to shush him, "William, mind your own business and let Mr. Snodgrass tend to his." For once, she hoped her husband would not obey but pry further. She was curious what could evoke such an outrage. Willie granted her wish.

"I'm tryin' to help the young feller out," he said to Daisy and turned his attention back to Toby. "That's a mighty firey little filly ya got. What's all the fuss about, why's she throwing a conniption fit?"

"Mr. Willie, you should ask what's all the fuss about today? It seems there's a different agenda every single day. It's enough to drive a man crazy." Before he went any further, the door to the store burst open with enough force to thrust the doorknob into the wall. Bethany stomped into the store like a raging buffalo in heat.

"You don't want me to have any fun! There's nothing to enjoy in this God-forsaken dink of a community. We could go by train and be back in five days. You never take me any place. I'm withering up into an old prune, and you don't care! I'm telling you, I need some culture and entertainment."

"Bethany, I said no, and I meant it. We are not going to Wisconsin. I'm trying to run a business. This isn't the place for a discussion." Bethany glared at her husband and shook her finger at him as she left the store. Willie, Daisy and Toby knew this discussion was far from being over.

Toby felt he owed an explanation. He shook his head, "I don't understand her lately. She wants us to take the train to Oconomowoc, Wisconsin to attend opening night for the première showing of a new movie, 'The Wizard of Oz,' whatever the heck that is. Can you beat that? She read about it and swears it is one of those things we absolutely have to be in on from the get go. Like I'd have any idea where to even look for the Stand Theatre in Oconomowoc or whatever it's called. I've never been to Wisconsin, and for that matter, I never want to go. I don't even know if trains run there! And I sure as heck don't want to drive all that distance. Holy Cow! What could possibly be worse than being pinned up in a car with Bethany from here to Wisconsin, especially with her moods of late. Just shoot me now."

Willie looked at his wife and waited for her to respond. He'd never heard anything more ridiculous in his life, for once he was quiet. Mrs. Daisy engaged her brain before her tongue, "You must admit that your wife seems passionate about going. It must be important to her for some reason. Maybe you don't understand the significance. Perhaps her family attended grand openings and she feels she's missing out."

"Mrs. Daisy, I appreciate your effort. I know you're trying to be diplomatic about her spoiled brat behavior. Bethany is passionate about everything under the sun these days! Nothing, and I mean absolutely nothing, makes her happy. She's lost her joy and replaced it with bitterness. She's always been headstrong, but to tell the truth, that is one of the things I admire about her. She is different than any woman I've ever known, in a complimentary way. But, she's never been this unreasonable and emotional. She cries at the drop of a hat and gets so upset with me, that she physically gets sick to her stomach."

"Mr. Snodgrass, it sounds to me as if your wife has the symptoms of a woman in the motherly way," Daisy said as tactfully as she possibly could.

Toby stared expressionless at Mrs. Daisy. "No! Could it be? Women act like that?" He headed straight to the living quarters leaving Daisy and Willie in the store.

"William, we just as well go on over to Darrell's and get fresh eggs and stop back here later. Those two have some talkin' to do." As Mrs. Daisy left the general store, she turned the 'Open' sign to display 'Closed' to offer a minute of privacy.

Two hours later, Daisy and Willie stopped at the general store. Toby was making change for a pound of coffee for Matilda Calhoun. "That's forty cents, Mrs. Calhoun." The nod and broad smile assured Daisy that she'd been accurate in her diagnosis.

As Matilda closed the door behind her, Willie slapped Toby on the back, "Congratulations, Poppa. Since ya didn't know what was wrong with yer woman, do ya know how she got that way? And I want to know right now, did she get off her high horse yet?"

Daisy reprimanded him, "William, stop that! I'll declare, I'll never teach that man a lick of manners. Does she feel better now, Mr. Snodgrass?"

"She isn't ranting and raving, at least not at this moment, but it could break loose any second. At least she agreed that in her condition, we have no business hauling off on a goose chase to Wisconsin for a movie. The timing of this child is very convenient . . . for me! That little baby saved me from a major battle. Not to mention, I'd have despised every single thing about such a trip. We struck a bargain on this one."

Mrs. Daisy compared three bolts of fabric before selecting one. Willie was preoccupied with a checker game with Old Man Burkett, who was six years younger than Willie, yet Willie always referred to him in this manner. Before Toby rang up the order, Bethany entered the store. "I have the most spectacular idea ever! And this would be for the entire community to enjoy! I don't know why I never thought about this before!" She hugged herself and danced before heading to the living quarters.

Toby shook his head, "Woe is me! I can hardly wait to hear this one. I shudder to imagine what she's cooked up."

Willie sympathetically chuckled, "That little woman stirs a stink better'n any I ever saw. If'n she was mine, and she cut them shines, I'd get goose bumps the size of hen eggs every time I heard her . . .", he cut it off abruptly when he heard Bethany approach the door.

She burst into the general store, all smiles and that special glow about her. The mere sight of her beaming made Toby a happy man. "I simply can't wait any longer to tell you!" Daisy and Willie halted in their steps to hear the basis for such excitement. "A jukebox! We'll order a jukebox for the store and everyone will enjoy it. I heard an advertisement on the radio and wrote down all the details." She waved the piece of paper over her head as if this scribbled bit of information sealed the deal.

After a long discussion that evening, Toby, relented to allow her to place the order. It seemed like the lesser of the two evils he battled that day. Perhaps she was right, the mountaineers may appreciate the luxury of music at their fingertips. Bethany presented a convincing argument, "The Depression is over. It's past time for everyone to act like we believe it's behind us." Bethany excitedly threw her arms around her husband, "Thank you! Thank you! This will be wonderful. You'll see. Oh, I can hardly wait."

Six weeks later when the jukebox arrived from the Rock Ola Manufacturing Company, it proved no small task for Toby to borrow a truck, enlist two strong men to drive to the train station with him, load the monstrous crate, and travel up and down the rough roads of the mountainous slopes to the store. The three men strained to unload the jukebox and position it in the store.

Bethany stood in awe with her hands tightly clasped under her chin, directing the men to 'take caution, move it a little to the left. That's way too much, now pull it out from the wall about 6". Perfect.' Toby took a step back and looked at the bright, shiny music maker with disdain. "Toby, what's wrong? Isn't it beautiful sitting there? It brings such class to the store! It's like we're standing on the first rung of a ladder, ushering in an exciting era." Bethany literally danced as she spoke.

"Bethany, I've never seen anything look more out of place than that, that, that 'thing' does. It's bright red, yellow, with shiny chrome and lit up like a war scene. Now, look around at the store." Bethany gave the rough wooden shelves and unfinished floor a quick glance. "It's just that it's . . . well it is ultra modern and the store has stood for generations. To tell the truth, it makes me uncomfortable to see it violating its humble surroundings."

"Well, Darling, that's a good thing. I'm proud that we are responsible for bringing a small piece of the modern world to this forgotten part of the country. Updating is long overdue! I couldn't be happier. You'll see. Everyone will love it." Toby shook his head in disbelief.

As patrons and spectators drifted into store the next day, most exhibited the same confused expressions, the jukebox was an affront. Few vocalized their feelings, but the shocked looks more than spoke their true feelings. At noon, Bethany pranced through the general store to admire her incredible contribution to society. "I haven't heard any music played yet. Toby, show them how to select a record and put their money in." She disappeared again.

Clyde, Lawrence and Darrell sat in the front whittling. "What'd she mean about puttin' our money in it?" Darrell questioned.

Toby waved it off as unimportant. The Brothers wanted more information on this mysterious piece of machinery. Money matters always held the utmost importance to the Brothers—money was too hard to come by. Clyde spent a lifetime sharing his motto, 'if you look after the pennies, the dollars'll take care of themselves.'

Lawrence stopped whittling and looked directly at Toby, "What'd she mean? That contraption needs money to run it? Ain't nobody on the face of God's green earth that stupid."

"Bethany thought the folks at Greenbed would enjoy hearing some, well, some different, more modern music, from time to time."

Clyde's interest was piqued, "Ya gotta be kiddin', that thing only works if ya put money in it? How much do ya' put in to hear this different, modern music?"

"Mr. Clyde, first you select the song, then drop the nickel in the slot." Toby pointed to the slot.

Clyde's voice bellowed across the store, "A nickel! That's a half of gallon of gasoline. That's the biggest mess of tomfollery I ever heard. I reckon that wife of yours ain't never noticed that the people living up and down these mountains is poor as Job's old turkey. They can't even buy play purties for their youngins at Christmas. It's hard enough to keep food on the table." Clyde closed his knife and ventured closer to inspect the jukebox for the first time. He stood peering down at the titles of the songs. "Lookie here, ya won't believe yer eyes."

Darrell and Lawrence joined him at the Rock Ola jukebox and stared at the songs listed. Lawrence shook his head, "What's the meaning of this? I ain't never heard of but one of these twenty four songs."

Willie entered the general store, allowing the door slam. He saw his three Brothers gathered at the jukebox with grave expressions on their faces. "Whatcha all lookin' at, battin' yer eyes like a frog in a hail storm?"

"This newfangled thing plays a song for a nickel. And we none ain't never heard of these songs. Can you beat that with a stick?" Darrell explained as he laughed at the ridiculousness.

Willie squinted his eye shut as he shuffled closer to the jukebox. He placed one hand on each side of the shiny jukebox to scrutinize it for himself.

"What da ya think, Brother?" They anxiously awaited Willie's response. They knew he would be painfully honest.

"Way I see it," he cocked his head to the right and peered at Toby with one eye, "that thing is as useless as a bottomless bucket. Why, lookie yonder, it ain't even got Wabash Cannonball! There ain't no Roy Acuff songs as best I can decipher. Sakes alive, nobody that's got his wits about 'im would want such a thing."

Toby rubbed his hand over his face. "I don't know what to do. Honestly, I find it unsightly. Mr. Lawrence, you haven't said much. What are you thinking?"

True, Lawrence remained quiet throughout the critiquing of the Rock Ola Machine. He shifted his weight from foot to foot, "We could load it on the back of my truck, take it up yonder a piece, to Stoney Path Cliff, and push it off the cliff. We'll run like a scalded dog back here. Ain't never nobody up there to see us and nothin's beneath it that it'd hurt when it crashed to the bottom. Tell yer little woman that somebody stole it."

"Mr. Lawrence, I wouldn't lie to my wife, furthermore, she'd know nobody in Greenbed would want the thing."

Lawrence looked Toby square in the eyes, "I'm a tellin' ya, boy, this thing is nothin' but the Devil's Instrument! I'd be scared to have it under my roof for fear of somethin' bad happenin' to me or mine." Lawrence backed up several steps, as if to remove himself from the presence of a demon. "A person ought not look upon such wickedness."

Word spread like wildfire about the Devil's Instrument being at the general store. Few risked associating with the Devil in any manner. Again, an unofficial boycott caused a drastic decline in business for Toby. Men didn't gather at the store for checkers or socializing. For the next two weeks shoppers were fewer than hen's teeth. Those risking to enter the store, hurriedly gathered necessities, departing with no fare-thee-wells.

The Preacher heard the rumors about the evil music-making machine at the general store; and how the Devil himself created this instrument and resided within it. His standard answer to the concerned patrons remained the same each time, "Don't give the devil that much credit. He doesn't create anything, except havoc," but his speeches fell on deaf ears.

Reverend Lawson spryly hopped up the steps at the general store calling out to Toby, "Hey, anybody selling merchandise today?" Since business was slow, Toby spent more time in the living quarters, and didn't hear the Parson enter the store. Reverend Lawson went straight for the jukebox to check and dropped a nickel into the coin slot selecting 'Blue Orchids' by Glenn Miller. When the music began, Toby and Bethany rushed into the store with alarmed looks on their faces.

Reverend Lawson removed his hat and waved, "You both look like you saw a ghost. Sorry, didn't mean to give you a fright. I thought the purpose of this thing was for hearing music. The next one I'm playing might be Will Glahe's lively Beer Barrel Polka. That should hit the rumor mill before sunset." The Preacher's humor brought relieved smiles to their faces.

"Reverend Lawson! Good to see you! It's been lonely in this neck of the woods, as I hear folks say. What's the word out there?" Toby inquired.

"Bethany, I commend you for your adventuresome spirit and your vision to introduce a new style of music. We, that is, you, Toby and I, grew up in areas where change occurred as an ordinary part of life. In fact, we expected change. The residents of Greenbed relish consistency in the same manner as we embrace variety. Truthfully, the people are spooked by the jukebox. You know, they believe you welcomed the devil's instrument into your home and into your lives."

Bethany's dark eyes flashed, "That is ridiculous! They'll get over it when they get used to it and they'll see how silly they've been. I hope they feel plenty foolish for dragging their feet."

Toby didn't interrupt her, "Reverend Lawson, you gave me excellent advice when I arrived here. I'm forced to ask again, what do you think we should do about the jukebox?"

The Parson pondered. "I came to see how you both were doing, certainly not to give advice. Since you asked, the way I see it, you have several options here. Keep the jukebox, and hope they learn to accept it, as Bethany indicated, before it runs you out of business. Or you might change the record choices to include songs they know, but I doubt they'll trust playing it. Thirdly, and I hesitate to offer this suggestion, but I know it crossed your mind, contact the Rock-Ola Manufacturing Company to ask if they'd take it back."

"I don't understand. Why would anyone be afraid of an apparatus designed to play records? Everyone listens to radios. What's the difference? This way you can control what you want to hear which is even better. What's the harm?"

"Bethany, I can't answer that question. I'm only addressing what I heard, and it seems when you first installed the jukebox and kept it playing on and off as customers came in, they felt the music far too worldly." Bethany started to interrupt, Toby held his hand up to halt her. "Please understand, I'm not saying I agree. I made numerous attempts to persuade their way of thinking. I must admit some of these folks, and I love every blessed one of them, born and raised with heads as thick as hundred year old maple trees and they'd stand there and argue with a fencepost. It's just their way."

"May I speak now," Bethany impatiently looked toward Toby. "There may be one other possibility." Toby's heart sank. "We could move it back to our living room. We could put it where the bookcase stands, maybe give it away. With the baby coming, I'll be spending more time in the back."

Shocked that his wife suggested a compromise without waging a major campaign, Toby beamed. Before she might rethink that decision, he responded, "That's a terrific idea. I'll do it this evening, soon as I can get muscles to help."

Reverend Lawson breathed a sigh of relief and adding additional levity to the situation, "I would offer to help, but being a man of God, it wouldn't be fitting for me to lay my hands on such a thing deemed as a Devil's Instrument." Bethany gasped, before realizing he joked. "Just teasing. Let me know what time and I'll be here to help. I may bring along another nickel and play the first song in its new location." He glanced at the other titles of the 78's in the music maker, "Here's one a Preacher should play, Glen Gray's, Heaven Can Wait."

With the absence of the fiendish jukebox, normalcy gradually returned to Formerly Known as Guthrie's General Store.

34

AN UNLIKELY MIDWIFE

After the morning sickness subsided, Bethany's pregnancy progressed without complication. Toby feared the constant mood swings even more than the morning retching. The next four months passed quite pleasantly. Entering her eighth month, she enjoyed great health and an uncommon happiness. Occupying herself with the preparations for a baby kept her planning, coping and happier than she imagined possible here in the mountains.

Toby accompanied her into the city to consult with the fatherly-type, Dr. Warren. The baby developed textbook perfect according to Dr. Warren. Toby viewed Bethany as strong, yet fragile. Throughout their courtship and marriage, it seemed Bethany had a knack for making every situation in life far more complicated than necessary. The doctor assured them that the last six weeks of her pregnancy would continue smoothly. He eased Bethany's concern that she would have ample time from the onset of labor to make the two hour trek from the mountain, through the valley, and into the city. He explained first babies take their time to make a grand entrance into the world.

The conversation in the general store on this beautiful day turned grim. Reverend Lawson corresponded with County legislators over taxation. The County proposed raising taxes on businesses and farmland alike, striking a devastating blow to the mountain community to further jeopardize the struggling farmers' livelihoods. Every set of ears in the general store listened to Reverend Lawson. "The only way to stop this is to fight it. Otherwise, if these laws pass, they can sell your land right out from under you if or when you don't pay the additional taxes."

Zachariah stood first, "I say we do jest that very thing, we fight 'em. Let's get our ammunition and hightail it right now and ambush em when they come out from hidin' behind closed doors. We'll show 'em."

"No, no, no!" Reverend Lawson quickly clarified, "That's not what I meant by fighting. You'd end up in jail, and lose everything for certain."

With fire in his eyes Zachariah turned to face the Preacher, "That's what ya said! Do we fight 'em or not?"

"Not with weapons. Fight by banding together and going as a group. groupeting to object. There's a meeting tomorrow afternoon. We could all go Furthermore, rather than everyone trying to speak, I suggest that you elect a spokesperson for the group to keep it organized."

Darrell immediately made his nomination, pointing to Reverend Lawson, "I vote for you."

"I'll go along, and put my name on the petition, but it would be better if it were taxpayers, better yet a business person." He glanced toward Toby to see if his expression gave any indication.

Toby shook his head, "I can't leave the store."

"If we're all at the meetin', whose comin' in to buy anything?" Darrell asked.

Bethany was also in the store, listening to the appeal. "Fiddle faddle, Tobias, I can mind the store while you're gone. Besides, more than likely, there won't be one person stirring. If they do, I'm perfectly capable of making a sale. You know, I have shopped a time or two in my life."

"Not to rush, but the meeting is at 1 PM tomorrow, it will take us two hours to get there. We need to leave by 10 in the morning. If you have any business at home to take care of, go get your ducks in a row. Tell your neighbors on your way home too. The larger our delegation, the more influence it carries to elected officials. After all, we vote them into office," Reverend Lawson reminded.

"Bethany, are you sure that you'll be alright? I'm afraid this will take most of the day."

"I wish you would have a tiny bit of confidence in my abilities. I am fine. The store can survive without you for one day."

The night brought anything but rest for Toby. He rehearsed what to say as the spokesman for the delegation, and worried about Bethany. After breakfast together, Toby gathered his expectant wife in his arms and pulled her tightly to his chest, "You can't fault a man for caring about his wife, who also happens to be carrying his first child."

"I feel just fine." She discounted the low ache in her lower back that she'd had for a couple of days. "Would you drag my rocking chair in here from the back? I promise to sit and read my book. This is the perfect excuse for me to do absolutely nothing." She placed Toby's hand on their baby, "See, the baby even agrees with that plan. She's been resting and quiet all night."

"She? Have you had a premonition about a girl? That's odd, I've had a boy feeling. Guess we'll have to wait and see. We'll know in a month which one of us is right. It doesn't matter. I only care about you and a healthy baby."

"Toby, you're going to be an awesome Father. I'm even starting to believe that raising a child here, in the mountains, is better than in the city. There is a certain peaceful beauty here." Toby beamed at this new attitude of Bethany's.

The delegation gathered outside the general store to finalize transportation plans. Reverend Lawson, Mr. Clyde, Darrell, and Lawrence rode with Toby in the shiny green Hudson. Reverend Lawson scribbled notes for Toby, the elected spokesman, as ideas bantered about as they covered the miles to the county seat.

Bethany settled with her book into the wicker rocker by the front window of the store. She relished the opportunity to help Toby in a tangible way, while enjoying a quiet day all alone. She knew most of the men left with the entourage to descend on the unsuspecting local government. She checked the wall clock every five minutes. She didn't intend to feel anxious about being alone for the day; but became unsettled and restless as the time slowly passed.

At 11:30 she stood to go to the kitchen and make a sandwich, more from boredom than hunger. Her appetite had diminished over the past three days. She gasped as she stood and felt a warm gush escape her. Immediately, she felt a heaviness in her lower abdomen creating pressure and discomfort as she slowly walked toward the living quarters. Within minutes, the dull, lingering back ache increased to full-blown sharp jabbing pains. Bethany forced herself to the backdoor and called for help. The panic of her situation was overshadowed with the rapidly increasing pain. She groped her way to their bed. After she flopped onto the bed she curled into a tight ball until the intense pain gripped her again. The moans and screams were intermittent with heavy pants as she struggled for a deep breath.

The intenseness of the labor pains dwarfed the voice calling out in the store. She didn't notice the heavy footsteps coming in her direction over her own moans. Her eyes were tightly scrunched shut during a long pain. When she opened her eyes, there at the foot of her bed stood Crazy Ike. She screamed from both fright and pain.

"I hollered out. Nobody answered. I brought more medicine for Mr. Toby to sell. I put 'em on the counter, in yonder."

"Get help! My baby is coming. Toby is gone. Hurry!" She closed her eyes tightly and clutched the quilt beneath her as she endured the next contraction which rendered her lifeless.

"Ain't no time for that. I done seen the puddle on the floor and tracked it like a hound dog to yer bed. Didn't see hide nor hair of nobody out and about. But I cin hep ya."

Bethany did not have the energy to argue with Crazy Ike. "Have you ever delivered a baby before?"

"Not 'xactly. Onct I hepped my dog, Fly, with a litter. She had five pups in that brood. Four of 'em lived. One I had to bash its head ag'in a rock. It was sickly." Bethany moaned and felt the tears welling up in her eyes from pain and fear.

Bethany closed her eyes to fight the hysteria she was feeling. That was not the answer she hoped to hear. Her precious baby delivered by Crazy Ike! Obviously, something was wrong for her to be delivering early, what if . . . Pain seized her entire body and interrupted the worries.

She felt Crazy Ike placing her hands on the bedposts. "Here. Hep yer self, pull and hold tight." He disappeared into the kitchen and she became vaguely aware of running water. He soon appeared with a washbasin and the tablecloth right off the kitchen table. He slid a couple of towels under her and took the pillows from the bed and placed under the small of her back. During the next pain he rounded the bed to her back and practically sat her up, coaxing in her ear, "PUSH, WOMAN, HARD! PUSH AGAIN!" When the pain ceased, he gently laid her back down, "Rest." She felt a refreshing, damp cloth on her brow, he squeezed a little of the liquid into the corner of her dry mouth. It seemed only seconds until the next intense pain began in her back and quickly worked its way to the front.

Crazy Ike lifted her shoulders again and repeated, "PUSH! PUSH!"

In exhaustion she screamed, "I can't! I don't have anything left."

He did not relent, "PUSH!"

For the next forty-five minutes they rotated between sitting up, with Crazy Ike supporting her back, laying down; pushing and resting; screaming and crying. Bethany's energy waned with each contraction. As Crazy Ike eased her down, she felt like a rag doll.

Finally, she said, "I'm going to be sick," turning her head sideways to throw up.

"That's the best sign that it's all over but the shoutin'! Ya can do it, Missy." He lowered her back to the bed. "I gotta hep ya now, we'll git through this."

Bethany felt a burning and incredible pressure. Crazy Ike looked at her with crazed eyes and said, "Scream! Hit'll do ya' right good and hep ya too." Ike was hollering, "Come on! Onct more. BIG!"

Just as Bethany thought she could take no more, she felt relief. She looked up to see Crazy Ike holding a baby up by the feet as he lightly patted the wet baby on the back. The silent tiny infant hung limply in midair. Bethany felt panic rapidly rising as she watched in horror, the motionless gray baby dangling from Crazy Ike's hand. He slapped the baby again, and turned it over, facing toward the floor and slapped the baby again, harder. A cough, a sputter, followed by a soft whimper developed into full-fledged protest. This time Crazy Ike was the one screaming, "Weee Ha! We done went and done it! God gived us a lil' girl!" Bethany uncontrollably sobbed, but this time for joy. The trauma she'd endured was already slipping from her memory as she viewed her beautiful daughter.

"Thank you! Thank you for helping my daughter. I couldn't have done this without you!"

Crazy Ike tied and cut the cord with his pocketknife, wrapped the baby in the tablecloth and handed her to Bethany. "That baby girl's tough and purty, jest like her Momma." Bethany held the baby close and kissed her little head over and over while Ike proudly looked on.

Bethany was overcome with emotion and gratitude. "I never want people to call you Crazy Ike again! You really are not crazy . . . are you?"

"Missy, call me anything ya want to, but it works better fer me if'n folks think I'm loony as a bedbug. They don't bother me none that way. I like it that way. Me and Ole Fly is happier than a pig in mud when peoples leave us be."

"How can I ever repay you for helping us?"

"Ya done all the work. If'n I can peep in the back yonder winder and see that lil' girl from time to time, that's pay 'nuff for me. I got a little somethin'

I want to give ya for the baby, but first I got to ask the Preacher. I swear to ya, it's somethin' real special and purty enough to charm a possum right out of a tree, even the Preacher done said so. It's somethin' I found, but the Preacher warned me aginst' sayin' nary a word 'bout it. I want to give it to that baby."

Bethany smiled into the small face of the infant. "I'm not naming my baby Ike, but what was your Mother's name?"

Ike smiled a snaggle-tooth grin, "Her name was Grace, a mighty fine Godly woman. She weren't like me, she wuz a refined lady, but she loved me anyhow, even with all my peculiar ways."

"I'm naming our baby Elizabeth Grace, in honor of your Mother."

Mr. Ike felt tears slipping down his cheeks. He was proud of his work for this day, yet unaccustomed to having thanks showered on him.

"That's mighty kind. My Maw would be proud of that baby and me. Lil' Lizbeth Grace'll be ok now. I'll mosey back home. Ya best stay put til yer man comes home. If I see anyone out and about, I'll send 'em here to look in on ya. Don't be a tryin' to git up. Ya might want to let the baby suckle a bit. Gotta git her some strength, she worked harder than both us put together." He turned to take his leave. "I ain't no midwife, but if'n I was you, since that lil girl come early, I'd be obliged to let her cry a right smart bit to grow them lungs." He chuckled, "It don't sound like she's a hurtin' for lung power though." Crazy Ike took his hand from the doorknob and turned with an afterthought. "Thar might be one thing ya can do fer me, if'n ya would."

"Anything. You just name it."

"Ya can tell yer husband and the Reverend what happened here today. I'd be beholdin' to ya if ya didn't tell another livin' soul. It's our secret. Me and that Preacher got us two good secrets."

"Mr. Ike, I'd love to give you the credit, but if that's what you want, I promise."

"Yessum, that's the way I want it. A secret. Another secret. One, two, three secrets!"

35

WILDFLOWERS AND HOPE

Reverend Lawson sat on the back steps of his modest four-room home, overlooking the mountain. Since arriving at Greenbed, he spent countless hours memorizing minute details of this unspoiled view. His open Bible lay in his lap, and an unopened letter from his cousin, Edmund Lawson, tucked inside his pocket. Today, he hungered for that peaceful calm as he struggled with a heavy decision. He'd been plagued for months now, searching for direction, feeling a further calling. He needed confirmation.

He understood from the locals, that the weather this past winter had been milder than most. He reflected on the bygone year: Tiny's marriage and baby; Jasper Thompson being abducted while in a drunken stooper and scared into religion by mysterious haints; the marriage of Mr. Willie to Miss Daisy. A sadness washed over him as he reflected on the love and hurt he felt over Rebecca. It was particularly painful that he never heard from her after she left Greenbed. He'd probably never understand that. He fondly recalled the days of substitute teaching, and considered that a highlight of his tenure. Sharing the poignant secret of Mr. Guthrie's failing heart had been a challenge. He needed time to grieve for his dear friend, but knew the community looked to him to carry them through. He smiled as he remembered the community's adjustment to Toby and Bethany; and the birth of little Elizabeth Grace.

The Preacher's eyes lifted from the budding trees to the blue skies as he recalled the day of Guthrie's death; being followed by the birth of Bertha and Homer Tyson, Jr.'s baby boy. Without fail, every time he saw the baby boy, he thanked God for Mr. Clyde's divine intervention. He mused as he recalled the Brothers countless times of teasing Mr. Willie about this or that. Closing his eyes he imagined the smell of the apple butter simmering and how marvelous that first taste treated the tastebuds.

He retrieved Edmund's letter from his pocket and unfolded it.

Dear Gerhart,

I apologize for not writing sooner. I hold fond memories of the Christmas Eve service at the little Greenbed church. I'll long remember the look on your face as we neared the manger and you realized baby Jesus was missing. What a delightful surprise for us to discover the doll was replaced by a real baby.

1940 promises to be a year of change. Wrestling with a decision that continues to disrupt my sleep, finally, I found peace. I'm putting aside my selfish notions and joining the army to fight for freedom. It seems war is imminent. I can't live in my comfortable home, while those abroad have their freedoms ripped from them, and their towns unwillingly annexed by opposing countries.

I expect to ship out in two weeks. I'll write you at my first opportunity. Please keep me in your prayers, and continue to pray for world peace.

Your cousin,
Edmund

He neatly refolded the letter inserting it in his Bible pages, bowing his head, "Thank you for the prompt answer to my struggle. Lord, you raised up mighty warriors throughout Your Word. Use me in whatever manner you see fit. I gave you my life once before to use, and I am renewing my dedication to Your leadership. Amen."

He resolved to tell the congregation the following Sunday. He felt an obligation to pay a visit to Mrs. Emma and Mr. Clyde before Sunday to break the news to them since they were members at Primitive Baptist Church. He wanted them to hear it from his own lips.

Mr. Clyde was walking from the barn to the house as the Preacher headed toward their farmhouse. "Hey Parson, what brings ya to this neck of the woods? Law Mercy, don't tell me yer comin' to preach!" They shared a good-natured laugh.

"No. I gave up. If you've been living with that Saint Mrs. Emma and it hasn't helped you, there is flat out no hope."

"Come on in here."

Mrs. Emma rolled out dough to serve as a topping to a sweet potato pie, wiped her hands on the apron and poured lemonade for the men. "Mrs. Emma, would you sit a spell with us? I'd like to talk to you both."

"I'm feelin' like ya've come here to rake me over the coals for committing caboogery or somethin' awful," Clyde jokingly admitted.

"Nothing like that at all. Actually, quite the opposite. I came to pay my respects."

"Alright, Preacher, yer makin' goosebumps run up my spine, we ain't neither one died."

Reverend Lawson wished for a smoother way to break the news, but this served as his practice run. "I know you attend another church, and I'll be making an announcement at my church this Sunday. I wanted you to hear this from me. This week I will be telling the congregation that I'm leaving Greenbed." There he said it for the first time. The words nearly choked in his throat, just as he feared.

Mr. Clyde broke the silence, "Headin' on to greener pastures?"

"Not exactly. I'm enlisting in the army."

Mrs. Emma gasped and put her hand to her mouth. Mr. Clyde grunted, "That's pure tomfoolery. Ya got no business in the army! There's others that can do that job. Have ya ever toted a gun in yer life?"

"The United States government will not send me into combat until they deem me fit and ready for battle, if it comes to that."

"I'd not put no stock in that lame idea. What's to become of yer church? What about all the people who count on ya'? Whatcha think we're gonna do without ya? Have ya give that any thought?"

"Indeed, I have. I struggled with this decision. I know we all listen to the news every night and the situation grows grimmer overseas with each passing week. We've got to rise up to this and put a stop to it now."

"Preacher, yer hearin' diff'rent news than I am. There ain't no stoppin' it. That Hitler feller is takin' over and runnin' ramshot over all them countries.

Ya' can't stop a pig from wallowin' in the mud. One man signing on the dotted line ain't gonna make no drop in the bucket of diff'rence."

"I can't explain it. I just feel the Lord's leading me in that direction. I want to help, in any way I can to bring about peace. I don't know where this will lead."

Clyde didn't relent, "Yea, that's all well and good soundin'; but if wishes were horses, then beggars would ride. Hopin' for peace ain't bringin' it. We got no business over yonder meddlin' in other countries' business. Ya've got ya a callin'! And it's right here under yer nose."

"I feel God is leading me, and as His servant, I must obey."

Clyde expelled a disgusted grunt, "Preacher, ya know good and well that ya' couldn't holler sooie if the hogs got ya' down. How do ya' expect to do any fightin' agin' them fellers?"

Before Reverend Lawson answered, Mrs. Emma spoke for the first time, "Clyde, let 'im be. He's got his mind made up, and he's answerin' to a higher callin' than the likes of Greenbed."

Clyde started to object, "But . . . . We're gonna miss ya somethin' awful. Yer the best thing ever happened to us," he paused and couldn't resist adding, "even if yer no more than a Jackleg Preacher!" Thankfully, the remainder of the visit took on a lighter mood.

As Reverend Lawson traveled the dirt roads and pathways back to his home, he marveled at the beauty of springtime in the mountains, the rhododendrons in bloom, dotting the massive hills with a delicate, almost lacy beauty. The grass was lush, soft and green with the promise of new life.

He vowed to take a detour and pass the field from which Greenbed derived its name. Here, he always felt rejuvenated, today was no exception. The colorful wildflowers filling the field produced a rainbow of vibrant colors while the aroma sweetened the air. As far as the eye could see, pinks, whites and maroon daisy-like flowers swayed in the mild breeze. The delicate thread-like leaves of these 3 ft. beauties could only have been crafted by a caring Creator. When first arriving at Greenbed, he learned these wonderful flowers were 'Cosmos' and from April to November, they spread a colorful blanket over this field.

He stretched his lean, muscular frame out on the soft bed of green grasses and gazed at the fluffy clouds against the backdrop of a blue sky. For the first time in months, he felt a peacefulness in his soul. Assured that he walked in the Will of God would make this announcement easier for him. Reverend Lawson spent the next half hour in fervent prayer for the community that he'd physically leave behind, yet carry in his heart wherever future travels directed.

The announcement made at the conclusion of the Sunday service was received in much the same manner as Clyde responded. At first, the congregation experienced shock, then anger for the desertion, and by the time Tuesday rolled around, a solemn, deep sorrow filled the community.

The Parson shared his innermost feelings with Toby, "There are times I feel consumed with guilt for disappointmenting them. Life is hard enough in these mountains without their shepherd adding to the weight of the burdens. Members pointed out to me that it isn't a preacher's duty to serve in the army, maybe they're right. At this point I wouldn't have to go."

Toby scratched his head, "Then, why?"

"To everything thing there is a season, a time to be born, a time to die; a time to plant, a time to uproot; a time to kill, a time to heal; and so forth. That passage ends with 'a time for war and a time for peace.' This is my season to serve and not take. I simply can't explain it."

Toby nodded in agreement. "I hate to see you go, I really do. Yet, you can't let yourself feel responsible for what happens overseas. It's admirable that you're willing to do whatever; but you have no control over that mess. Don't bear guilt for leaving Greenbed either, or you'll be defeated before you even put on the green uniform."

Bethany cuddled the small babe in her arms, "Well, I for one thank you for going." Both the Preacher and Toby looked shocked. "I mean, of course, we're going to miss you, and all. But I look at it like this. You're doing this to insure Elizabeth Grace will grow up with the same freedoms that we take for granted. I thank you for that."

"Bethany, when I sense a shadow of doubt creeping upon me, I want to recall this beautiful picture of you cradling that precious miracle in your arms." Almost as if Elizabeth Grace knew she was being talked about, she sighed and expelled a soft coo. "That—right there—is the face that launches a thousand ships."

He prayed for strength and courage to get through that final sermon. Following 'When the Roll Is Called Up Yonder I'll Be There,' he placed his hands on each side of the wooden pulpit to calm the uncontrollable shaking. He squeezed the wood hard. "Friends, this is the most difficult sermon I've ever preached. The truth is, I don't have a sermon." He looked into the faces of the awaiting congregation. He saw the members of the Primitive Baptist

Church seated mid-way back on the left side. He saw Mrs. Emma's sweet smile and Mr. Clyde's nod of approval.

"On this blessed spring day, I would like to speak to you about hope. It is never too late to grasp for hope. Following the gray days of winter, when it seems the sun may never shine again, the bitter cold fades into a crisp chill. If you brush away the dead grasses and weeds covering the flower beds, you find the tiny budding of purple, pink and yellow crocuses, ready to push the rest of the way through the frozen ground. Spring produces new hope. The day I made this decision, I spent time alone at Greenbed and looked around me at the magnificient signs of new life and hope.

'Hope.' How does one embrace or give hope? As with any circumstance of life, the best instructions can be gained from God's Word. I refer to the Book of Job. Job declared 'though he slay me, yet will I hope.' Job remained faithful to God in the midst of terrible circumstances. He held onto 'hope' for a brighter future. David, in the book of Psalm writes, 'my hope comes from God,' and from Romans 15:13, 'May the God of hope fill you.'

As I studied the many scriptures about 'hope,' it became clear to me that hope is an active word. It's more than a desire. It is a confidence. As Christians, we can be certain of forgiveness and for eternal life.

I am confident that Greenbed will survive and grow. I see amazing promise." Unconsciously, his gaze rested on little Elizabeth Grace peacefully cradled in Bethany's arms.

I will pray for each of you every day. I'd be honored if you keep me in your prayers. Toby volunteered to post my letters in the general store. My final words to you are a charge and a blessing that Paul gave the Church of Philippi:

'Grace and peace to you and yours from God our Father and the Lord Jesus Christ. I will thank my God every time I remember you and I will find joy when I think of each of you.'

Please welcome our guests today, seated in the back, Elihu and Willamae, and their son his wife, Shad and Annie Fisher." Everyone turned to see the black family seated uncomfortably on the last pew. "These fine people are good friends. God doesn't see your white skin any more than he sees their black skin. I made a promise, shortly after arriving in Greenbed to destroy that tree behind the schoolhouse, the killing tree. Following the service, I'm burning that horrible reminder of death to the ground. You are welcome to join me." He looked back to the black family, "I'd be honored if you'd set the burning torch to the tree." Elihu nodded.

He left the pulpit and assumed his usual position at the door.

He broke two of his own rules: not being overcome with emotion while in his professional role; but he had broken that promise to himself many times since coming to Greenbred. Secondly, not initiating hugs toward parishioners. He needed the warmth of those hugs to fill his memory bank for future days. As the congregation filed past him, wishing him well, shedding tears, offering words of wisdom, the Reverend was relieved that no one made him feel that he deserted them.

36

THE LAST PROMISE

The procession marched straightway from church directly to the little school. More than two-thirds of the congregation gathered for the solemn ceremony. No one spoke. The Parson handed the pack of wooden matches to Elihu, who lit the torch. He then handed the flaming the torch to Shad and allowed the next generation to ignite the branches of the killing tree. The thick dark smoke billowed upward to the sky toward the heavens. The assembly watched until the tree burnt and tumbled to the ground, leaving a mere stump with glowing embers. In his Sunday-best clothes, Reverend Lawson grabbed the shovel, pick and axe to destroy the last bits of the stump. The only words spoken throughout the procedure came at the conclusion, when only smoldering ashes remained. Elihu walked past Reverend Lawson and extended his hand for a hearty handshake and looked the young preacher directly in the eyes for several seconds before proclaiming, "Ya done a good thing here today, Preacher. We thank ya'."

"That hatred ends here. Today. For once and for all." Reverend Lawson felt this act served as one of his greatest accomplishments in Greenbed. Yet, he could not produce a smile for the remainder of the day. A great sadness consumed him as he imagined the generations that lived under this curse, rather than ridding the area of this awful injustice for healing to begin. Wasted hatred. Useless hatred. Wasted years.

His last promise fulfilled, he could now move on ... with only one regret. His heart longed for Rebecca to be by his side and witness the demise of the killing tree.

37

PENNIES IN MASON JARS

Bethany insisted she and Toby were the logical ones to drive the Reverend to the train station since they owned the most dependable mode of transportation. The shiny green 1939 Hudson was the only new vehicle in the community. Bethany pressed the argument that, 'you realize, of course, that the Hudson is advertised as America's Safest Car.' Reverend Lawson secretly hoped for an invitation from one of the Brothers. He would've gladly accepted an offer from any one of them, to ride in their unreliable trucks or cars that rattled and often stalled along the way. He longed for that one last touch of the simplistic, down-to-earth lifestyle of Greenbed. The invitation didn't appear forthcoming. He accepted the ride with Toby and family.

The conversation to the train station centered on the baby, the three adults obviously wanted to prolong the inevitable goodbye to the last possible moment. The Hudson did hold true and produced a smooth ride up and down the steep elevations. In contrast to some of the jiggling, noisy rides down the mountain he'd made with well-meaning parishoners.

They granted his one request along the way, to visit Guthrie's grave. He walked the distance past his beloved church, down the dirt path to the graveyard. He recalled the cold day of the funeral, the sleet pelting them in the face as they followed behind the three roaring John Deere tractors carrying Guthrie to his final resting place. Reverend Lawson knelt and touched the simple grave marker. "My friend, the General Store is in good hands with Toby. You'd be proud of your nephew. He's a man of integrity; it must run in the family. I wish you were here to talk this decision over with, but wouldn't wish you back. I know you're strolling down streets of gold and arranging merchandise on marble shelves."

Returning to the car in a solemn mood, he spent the remainder of the trip committing to memory every minute detail along the road, the sights, the long and winding lanes leading to the simple farmhouses, the leaning mailboxes, and silently offering prayers for the families they represented.

As the Hudson pulled into the train station, Reverend Lawson stared in disbelief. Parked haphazardly in the station lot, there sat the aged vehicles of nearly every resident and parishioner from Greenbed. They'd formed a semicircle around Mr. Willie's Model-T pickup truck. Several of the men, waved for the Parson to join the delegation.

"You all made the trip to see me off! I don't know what to say."

One of the men shouted, "Mark it down. This is a first if a Preacher cain't talk," good-natured laughter followed. "Jest kiddin', Preacher, ya know blame good 'n well, we'd give our eyeteeth if'n ya'd stay for a spell."

Mr. Clyde served as the spokesperson, "We want to show ya somethin', Preacher. None of us is ready or willing to make this a farewell. As soon as ya' finish doin' whatever ya' need to do, we want you back here! The Army won't give ya much money to travel with, so we started raisin' money so's to buy yer train ticket to git ya back to where ya rightly belong." Right on cue, the crowd parted to expose the bed of Mr. Willie's truck and there lay what looked like fifty to seventy-five mason jars. Several of the jars halfway filled with pennies. A makeshift sign hung across the back of the pickup:

"Pennies to Bring Back the Jack Leg Preacher."

"We're leavin' a jar in the general store, one at the mill, one at the lumber yard, and we got promises to keep jars in nigh unto ever' home hereabout. We want ya' to know, our homes are yer home, we'll be a waitin' here with open arms."

"Now I am speechless." His throat closed for several seconds. "I thank you. I've never felt such an outpouring. During my time here, I heard many a tall tale bantered about at the general store, but I also learned heartwarming truths. Truths about how you relied on each other during the Great Depression, and I see how you continue to be Good Samaritans. You," he pointed his finger at all of them, "are the preachers. You preached to me. I feel blessed to know every one of you and your wonderful families." The train whistle interrupted with a shrill blast. He slowly turned to board. No need to delay this agony; after all, he felt confident that he was following God's Will for his life.

Mrs. Daisy pushed her way through the crowd and grabbed the Reverend by his sleeve and pulled until he faced her. She stepped forward and took both of his hands in her small, frail hands. She seemed to savor the moment as she retrieved a letter from her dress pocket and pressed the envelope into his hand and looked up at him with a mischievous twinkle in her faded blue eyes. She gave him a knowing wink, clutching his forearm with all her strength, "It arrived yesterday, in the nick of time." Reverend Lawson locked his eyes on the familiar penmanship of Rebecca, 'Gerhart' neatly written on the sealed envelope. He tucked the letter in his shirt pocket to keep it as close to his heart as possible, until he had the opportunity to read each precious word in privacy once seated on the train. He knew he'd memorize it before ever reaching his station of call. He grabbed Mrs. Daisy and squeezed her close, planting a kiss on her wrinkled cheek. He'd learned a valuable truth from this community: Many times in life, words are not necessary.

CPSIA information can be obtained at www.ICGtesting.com
Printed in the USA
LVOW120020010313

322163LV00002B/132/P